A Bridge To Eden

A Bridge To Eden

by
David Turrill

BONNEVILLE BOOKS ™
Springville, Utah

ISBN: 1-55517-548-1
v.1

Published by Bonneville Books
Imprint of Cedar Fort Inc.
925 N. Main, Springville, Utah 84663
www.cedarfort.com

Distributed by:

Typeset by Virginia Reeder
Cover design by Adam Ford
Cover design © 2001 by Lyle Mortimer

Printed in the United States of America
10 9 8 7 6 5 4 3 2 1

Printed on acid-free paper

Library of Congress Cataloging-in-Publication Data

Turrill, David A.
  Bridge to Eden / by David Turrill.
    p. cm.
  ISBN 1-55517-548-1 (pbk. : alk. paper)
  1. Psychiatric hospital patients--Fiction. 2. Abused wives--Fiction.
3. Widowers--Fiction. I. Title.
  PS3570.U756 B75 2001
  813'.54--dc21
                        2001001973

To Jannie

Acknowledgments

Special thanks to my sister, Janet, and my brother, Doug, who helped me to remember what our extraordinary parents taught us by word and example; to my children and grandchildren who never let me feel alone; and to John Klapko and Pauline Jones who listened to my countless discourses on Edenic time and metaphorical dynamism, edited and criticized, and always, always, kept their faith in my work, even when I didn't.

"When a writer calls his work a Romance, it need hardly be observed that he wishes to claim a certain latitude, both as to its fashion and material, which he would not have felt himself entitled to assume, had he professed to be writing a Novel. The latter form of composition is presumed to aim at a very minute fidelity, not merely to the possible, but to the probable and ordinary course of man's existence. The former . . . has fairly a right to present that truth under circumstances, to a great extent, of the writer's own choosing or creation."

—Nathaniel Hawthorne, Preface to *The House of Seven Gables*

"When I have fears that I may cease to be
    Before my pen has gleaned my teeming brain,
Before high-piled books in charactery,
    Hold like rich garners the full ripened grain;
When I behold, upon the night's starred face,
    Huge cloudy symbols of a high romance,
And think that I may never live to trace
    Their shadows, with the magic hand of chance;
And when I feel, fair creature of an hour,
    That I shall never look upon thee more,
Never have relish in the fairy power
    Of unreflecting love—then on the shore
Of the wide world I stand alone, and think
Till love and fame to nothingness do sink."

—John Keats, "When I have Fears That I May Cease to Be"

Introduction

July 1, 2021

My father did not intend for anyone, other than his two friends, Dr. Kim and Jack Csinos, and Shelly and I and our families, to read his manuscript. It's about a miracle, and only those who have seen such a thing, or trust its witnesses, can really ever accept it. Dad thought of it as a personal testament and, as he occasionally reminded us, a condition of liberty—nothing else, really.

I am his son, Tysen Riveridge. My sister, Shelly Rose, and I are his only heirs. And acting on advice from Dr. Kim, we have decided to make Dad's manuscript public, if for no other reason than to serve as evidence that magic still exists in the world and requires no more faith than its opposite.

Dad's real name was Ebenezer Riveridge. He hated his first name, and I've never heard him referred to as anything except Ben by his friends. Only our mother, Morgan, was allowed the use of the more familiar *Benny*. Morgan was allowed anything.

Dad and Morgan moved to the little town of Eagle Harbor, in the upper peninsula of Michigan, shortly after his release from Ypsilanti State Hospital in November, 2000. It's a picturesque fishing and tourist village, located on the Keewenaw Peninsula, a jut of land that arcs out in a half moon from the larger peninsula into the waters of Lake Superior. The place is nestled among giant pines, protected from the storms of the larger world as fully as the aeries of the splendid birds for which it's named.

Dad and Morgan crossed the Mackinaw Bridge almost exactly twenty years ago, with a few meager possessions. They headed north as far as they could go by land. Eagle Harbor is where they stopped. Dad bought the sprawling, clapboard house where he and Morgan took up residence in the upstairs rooms. The lower floor was converted to a bookshop and became their means of support. Dad loved books more than money, so it was enough.

They never crossed the bridge again—not alive, at least—not even to visit Shelly or me, or their grandchildren, who lived in the lower peninsula. It was always up to us to visit them. We understood. Even paradise has its borders, and Eagle Harbor was as close to Eden as Dad could imagine.

The trip wasn't much of a burden, really, though the distance to Eagle Harbor from Detroit, where Collette and I live, is over four hundred miles. Our children have always loved Grandpa's house, especially at Christmas time when Shelly and her husband, Charley Rose, and their children, were there too.

Shelly and I seldom visited at the same time. Though we missed each other, it was intentional scheduling. Alternating trips gave Dad and Morgan more individualized time to devote to each grandchild, and many more visits for them to anticipate.

Dad's passing was made more difficult because of this Christmas tradition. Shelly and I and our families would always meet in Eagle Harbor on December 20th. Shelly, because she lived in a small town near the Straits of Mackinac (you can see the Mackinac Bridge from her porch), arrived first at the house in Eagle Harbor, her journey being about half the distance of mine.

She told me that as soon as they arrived, she sensed that something was wrong. They got there in the late afternoon. It was already dark. The only light was in the bookstore downstairs.

The walkway leading to the entrance to the shop was filled with snow and Dad always kept it shoveled for potential customers. The sign in the window read CLOSED although he normally kept the store open until 6:00 on every night except Sunday.

Shelly told Charley to keep the kids in the car. Part of the magic was that she knew, without really knowing. She discovered Dad lying on the floor among the shelves of books. He'd probably been there since early morning. He'd put the cash drawer into the register, but had not yet turned the sign to OPEN. Shelly told me that she sat beside Dad for a long time, cradling his bald head in her arms, before Charley finally disobeyed and came to check on her. She didn't cry, she said. She was remembering, silently.

We're still mystified, as we'll always be, by the impossibility of all that has transpired.

Dad showed us the power of faith and the magic that could happen if one loved well enough. He'd died among his beloved books, the books that had taught him what he knew. But his application of what he had learned had been the amazing part of it. He'd learned that the world was full of mysticism, and he had taught us to believe it, so that we could never despair—not even in death.

He was seventy-four when he died. Except for an interruption of exactly four years, he and Morgan were together for over half a century. She disappeared when he died.

Their story is in the manuscript that follows, and people who are tired of desperation must read it to see, in cloudy symbols, what faith can accomplish.

Chapter One

One Hand, One Heart

Guided by his sense of beauty, an individual transforms a fortuitous occurrence into a motif, which then assumes a permanent place in the composition of the individual's life.
—Milan Kundera, *The Unbearable Lightness of Being*

I never connected the heart with anything physical, so when the cardiologist told us an eighty percent block needed to be routed and flushed, I couldn't seriously envision the procedure as applying to anything but a toilet. Morgan actually snickered, although it was her plumbing that the doctor was admiring in the x-ray photos he held pinioned against the boxes of artificial sunlight mounted on his office wall.

He looked at them with the same wistful expression that Blackbeard must have used when gazing at his treasure maps. There was gold there, somewhere. This blocked river of Morgan's geography was a clue.

Our general practitioner had told us that Dr. Singh was one of the best. He was Indian and his family had immigrated here from some place called Madras. I remembered this only because I connected the bleeding Madras shirts I used to wear—that had to be laundered separately from everything else—with Morgan's bloodpump. Dr. Singh was a Sikh. He sported the mandatory turban of his faith, which was so incongruous with his expensive, American suit and silk tie, the knot of which disappeared under the bushy whiskers protruding from his face. I thought he did, indeed, resemble a pirate, or an evil wizard, but quickly dismissed my impressions, inwardly chastising that part of me that could be so basely ethnocentric.

I had read somewhere that Sikh means he wishes to learn.

"Does this have to be done?" Morgan asked. She hated the idea of surgery, having experienced it only once in her fifty years. She'd had her gall bladder removed only a few weeks after giving birth to our daughter, Michelle, in 1970.

We sat in leather chairs on the side of the desk opposite the cardiologist. It was June, the last week of classes at Swan's End High School where we both worked. We were almost as eager for vacation as the students.

"I'm afraid so, yes. The only other possibility is to let it remain as it is and try to combat it with diet and medication." He glanced again at the treasure maps.

"And if we did?" I asked this because I knew Morgan wanted to, but wouldn't.

"Then you'd be playing Russian Roulette."

Morgan's small hand squeezed mine with unnatural power. She'd forgotten about my arthritic knuckle. I winced and bore it with a martyr's satisfaction.

After scheduling the procedure, we stopped at a restaurant on the way home. She stared at me across the table, always sounding the depth of my comprehension of her. Morgan had the darkest eyes I'd ever seen. Though brown, they appeared to be black, like strong coffee. The Sikh's seemed pastel by comparison.

I reached across the table and engulfed her small hands in mine. They were ice. She read my reaction. "Cold hands, warm heart," she quipped.

Her cliché made me think about the first movie we'd ever seen together. It was *West Side Story*. We were eighteen. Years later, one of my students would call it a "chick flick" and I would become unreasonably angry, raging into a harangue against the poor kid that had something to do with the imbecility of equating sensitivity with estrogen.

After the movie (it was in 1965, I think), in the privacy of my father's '63 Chevy, we sang *One Hand, One Heart*, Maria and

Tony's love duet. Morgan had the gift of harmony.

It became motif. It was sung by her father at our marriage ceremony. "One Hand" was engraved on my wedding band, "One Heart" on hers. We sang it together at our twenty-fifth wedding anniversary party, given us by our children. We sang it on the way home from Dr. Singh's office. It is etched beneath two conjoining rings into the rose marble of our headstone. A fortuitous occurrence that grew into motif.

The Sikh cleaned Morgan's artery, collected his treasure from Blue Cross Insurance, and pronounced her "as good as new." Twenty-eight days later she died of a massive heart attack.

That was the last day of July, 1996. On the first day of that month, Morgan had turned fifty. We'd been married for thirty years. I didn't see her again until the passage of the new millennium.

Chapter Two

The Palace of Cracked Heads

I stand for those who have made themselves up.
—Tom McGuane, *Panama*

Dr. Kim told me that what I believe is impossible Others have called me "delusional." When one has been identified in such a manner, the real and unreal are neatly divided and everyone, except the labeled, can go on living as they please. Love is a mystic doctrine of forceful experience.

At our first meeting, I told Dr. Kim, who is not very familiar with Carl Sandburg, that this place is the "Palace of Cracked Heads" and that they won't allow me to have an alarm clock because I will feed it to the goats or crocodiles. He takes this as conclusive evidence of my need for counseling. I see it as wit. I told him to substantiate my metaphor by reading Barrie's *Peter Pan*. I don't think he has. He's grown up, and we live in different worlds.

Dr. Kim is Vietnamese. My initial impression was that he wanted to discover some new approach to his discipline—to emulate Freud or Jung, Skinner or Adler. He doesn't want to diagnose by the book. He wants to write the book.

I think he equates neatness with authority. He wears little wire-rimmed glasses and is defaced by a wispy beard. It erases his features and appears to be drawn on his face, as if some imp had marred his photograph with an ink pen. He wears a white coat. I thought, at first, that it was to protect him from insanity. Like Pilate, he is forever washing his hands.

He told me I was ill. I told him that, like my father before me, what I have is faith. Because I see what he does not, he says I am wrong. I tell him we are "clay in the potter's hand." His impatience leads me to believe that he is not familiar with the passage. He sighs, as if to say that surely I must know that he understands me better than I do. It offends him deeply that I do not accept his premise. He has been reading *The Three Christs of Ypsilanti*. It is lying on his massive desk with a bookmark in it. It catches my eye because this hospital is in Ypsilanti. The town, for which it was named and in which it resides, bears the surname of two brothers who were heroes in the Greek war for independence. What could be crazier?

The desk is too big for Dr. Kim. I originally thought, before he became my friend, that all the desks of his life had been too big. He didn't seem to sit behind it so much as to compete with it for my attention, as he probably did with his teachers. At that time, I believed, the belittling desk had a higher purpose.

He began our first interview by calling me by the wrong name, damaging our relationship before it had begun. I relate that conversation now, as well as I remember it. Forgive me, Dr. Kim, I was in a poor frame of mind.

"Ebenezer," he said, "do you know what the term 'obsessive-compulsive' means?"

I was admiring the desk. I think it was made of mahogany—imported, I was certain.

"Ebenezer?"

"I prefer Ben."

"All right, Ben. Do you understand the term?"

"Yes."

"What does it mean?"

"It describes passion."

"You mean, for example, Christ's passion?"

I pointed at the book-lined wall to my right. "There's a *Dictionary of Psychological Terminology* right there. Why don't you look it up?"

"Could you answer my question?"

"Like Christ? Sure. It refers to his death. Was he compelled to it? Yes. Was he obsessed with it? Yes. Was he obsessive-compulsive? No. He was passionate."

"Your attorney argued that you have this problem and that you might be schizophrenic. You should be grateful. It kept you out of jail."

"Did it?"

He ignored my question. "It's a common psychological disorder. My task is to determine if you have it. Delusion is one of its symptoms." I remember he pumped up his chair with the hydraulic handle beneath it. I assumed, then, that like the blow-fish, it was to make himself appear less appetizing.

"Why do you call it a 'disorder'? Because it isn't tidy? Passion isn't neat, you know. It's the sloppiest part of life."

"Is that how you see it?"

"It's the truth."

He shifted upward again. "You teach literature?"

"I did. Yes."

"Fiction?"

"The only truth is in fiction."

He smiled. "Sounds like Orwell's double talk."

"It's doublespeak, and I didn't say truth *is* fiction. I said the only truth is *in* fiction. Big Brother needs to pay attention. It wasn't paradox."

Dr. Kim frowned darkly, but continued in spite of my antipathy. He asked me if I knew what stalking was.

"Unwanted attention."

"Do you think that you were guilty of this 'unwanted attention'? With this woman, I mean?"

"No more than you are now."

Dr. Kim sighed. He wrung his hands. "Perhaps we should continue this another time, when you're feeling more cooperative."

"If you feel compelled to do so."

That was the substance of my first meeting with the man who was to become a valued friend. I shouldn't have judged him so quickly, but I was raised to understand that all is possible.

Coincidence does not exist for me. Things hold meaning. As a child, I told my mother that I disliked intense sunlight. When she asked me why, I told her it was for the same reason that I abhorred utter darkness—both blinded me so that it was necessary to close my eyes to really see. She smiled and told me that I was learning.

I believed in Santa Claus far longer than my schoolmates and I wept when my mother finally confirmed what all the kids had been teasing me about. When I became a father, despite the remonstrances of the Lutheran Church, I fostered the heresy of St. Nick in my own children. I was truly mystified when they surrendered their convictions so readily and, apparently, without remorse.

I was always big (over six feet by the time I reached the eighth grade). My dad often chided me for "rolling on the lawn" with my younger brother (eight years my junior), and his neighborhood playmates. I concocted imaginary scenes with them, which they loved. I was always the dragon, or the ogre, or the troll under the bridge. My size made it real to them and they would flee from me in delighted terror.

Dad thought me childish and admonished me. He told my mother that he suspected that my actions might be construed as pedophiliac by our neighbors. It never occurred to him that I might be practicing to become a teacher—and a father.

We give things names to make them real. My father wrote "Ebenezer Riveridge" on my birth certificate so that I could be born. That was in January of 1946, which should have made me a baby-boomer, but Dad worked in a General Motors plant which manufactured jeeps and tanks, so he didn't have to come back from taking life in order to give it. Consequently, I never considered myself a real member of my generation, since the name of *baby-boomer* implied what did not occur. I walked through my high school graduation with a sense that I was the only one of the 914 seniors whose father wasn't a warrior. Misnomer is at the heart of existentialism.

Even though it made me alive, I hated the name of Ebenezer. Like everyone else of my surreal generation that had matured while watching Alistair What's-His-Name on his or her first television set persecute Bob Cratchit, I matured into bigotry, knowing that anyone named Ebenezer was a grasping old skinflint who despised children (especially crippled ones), and humbugged Christmas. I hated being identified, however remotely, with someone who had murdered romance and saw only the coincidence of life.

Dad had insisted on crippling me this way because there were many Ebenezer branches on our genealogical tree. Since our Puritan ancestors had first arrived from England to settle in that little WASP's nest called Massachusetts Bay (freed, then, from intolerance to practice it), there had been five Ebenezers. In fact, the first non-Ebenezer, Captain James Riveridge, had been born about ten years after old Boz had raised the dickens with the name and his parent, cursed himself, hadn't the coldness of heart to inflict that kind of reality on his son. The father of the current Ebenezer had had no such qualms (though he had escaped the curse himself). Dad was dubbed George Washington Riveridge. As a child, it was the only luck he would ever have.

When I started school, I began to deny my existence. I came to see my name not only as a negative metaphor that was breeding into a virus of motif, but also as an obstacle to individuality and, therefore, imagination. I became, to myself at least, simply "Ben." But there was always the omnipresent roster, that list that holds us up to the glaring light of social stigma and perpetuates the reality that some call "truth." So it was that some insensitive wretch who knew nothing of child psychology, (usually a teacher), would betray my identity to the mob, merely for the purpose of discovering my presence. The fortress of my pretense would then be assailed with such missiles as "scrooge," "stooge," "wheezer" and "geezer." Oddly, I've played those parts, at least the first three, in my life. I'm rapidly approaching the last.

I had to tolerate this abuse until a sudden growth spurt in the eighth grade taught me that a name is a façade and terror is a substance. George Washington Riveridge never knew that the son he saw frolicking with children was a real dragon to any peer who dared to use his given name. A bloody lip was, generally, the price of such folly. By the time I arrived in high school, I had become "Ben" to everyone, even Dad, who had only just returned from the state sanitarium for the first time and didn't care about reality anymore. I was born again—not by water, but by word. I didn't know that I would follow my father to Ypsilanti.

Chapter Three

The Tutor Dynasty

The Child is father of the man;
And I could wish my days to be
Bound each to each by natural piety.
                    —William Wordsworth, "My Heart Leaps Up"

After she died, I found what we used to call a "baby book" in a box my mother had marked with my name, 'Ben.' It had pictures and measurements and ink footprints and records of my first smile, my first Christmas present, my first word ("Mama"), and all the other paraphernalia (locks of wispy hair, etc.) that proud, young mothers preserve, as if they might always keep their children. She had written, on the back cover, a few words that must have been added long after I was an adult. In the poor-vision scratching of old age she had scribbled: *I love you, Bennie, I have from the beginning.* Such words! The loveliest things often hurt the most.

She was the one who taught me—if such a thing is possible—to be a romantic. She was the first to love me. She was the first to call me "Ben." I knew that she had fought to save me from my name before I was born. She reminded me about something that everyone overlooked—Scrooge had become a good man. He had saved Tiny Tim. Such things counted.

Before I ever stepped inside a school, she had read Shelley, Byron, Wordsworth and Keats to me. Before I could walk, she would sit me down in her flower garden, just beyond the kitchen window of the old house where I grew up, and tell me the names of each flower she picked. She thrilled to the aroma of lilacs. She told me stories of the Easter lily and the pussy willow, how they got their names. She filled my world with unseen characters. She drowned my senses in beauty.

Her name was Jennie. Her father could have sent her to Michigan State University. Their house in Lansing was only a few miles away. She was a National Honor Society student at Eastern High and the President of the Drama Club. She kept the pins commemorating these offices in a little box, along with the birth certificates of her four children, the treasures of her life. Her father would not allow her to go to the university, even though he had the money. College was, he told her, for men. He kept the money for my Uncle Bert, who would squander it away. He was a hedonist who could not hold a job or wife.

Mom met my father and married him, as she was supposed to do. She loved him once, I think, but not always. His mania drove it from her. Neither her father nor her husband, however, could keep her from books. While George Washington Riveridge was at work, and my older sisters Ruth and Ella were at school, Mom would bundle me in scarves and mittens and we would tramp through the snow to the public library. We'd spend hours selecting the right tomes, then pack them in grocery sacks for the journey home. Once there, over a bowl of hot soup and warm bread, in our massive kitchen, she would read to me everything from *The Eskimo Twins* to *The Deerslayer*. She knew that it didn't matter if I understood it all or not. No one completely understands another's book.

Strangely, she did not do this with my sisters. Perhaps she believed that they would never be allowed, as she had not, to further their educations. Perhaps she felt that women intuitively knew more and did not need such tutelage. Ruth, the oldest, was very bright, but possessed such energy that sitting still was agony for her. She would learn to concentrate on the physical side of things. She was a natural athlete in a world where it was not yet fashionable for women to be athletic. My other sister, Ella, had worked open the basement door and tumbled down twenty-five steps in her stroller, striking her toddler's head on the concrete floor when she was less than two years old. Her painful shyness, slow thinking, and frequently odd behavior both then and now, were attributed by my father to this accident. Mom believed that Ella had been strange from birth.

Jennie was a housewife in the truest sense of the term. She was married to the house in which we lived. She rarely left it. She had few friends. She focused on me. She believed that I could create my own life out of imagination. She spent one whole summer, when I was eight, trying to get me to understand *Ode On a Grecian Urn*. Then she read William Faulkner's story, *The Bear* to me. She would say things like: "Gertrude Stein has no soul. A rose is more than a rose." She referred to William Carlos Williams as "the pediatrician who had never been a child."

It was all lost on me—then.

She wasn't a tyrant. I adored her. She was always full of excitement for what was beautiful. My dreams were filled with possibilities that she made me believe. From her, came *Peter Pan, Ichabod Crane, Natty Bumppo, Aladdin, Br'er Rabbit, Toad of Toad Hall, Alice in Wonderland, Black Beauty,* ad infinitum.

When I began school, Mom supplemented my education. While the teacher talked about Teddy Roosevelt's administration, she told me of San Juan Hill and big-game hunting and piranha-filled rivers and boxing and assassination attempts and how teddy bears got their name. A reading of *Annabel Lee* at school prompted stories at home of Poe's dark dreams, his alcoholism, his wicked stepfather, his incestuous love. She taught me about Cochise and Geronimo, Crazy Horse and Sitting Bull, Sojourner Truth and Nat Turner before they ever became visible in the textbooks of American public schools.

Jennie Riveridge loved everything of beauty.

"Oh, look at the hummingbird, Bennie, do you see it? No? Over there Honey, by the forsythia bush. Remember John Keats? *Beauty is truth*? Look at how the sunlight comes through the window. See how it touches the floor there? It's faded the wax

15

shine. Emily Dickinson wrote a poem called *A Certain Slant of Light*. One light diminishing another. Thomas Jefferson was the real force of the revolution, I don't care what your teacher said about George Washington. He was only the muscle. Ruth! Sit down and eat your breakfast! Yes, Daddy's name is the same as.... Ella! Quit playing with your cereal, Sweetheart, and eat. Well, they're both on Mount Rushmore. Gutzon Borglum carved those faces, you know. They should make a monument to him. Artists never get the credit of politicians. George, could you put down the newspaper for a moment and help Ella to eat? She hasn't had a bite! Ruth! Sit!"

All this while she fried eggs in an iron skillet and kneaded dough for cinnamon rolls. Dad silently read the paper through it all, seemingly unaware of any member of his family, though I would come to understand that he was acutely aware of everything. Silence indicated consent.

When I was eight and my mother was forty-five, she gave birth to the fourth of the Riveridge children. To no one's surprise, she named him Thomas Jefferson Riveridge. Dad didn't care. He had his Ebenenzer. Tommy-Jeff was allergic to everything from mother's milk to chocolate. The doctors determined that he had severe reactions to sixty-eight different foods and milder responses to a hundred more. He was extremely thin, cried constantly, and was incessantly scratching. As he grew into early childhood, his clothes were always stained with the blood of his aggression against the itching that didn't stop until he began to take a series of weekly shots, beginning at around the age of seven. That was the year that Lee Harvey Oswald tried to rearrange the United States. It was also the year that my sister, Ruth, gave birth to her first child and George Washington Riveridge began to converse with God.

Chapter Four

The Sanctity of the Home

O my people, hear my teaching; listen to the words of my mouth. I will open my mouth in parables, I will utter hidden things, things from of old.

—Psalm 78:2

My father was born in Lansing, Michigan, not too far from the dome of the state capitol building. His mother, Belle, had been a beautiful woman in her youth, who gave parts of herself away until she ceased to exist. She gave her body to my grandfather (another of the unfortunate Ebenezers), her heart to her son, and her soul to the Holy Gospel Church of the Right Brethren. Her mind she retained, but only in the reduced condition that her parents, German immigrants, had considered proper for a young woman.

The Holy Gospel Church of the Right Brethren gained her as a convert when my father was still in diapers. She knew that her husband was seeing other women. She saw her own failure in it. She turned to God for comfort and hope. Instead, she found religion.

The ministers of the church did not have homes. They lived with the families of their congregation, moving from place to place, staying for days, or even months, at a time. My grandmother welcomed them often, but only when Grandfather was gone for extended periods on his "business" trips. Out of fear, she never asked what business he was attending to, but only when he would be back, so that she could tell the brethren that they must move on for a while. When they were there, she convinced herself that she was like Mary or Martha, housing the Lord's servants.

My grandmother adored her little Georgie and thought him

fortunate to have the ministers of the gospel on hand so often to instruct him in the ways of righteousness. To my father, however, the brethren were like wraiths that would appear and disappear with nightmarish regularity. As soon as he was old enough to think, they would require him to commit long passages of scripture to memory, most of it having to do with law and condemnation. If he failed in this holy task, he would be backed into a corner by the dark brothers, who then screamed hell and the devil at him until he was so terrified that he couldn't sleep. Belle would feel the natural urge to protect him, but she knew that what was natural was sinful, and she held back for the sake of Georgie's soul, leaving the room in tears and covering her ears to block out the sounds of his cries. I would find out as a man, when Dad was in Ypsilanti State Hospital, that when he was six years old, grandmother had returned from the meat market only to have Georgie fly into her arms when she opened the door. He was naked and terrified and was, apparently, being chased by "Brother Aaron," who suddenly appeared behind him, breathless from pursuit. The good brother explained that he had been attempting to give Georgie a bath to illustrate how God can remove the soil of sin just as man can cleanse a dirty body. My father had told his psychiatrist how he had screamed and cried and trembled in his mother's skirts, begging her to save him. She knew what salvation was. She handed him back to Brother Aaron and began to unpack the groceries as Dad was hauled back upstairs, too overcome by betrayal to scream anymore. It never occurred to grandmother that the water was not running. Subdue the natural. Erase the mind. Georgie would be saved in spite of herself.

From that point in his life, my father lost trust—in himself, in God, in people. He became introverted. He didn't tell anyone about the molestation until he had his third or fourth mental breakdown. I don't think he was ever sure, as a child, that what had happened to him had been wrong. Everyone around him revered the brethren. Nothing was ever mentioned. And an act must be openly condemned in order to be bad. Fornication was something that happened between a man and a woman. That was clearly wrong. Fellatio wasn't mentioned in the Bible. It wasn't until much later, as an adult, that he discovered that it was pedophilia—immoral and criminal. He had always sensed it, but naming it made it real. By the time he figured it out, Grandfather Ebenezer was in prison for selling false bonds, apparently the focus of the "business" that so often took him away from home.

Dad broke with the church the day after his high school graduation. My grieving grandmother couldn't understand his insistence that the brethren not be allowed into their home anymore. She continued to attend services, which he did not object to, but she could not cajole him into accompanying her. Then he met my mother, fell in love as well as he could, married, and moved to Saginaw. The wraiths, however, never left him.

Although Mom wasn't much on religion, she felt that her children should be baptized and have some Christian training. She joined the Presbyterian Church, located only a few blocks from the house. Dad attended for her sake, but insisted that the ministers would not be allowed to live in our house. Mom laughed. The ministers had their own homes and families, she said, a concept which was novel to my father.

Dad came to understand, over time, that our minister, Reverend Peterson, was in fact, a good man. Dad listened to his sermons with interest. The cleric's voice was calm, his sermons comforting, and his emphasis was on the New Testament rather than the Old. Dad even went to the minister's office one Saturday and talked with him extensively about the Trinity. It was there he discovered that God and religion were not necessarily antithetical.

He went to Bible class, became an Elder, and ushered twice a month, but he didn't let God get past his intellect. In 1956, Grandpa Ebenezer was released from prison, and, since he had been born in Canada and had a felony on his record, he was deported as an undesirable alien. Grandfather and Grandmother

Riveridge went to live in Vancouver, British Columbia, where the old man joined the Holy Gospel Church of the Right Brethren and began to atone for his life—a preparation for dying. He never knew what the brothers had done to his son.

Mom and Dad went to visit them once before the old man died. Grandma had a stroke shortly after. They brought her back to Michigan and placed her in a geriatrics home. She was bed-ridden and her speech was so badly slurred that only my dad and I, who visited her together, could decipher what she said. Mostly it had to do with how much she loved God.

Dad returned to his introversion after Grandpa's death and Grandma's return. A deep depression overtook him, and he would seldom speak. I had just turned seventeen and I was confused by Dad's withdrawal. He had always been the perfect father to me. He was active with me in the scouting program, serving as a pack leader. He played innumerable games of "catch" with me. He once took me to a baseball game in Detroit, where he caught a home run ball hit by Al Kaline. Although my mother probably had the strongest influence on me, Dad was a conscientious parent. That is, until 1963.

When his depression set in, no one could reach him. He quit going to church; he was fifty-one and his mother was dying. Ella hid in her room. Mom had gained seventy pounds and seemed interested only in teaching Tommy-Jeff, who had replaced me as the primary target of Mom's aesthetic campaign. My sister Ruth was married. Dad kept reliving the horrors of his childhood. Fear overtook him. Every visit to the geriatrics home made it fresher, more vivid; he wished his mother would die so that he wouldn't have to go there anymore. He saw, in his dreams, the brethren unbuttoning their pants. Brother John, Brother Aaron. *Open that sweet little mouth, Georgie. I've told you how nice you can be, now you do it for him too.* Grandma would ask him why he was feeling so bad—such a bad thing, to wish your mother dead.

Then, one morning in January, Dad's depression changed to

euphoria. God had come to him in the night and invaded his heart. The almighty had spoken directly to him in a blinding light, like He had to Paul on the road to Damascus. Unlike Paul, however, Dad's sight was not interrupted. He could, he said, see clearly for the first time. He found two things that had been lacking: forgiveness and direction. Jesus Christ had returned in the person of George Washington Riveridge. He must gather to him a new Twelve and announce the eminent Kingdom.

At his "trial," as Dad called the proceedings that would commit him to the hospital, he asked the judge (a friend of the family who was an amateur pilot), if revelation was against the law? If so, he argued, then he, like God's Son before him, would take up his cross. I was impressed by Dad's complete self-possession—a term which inferred not only his confidence, but indicated a spiritual take-over. The judge, whose sympathy was apparent, attempted to bring his friend back to earth. But Dad insisted on martyrdom and the judge washed his hands of it. He signed the commitment papers, his arm around my mother as she wept.

Ruth and her husband, John, drove Dad back to the house, silently tolerating his diatribes. Mom held his hand, but he didn't seem to be aware of it. I remember he was very calm as he packed his suitcase. He kept turning to look at us, his Judases. The attendants from the local hospital arrived with the court order in hand. They put him in a straitjacket, which made Mom cry again and outraged Ruth and me (Ella was in her room reading *Gone with the Wind* for the hundredth time and Tommy-Jeff, mercifully, was at school). The attendants would have no need of this restraint on the trip. Dad would first have to be taught the necessity for defending himself, and that was yet a year away. He smiled sadly at us from the rear window of the ambulance. Then, he was gone.

Mercywood Sanitarium in Ann Arbor was a private hospital, which was run like a country club. It contained a golf course, tennis courts, swimming pools, and spas, so that its rich patients, most of whom had been driven crazy by the pursuit of money to sustain such luxuries, would feel at home. We could not afford it, but Mom would not have him at the state hospital. Dad loved it at Mercywood. He was away from his dying mother, his monkish, emotionally crippled daughter, his fat wife, his disappointing sons. He was away from responsibility for the first time in his life and he could listen to God at his leisure. All he had to do was to talk with a psychiatrist every morning. The rest of the day, he was free to play tennis, use the spa, golf, or recruit his disciples—which he did, in large numbers.

The doctor had suggested that our family not visit for the first two months in order to get Dad "acclimated" (I couldn't help but think of tropical fish when I heard that word), so we didn't make our first visit until spring. By that time, Dad had converted most of the patients on his floor and was holding daily worship services on the front lawn of Mercywood.

Pregnant Ruth, her solid, soft-spoken husband, John, Mom, Tommy-Jeff (now age seven), and I, took a picnic lunch and drove in silence to Mercywood. Ella stayed at home, engrossed once again in Margaret Mitchell.

Things went well at first. Mom was pleased with the beauty of the place—the sloping lawns, the pillared, brick mansion that was home to about two hundred patients—all with private rooms. Dad was waiting for us, unattended, on the front steps. He beamed as John's old station wagon labored up the circular drive and pulled into a space between a Mercedes and a Cadillac. He seemed uncharacteristically happy. I noticed that a healthy tan had replaced his normally sallow complexion and he looked as though he had acclimated quite well.

After an emotional reunion (only Dad kept a dry eye), the family migrated to one of the picnic tables that were scattered across the expansive lawn, and Mom unpacked the food. We all watched in awe as Dad devoured the cold chicken, potato salad, and lemon pie that Mom had so lovingly prepared the night before. He seemed intent on getting through it, as though he couldn't speak until that duty had been performed. "Delicious, Jen," he pronounced, and wiped the grease and meringue from his chin with a paper napkin.

He began to stare at me. I felt studied and nervous. I think he was looking for himself in my youthful face, and saw only Mom. If he had bothered to look closer at Tommy-Jeff, he would have found what he was looking for.

He stood up rather grandly. I almost expected him to pull his robes about him. "Come with me for a minute, Ben," he said.

Mom must've looked concerned. "Just for a minute," he reassured her, sensing the distrust that the sane have of the committed.

He put his arm around my shoulder as we walked. He had to reach up to do it, since I was now three inches or so taller than he. We moved only a few feet away, into an open area, out of the shadows of the trees. Tommy-Jeff was fighting with Mom behind us, protesting his inferior status as a Riveridge male.

The sky was flawlessly blue. The sun was at its fiercest angle, having burned away the clouds.

"Ben," my father whispered. "I want you to look at the sun and tell me what you see."

I wanted to tell him that I wouldn't see anything; that the sun was too bright to bear; that both light and darkness could blind you. But I sensed that this would spoil the moment somehow, perhaps turning my father further away. I complied. I had to close my eyes almost immediately. They were stinging and filled with tears. Several minutes passed before I could rid myself of the little suns that floated across my universal vision. Years later, I would read that one of the symptoms of manic-depression was an extreme sensitivity to light. I think Dad knew it then.

"Now watch me," he said.

He turned his grinning face to the firmament and opened his blue eyes. He gazed casually and directly at the burning mass over his head as when Moses saw the bush or Peter beheld the fires of Pentecost.

"Stop it, Dad," I shouted. "You're going to blind yourself!" I could see his retinas melting like old film, jammed in a projector.

He stood there, immobile, his thick, white hair, too long uncut, moving like wheat in the soft breeze. His eyes were wide and dry. He didn't squint. John had risen from the table and was approaching us when Dad suddenly turned to me and looked deeply into my still-watering eyes. I could see well enough to know that he saw no spots, no shadows. His eyes required no adjustment to the shade.

"God protects his prophets, son," he whispered.

I felt an obligation to disbelieve, to argue my father out of his delusion. "You're not Elijah, Dad."

"You're seventeen."

"I know who I am."

"Oh? Who are you?" His eyes expanded. His white brows raised.

"Ben Riveridge. Your son."

"You're Ebenezer Riveridge." He laughed. I think it was meant to wound. "If you can recreate yourself, why can't I?"

"I thought God did this."

"He did."

"Then who are you now, Dad?"

He paused. I could see that he was considering his response. A prophet is never welcome in his own country. "I am."

"You are what?"

"I am."

"I don't understand."

"No, you don't. There are no metaphors." He looked sadly at the little family group huddled under the pine tree behind us. To me, the scent of pine was another fortuitous circumstance that would alert me to the aromas beyond my borders. All eyes could be felt.

"How's your mother, Ben?"

"She wants you to come home."

"I didn't choose this."

"You can *not* choose it."

"Even that's not a choice. You can't defy God, son, not without losing who you are." Dad put his hand on my cheek. He felt the unfamiliar stubble of maturity. "Someday you'll know what all this was for. When I'm dead, most likely." Tears that could not be forced from him by one sun, were drawn by another. He looked desperate. "You are my beloved son," he said gently, "in whom I am well-pleased."

Six months later, Dad hadn't changed for the better and his ravings to Mom in his letters had grown worse. He wrote that God had instructed him to establish a harem in order to begin a new nation and he hoped she wouldn't mind since she would still be his "number one wife." The psychiatrist had nothing but praise for Dad as a model patient. He liked him, he said, and hoped that he would 'come around' within the next year or so. In the meantime, they enjoyed each other's company and the doctor was learning a lot about theology while Dad was reducing the wrong handicap.

At home, things were not so pleasant. By February, Dad's financial resources had run out. Though General Motors was generously paying eighty percent of his normal pay to Mom, and I had taken a job selling shoes after school to help make ends meet, the cost of the private hospital, most of which the insurance would not cover, had drained all of Dad's savings and now posed a real threat to paying the mortgage. John and Ruth convinced Mom that a change was necessary, that she should transfer her messianic spouse to the state-run psychiatric hospital in Ypsilanti.

She didn't want to. Dad's uncle, a brother of my philandering grandpa, had been incarcerated there for years. In fact, he had died there. Mom had gone with Dad several times to visit him. She'd been horrified by the insensitivity, the cages, the Bedlamesque atmosphere of the place. But by the end of the summer, there was no longer any other possibility. She still had children at home. Ella continued to read *Gone with the Wind*, rarely venturing from her room. Tommy-Jeff cried for his daddy and refused to go to school so that either Mom or I had to walk him there, often dragging him by the collar. Mom's sympathy for Dad was swallowed up in adversity. Corners had to be cut. She acquiesced. Dad was transferred to Ypsilanti. There, at the state hospital, he was reintroduced to the devil.

He wrote to me, because Mom refused to read his "rantings" anymore.

Dear Ebenezer:

They won't let me out of this cage, even to walk the hallway. I am by myself all the time. They fear my powers of conversion. It's too early yet for martyrdom. I seek God's wisdom in this, but He has been silent thus far. You must help me. You will be the instrument of my liberation. I must continue my ministry. I miss you all so much. In literary terms, which you understand best, being alone like this is a broken metaphor, gone plain. It's like being narrowed and honed to simplistic sorrow, edges removed, in preparation for the eventuality of disappearance, water running over a stone. I am evaporating! Free me, my dear son! You will. I have dreamt it.

Your loving father,

I AM

He didn't write anymore after the electric shock treatments began. The first time they came for him, he went with the attendants eagerly, delighted to escape his solitary cell, convinced that I had somehow arranged for his release. The second time, he had screamed and struggled all the way down to the therapy room on the main floor. The third time, they had to shove a rubber biter in his mouth before they wired him, since it diminished the effect the screaming had on their nerves.

After a dozen "treatments," his hands began to shake. His heartbeat became irregular. His memory clouded. He made up his mind not to be electrocuted anymore. Though he was fifty-one, and a gentle man by nature, he fought them off one September day with a pipe that he had worked loose from the drain in his bathroom. It had taken them three hours to get him out of the room and downstairs. Two of the six attendants had been badly hurt—one with a fractured skull, the other with three broken ribs and a punctured lung. Dad's God was Old Testament that day.

After that, the doctors at Ypsilanti put tranquilizers in his food and wheeled him to his torture, strapped to a gurney. He had seventy-two shock treatments before he admitted that God's visit was an illusion. They let him come home. Mom never believed that he was cured. He simply returned to the abysmal depression that had preceded his mania. You can make a man *say* anything, but he'll believe what he wants. Somewhere inside George Riveridge, God was still talking, albeit with a still, small voice.

I knew that Dad's return to his job and family was a most extraordinary act of courage. His work drained him, and at home at night, he only sat and stared at the television. Grandma had died in his absence. He never spoke of her. He would nod when I talked to him, smile when he was supposed to—as on his birthday, or Christmas, answering questions in laconic brevity. He would not be engaged in any kind of meaningful dialogue. That was reserved for God.

The rest of his life was like this. Euphoria, institutionalization, release, depression, euphoria again. He went back to Ypsilanti in 1968, 1970, 1973, 1976, 1984, 1989. He couldn't let go of the vision. Under the influence of drugs, he finally told one of the doctors about the abuse he'd suffered as a child. Mom was flabbergasted when the psychiatrist told her. Ruth and I were appalled. Although he was pronounced cured several times and, after 1973, kept on a reasonably even keel by a drug called lithium, he never ceased to be a manic-depressive, the label for his hope. When he died in a nursing home in 1990, he still believed in his vision.

Chapter Five

Fata Morgana

I cannot express it; but surely you and every body have a notion that there is, or should be, an existence of yours beyond you. What were the use of my creation if I were entirely contained here?

—Emily Bronte, *Wuthering Heights*

Arthur Hill High School was named for a lumber baron in Saginaw who had become enormously wealthy by ruining forests. Consequently, Mr. Hill had funneled a part of his considerable fortune into building the school so that he would be remembered for something else. Theodore Roethke, the poet, was one of its distinguished alumni. His sister, June, had been my English teacher. I met Morgan in this place.

It was her dark eyes that turned me away from childhood. She saw through me, into me, somehow. My privacy was corrupted at first glance. I couldn't do secret things anymore, because Morgan was watching with God's eyes. I didn't understand that it was because of the image of her face, omnipresent in my mind.

She looked at me, that's all—and smiled. But the smile was more a part of her eyes than her mouth. The rest of her was incorporated into her eyes, like the moon draws the firmament to its glow and dominates the night. I wasn't surprised to learn later that she was already in love with me. Although Morgan wouldn't live to see it, both of our children eventually divorced their spouses, believing that their love, as we had told them of ours so many times, should also have been that spontaneous. Perhaps it is, or perhaps it's not allowed for everyone.

In January, 1964, I followed Morgan Woodson out of the door of our American History class into our own. I fought through

28

the crowds, desperate to keep sight of her, like a vision at sea. She wore a bright yellow dress. Otherwise, I would have lost her. I would have seen her in class the next day, of course, but I felt then, as I do now, that what happened had to happen that day, or not at all. It was a thing predestined, and time would corrupt it. I didn't think this out. I only sensed it, like a deer feels the hunter. I understood it purely—to the point of panic.

I pursued the swatch of color, leaning to it like a flower to the sun, afraid that its sudden disappearance behind the dark cloud of students would cause me to wither, shutting down the photosynthetic chemistry that I now felt dying in my green veins. I sensed that I was changing myself. If she escaped, I wouldn't be able to think or feel anymore. She stopped, and began casually working the combination to her locker door, fully aware that I was approaching to change us forever, though she did not, never would, look back. I sensed the rivers in my veins beginning to flow again.

I stood behind her, breathless, like some obedient dog. I only lacked the stick in my mouth. I could smell immortality. Still facing her locker, she said: "You're Bennie Riveridge."

I couldn't understand how her voice could be so unremarkable, especially when she turned, and in the dark windows of her eyes I saw my own reflection, quivering in the half-light of morning that joins opposites. I looked down at my hands because her eyes were too dark and too full of light to sustain the image. So I missed the tragedy, though it was there, waiting. "You know my name," I managed. "How?"

"I asked around."

"Why?"

"I had to separate you."

"From what?"

"From the rest."

"Why?"

"Because you're in love with me," she said.

She laughed in a way that identified her. It would become a

signal, a kind of radar. I would find her in department stores, airports, and other crowded places, by honing in on it. She laughed every day, including the last time I talked to her.

The eyes. She knew me already. It occurred to me that I ought to tell her that she was being egotistical, presumptuous. Maybe the whole world didn't think she was God's gift. But I knew she was. "I need to know your name," I heard myself say.

"You're behind in this courtship, Bennie."

"What?"

"I'm Morgan Woodson and I won't marry you until after graduation, but that's only about five months away. The rest is up to you." Then she strolled away, leaving me to consider how I had lived to be eighteen as only half a person. The waters inside me clouded, grew murky, slowed to stagnancy.

The eternity of that night almost killed me. The next day, we began to erase what we had been. I ceased to be Ben or Bennie or Ebenezer. I would not be referred to individually again for thirty years. I became one half of us: Morgan and Ben. I didn't mind at all, no fuss about lost freedom. My survival was not the perpetuation of my species anyway. It was, more likely, the endangerment of everyone else's. It's all point of view. It's how we name the thing. Devotion or slavery is up to us. In my case, the river had to flow.

Morgan told me that she had dreamt of me before she had known who I was—not in a figurative, but a literal way. She had not seen Prince Charming, but my face, the face of Ben Riveridge. In other words, her dream was specific, not misted over in generalities. That was how she knew, and she had accepted it without understanding, much in the way she accepted the possibility of such things.

She was not an intellectual, but metaphors were not lost on her—only clichés. She could never get them right. "It's like looking for a straw in a haystack," she would pronounce while searching for a missing shoe. Or, "that's the needle that broke the camel's back," while instructing me on the amount of detergent to put in the washing machine. She recognized romance and was, at heart, a poet. We moved through the world in fluid rhythm like the liquid that flows through all things alive—milk, sap, blood, water. We each felt the other in the pulse.

We believed in each other in the same way that my father believed in his vision of God. Truth was truth, and the apathy of others didn't matter.

To me, Morgan was Eve, Helen, Sophia and Mary. She was the seductress, the emotive beauty, the wisdom, the virtue of woman. No qualities had been denied her and so distraction by another was impossible.

I was astounded then, when my mother raised objections to our marriage. Her primary argument was that Morgan had no interest in furthering her education beyond high school (which was true), and therefore would prevent me from attending the university (which was not). I was baffled that Mom should betray her own philosophy. She had taught me to believe that *Green Mansions* and *The Woman in White* and *Jane Eyre* were real. How could she now deny all that, when Morgan was the culmination, the practitioner of my education. But Jennie abandoned her role as teacher and became Mother. That is to say, the psyche was enveloped in the heart.

It didn't matter. Mom had taught me too well. At a drive-in movie, in August of 1964, I told Morgan that I loved her. It was no surprise to her that I should state the obvious. I remember the details of that night: the way that my hand rested on the soft skin just above her knee and below the hem of her shorts; the gentle thickness of her dark hair, like silk, against my face; the lovely aroma of her neck; the sigh when I kissed her, her breath, sweet with Juicy Fruit gum; my hand on the swell of her breast, incredibly pliant beneath the blouse and lacy bra. But of all things, the sense of coming home. Whatever else should happen, I knew I had found what I had to have. Epiphany. Revelation. As great a message as God could give. Truth, beauty, love.

"I want us to get married, Morgan," I told her.

She studied my face for a moment, but she had it memorized from dreams. Her eyes penetrated, full of self-abnegation. "Do you know, Bennie? Do you really *know*, like I do?"

"Yes."

"Do you?"

"Yes."

"How?"

"When I saw you, when you looked at me, I knew. I saw completeness, wholeness, like a path heading home. Am I making any sense?"

She kissed me. Behind misted windows, we lost our virginity. Morgan would later laugh about it. How can a person lose something that they were never intended to keep? She said it was like an infant nursing for the first time. Should the world mourn over its appetite?

* * *

Morgan died four years ago. For me, every day after that opened like a lion's jaw, imploring me to get a firmer grip on mortality. Tomorrows, for me, became obsolete, but I didn't run out of yesterdays. I remembered everything and my grief was Promethean, the tearing of my soul by the talons of memory. It's a high price to pay for a little warmth.

Until I saw her again, standing there by the creek, I looked at rain differently. I could see in the dark. Silence was not something I envied anymore.

A rainbow had arched across the skyline of downtown Grand Rapids on the morning of her death. I saw it through the hospital window. I had held her hand all night. It was, I remember, strangely warm. We had rushed here in the dawn of the previous day, when I woke to hear her struggling for breath and felt the fierce grip of her hand on my careless arm. The EMTs recognized it immediately as cardiac arrest. They'd shoved me aside as they pumped electricity into her on our bedroom floor. They brought her heart back but, as my father could have told them, you can't save the mind with electricity. All night, she was hooked to machines that couldn't restore her, while she slept in another country. They wanted me to donate her eyes. I said: "No, they belong to God."

* * *

When I met Morgan's mother for the first time, Elyda Woodson had disapproved of me. Like my mother, she didn't want her child to get married at such a tender age and, she told me, quite frankly, that her daughter didn't really love me at all. She was just in love with the idea of love. Elyda was, I later discovered, confused about the subject because she didn't know what love was and assumed that everyone else was equally mystified.

She was a tiny, small-boned woman, who had suffered a good deal in her life as was evidenced by her pinched smile, which was more fortitudinal than a manifestation of any inner joy. As a child, she had contracted polio and her right leg was withered. She walked with a decided limp. Her father, an alcoholic cop, had been killed in a high-speed chase when Elyda was a teen-ager. She had two older sisters, both of whom were great beauties. One became pregnant before marriage, the other had been raped. Elyda's mother had lost a long, terrible struggle with cancer. Shortly after, Elyda had suffered the death of her first daughter, only weeks after its birth. The infant would have been Morgan's older sister. Elyda's greatest tragedy, however, was marrying Morgan's father. Except for the atrophied leg, Elyda Schmidt, like her sisters, had been beautiful. Because of the leg, she had settled for the first man to show any interest in her—Harlan Woodson.

Harlan's people were from Iowa. His father had been a butter-maker and a bona fide member of the Ku Klux Klan. When Harlan was in his twenties, he had died of pancreatic cancer. The Woodsons had moved to Michigan when Harlan was a boy. He grew into a big, homely, almost effeminate man who, like every bigot, completely understood the world. He hated all minorities and was the worst kind of hypocrite—always publicly polite to those he casually referred to privately as 'chinks,' 'coons,' 'kikes,' 'spics,' and 'micks.' I always thought it remarkable that Harlan's racism and bias had never taken root in Morgan. I thought it an even greater miracle that she loved her father.

The first conversation I ever had with Harlan involved what he called the "inability" of African-Americans to be swimmers and divers. The Olympic trials were being televised and I was sitting in the Woodson living room, waiting for Morgan to finish primping. Harlan had just awakened from his after-dinner nap. Elyda was washing the dishes.

"See there, young man," he said, pointing at the television. "There's not a single nigger on the American swimming team. You know why?"

I was, as yet, blissfully unaware of Harlan's world-view. I shrugged my shoulders. "Discrimination?"

"Naw, use your common sense. Them days are over. They go out of their way now to give niggers whatever they want. Keeps 'em from rioting." "They," was Harlan's favorite pronoun. When used in a conspiratorial sense, "they" was usually synonymous with "the Jews." Otherwise, "they" served as the supreme philosophical authority for his own arguments. "No, it's their glands," he said.

"What?"

"Yeah. They don't have the same glands we do, to make 'em float, you know? Most of 'em are scared to death of the water. That's why they don't bathe."

"Where did you hear about this?"

"I dunno," he mumbled as he lit a cigarette. "It's common knowledge. Heard it ever since I was a kid. It's kinda like men having one less rib than women—because of God taking one to make Eve, you know."

Eventually, I would learn to ignore him, but this was the first time I'd had to deal with Harlan's tripe and I couldn't let it pass. "Isn't it possible that most black people in America can't afford swimming pools for their children to train in? They've been denied jobs and education. Olympic contenders start early. Swimming is an expensive sport. You don't see too many black golfers either. Not a lot of country clubs in their neighborhoods."

Harlan sighed. His expression said he was trying to be patient with an ignorant child. "You obviously got to read more, boy. This here's been scientifically proven. It was in the National Geographic or some such magazine."

Fortunately, Morgan appeared and I was rescued. In the years to come, I would have to suffer Harlan's pontifications on why the Roman Empire fell (lead poisoning), why Hank Aaron beat Babe Ruth's home run record (the pitchers were instructed by "them" to throw only gopher balls), why there was increased immorality in movies (Jewish film producers trying to corrupt Christian children), why Bobby Kennedy was assassinated (a Muslim crusade to destroy Catholicism), etc. All this came from what Harlan called "ancestral knowledge" and "common sense."

To give him credit, Harlan made a good living, at least in terms of money. He'd become a real estate salesman, then a broker, at a time when getting a license could be done through the mail. He ran the Harlan Woodson Real Estate Agency out of his home and he did know how to "wheel and deal," as he put it. It was fortunate that he didn't have to work anywhere that would require him to take orders or get along with people who didn't believe as he did.

In addition, he had his own band. His mother had taught him to play the piano and he was pretty good, as long as he didn't have to stretch much beyond chording. His band played in bars across the state. The biggest draw was his voice. He could sing in a beautiful baritone that would bring tears to his audience's eyes. It always amazed me that there could be so little depth of feeling behind it. He could sing *Danny Boy* with what appeared to be profound empathy and, immediately following, talk about how the "Micks" were ruining the country and that Lee Harvey Oswald had done the USA a big service when he shot that bead-fumbling asshole in the White House. He didn't know that *Danny Boy* was the Irish tune, *Londonderry Air*. When I told him, he said that it figured that the Micks would call it that, since Ireland was the ass-end of the British Empire. I was surprised that he knew what a derriére was.

He also owned what he called the Harlan Woodson Entertainment Agency. For a ten percent fee, he booked shows, mostly striptease, for private parties. Neither his racism, nor his questionable moonlighting affected his community standing. He did what was important to most people: he made money and he went to church. He'd become a Lutheran for Elyda's sake; the conversion made easier when someone told him that the Great Reformer had been anti-Semitic. He sang in, and later directed, the church choir. He was always chagrined because, despite his stature, no one ever asked him to serve on the Board of Elders.

He'd been in the army during World War II. He was proud of the fact that he'd been with Merrill's Marauders, building roads, mostly in India and Burma. Fortunately, he'd never seen service in Europe. If he had, he might have gone over to the Nazis. To me, the only downside to that would have been that Morgan would never have existed. Harlan admired Hitler and could never understand why such a great man would have allied himself with a "bunch of chinks."

He privately explained to me, after Morgan and I were married, how he'd had sex with an Indian whore in the middle of a busy street in Calcutta. He'd done it on a dare, he said, while his G.I. buddies watched and cheered him on. He'd won twenty bucks for his infidelity to Elyda, who waited for him in Michigan with, I was sure, little anticipation. I told him that I found his story taste-less. Harlan had responded angrily that the woman wasn't white, after all, and thus, didn't count. He didn't expect anyone who loved poetry, he said, to understand the manliness of his actions. Poets had "too many female hormones." I asked him if he wanted me to behave similarly, as Morgan's husband. He said he wasn't worried. He doubted if I could do it anyway. Occasionally he could be right, although almost always by accident.

Elyda objected to me because she hated her own marriage. She drank excessively, probably to anesthetize her soul. Under the influence of both liquor and unhappiness, she often said things she didn't want to mean. She hated her life with Harlan. He was crude, unfaithful, bigoted, vulgar and ignorant. She had none of these Pecksniffian traits, but she tolerated her slavery to Harlan in order to be emancipated from her family's pity. Her withered leg ruled her.

She had been determined, when Morgan was born, to prepare her for a life of dependence on the right man. She used Harlan's money to send her to private elementary schools, to associate her with the most influential people. She insisted that Morgan be beautiful, a directive that Morgan fulfilled without effort. She trained her to look for the right man. I was not that man. Nobody was.

Unfortunately for Elyda, Morgan could not be intimidated or deterred, once she'd made a decision. I could not be removed. Consequently, Elyda rolled up her maternal sleeves and went about the challenging work of trying to fit me to the right-man image, to reinvent me. The first order of business was religion. I must be a Lutheran.

I was invited to dinner at the Woodsons the day after Morgan had told her parents that she was going to marry me. I didn't know that I was to be the entrée. They said Luther's Common Table Prayer, which allowed one to thank God without really having to talk to him. We were munching on salad when Elyda raised the question. Her face was pinched as she spoke, and she didn't look up. It was her habit. She didn't like to see Harlan, who resembled a pig at trough, dropping lettuce and salad dressing on his shirt. "What faith are you associated with, Ben?"

It seemed both a presumptuous and an innocuous query.

Morgan rolled her eyes, but didn't rescue me. "Christianity," I answered. "I was baptized a Presbyterian."

"Are you still?"

"Presbyterian? Not a very good one, I'm afraid. I don't go to church much."

Elyda seemed pleased rather than upset, perhaps believing that it was easier to convert a confused wolf than a convinced sheep.

"Do you believe in God?"

"Mom!" Morgan was getting annoyed by the interrogation.

"Well, if you want to get married, Darling, it will have to be in our church. You know that, unless you want to get married in a civil ceremony. Pastor Himmelsbach will ask the same things. Benjamin..."

"Ben," I corrected.

"Ben will have to know the right things to say."

I wondered how she would react if I told her that my father thought that he was Jesus Christ. Instead, I said: "Yes, I do believe in God. I read *Thanatopsis* once and didn't get much comfort from knowing I'd be mulch in a gigantic graveyard. That's when I decided there must be a God."

"I'm not familiar with that, um, book."

"It's a poem."

Harlan snickered.

"That poem then. Have you read Luther?"

"Some. My mother wanted me to read everything."

"What did you think?"

"Faith alone. Scripture alone. That confused me."

"Why?"

"Because only one thing can be alone."

Morgan laughed. Harlan was trying to wipe steak blood off his chin and work a monstrous bite of sirloin down his throat. "Listen, Ben," he said, the half-chewed meat quite visible in his open mouth, "the only thing you have to worry about as a Lutheran

38

is to believe what the Bible says. You can do that, can't you? That's what I did. Simple thing."

I didn't know if he was referring to the process of belief as simple, or to himself for doing it. "You mean literally?"

"Please keep your mouth shut Harlan...when you chew," Elyda said, twisting a finger through her bleached hair. She turned to me. "Everything in scripture is based on the testimony of eye witnesses. It's meant to be taken as literal truth."

"I don't mean to be argumentative or disrespectful, Mrs. Woodson, but what about, say, Cain's wife? I remember Darrow asking, in the Scopes Trial, where she came from. No one ever gave him an answer."

"I don't know, Ben. But absence of explanation doesn't necessarily indicate error."

"It doesn't mean truth, either."

Later, when we were alone in my car, Morgan asked me if I really wanted to marry her. I said that I did.

"Then turn Lutheran," she said. "We'll sort it out later."

"You want me to sacrifice my conscience for a wedding?"

"No. It's much simpler than that. I want to know that you'd do anything for me. I want a big wedding. This is the only way to get it. Your parents aren't going to pay for it and you can't afford it. It'll keep the peace."

"Fundamentalism puts God in a box."

"Then don't be fundamentalist. They're the only ones who argue over whose religion is correct. I know we were brought together, by God." She kissed me. "Do you think it was God?"

"Yes. Morgan. If I said I couldn't do what you're asking, what would happen to us?"

I saw the street lamp reflected in her eyes—a dim, half-light. "I'd probably lose my family. I wouldn't get my wedding and I'd be pissed."

"But it wouldn't keep us apart?"

"No."

"We'd still get married?"

"Yes. But the honeymoon wouldn't be nearly as much fun."

We were wed on a Saturday in February, shortly after my confirmation. We had to be back on Tuesday. I'd gotten a job in the GM factory, below the offices where Dad continued in his role as Supervisor of Production Control and, secretly, as Messiah. I was also enrolled for night classes at the local junior college. Morgan took a job as a teller at a savings and loan. Neither of us could be gone for more than a few days.

We rented a house on the south side, too close, in Harlan's opinion, to what he referred to as "niggertown." The wedding was a sad affair for both mothers who commiserated over the mismatch, each carefully concealing her belief that the other's child was not worthy of hers, and couching that thesis in expressions of general regret—too young, not educated, etc. Dad said very little, although I knew that he disapproved. He loved Morgan, I think, but he thought she would prevent me from obtaining my education, and he believed that I must have it or, to use his phrase, "spend the rest of your life working with your hands." This, to him, was a backward slide down the ladder of human evolution. But he was too lost in his own forest of musings to raise any serious objections. The future was something too vast to consider. For him, looking back was the only way, no matter how painful, to ever see what was ahead. Harlan reveled in the pomp. As father of the bride, he loved being the center of attention. He accepted the accolades of his friends for his touching rendition of *One Hand, One Heart*. He ignored Morgan because he was too busy entertaining. He sang several songs at the reception that were moving—to everyone but him. He didn't notice when Morgan and I left for our honeymoon.

We drove a hundred miles to Detroit in the worst snowstorm I could remember. I could barely see through the massive white curtain that blanketed Interstate 75. Few motorists braved the late hour and the blizzard conditions, and most of those few were pulled off the road. Morgan was oblivious to the danger. She had one thing on her mind and she was enjoying torturing me as I struggled to keep going, even at twenty miles an hour. She kept rubbing my leg, whispering in my ear, kissing the sensitive skin just under my jaw, all of which I found wonderfully frustrating.

"If you don't stop that, Mrs. Riveridge," I moaned over the whirring of the heater fan, "we'll be dead soon." I'd only heard two people referred to as Mrs. Riveridge—my mother and grandmother, and I didn't like the sound of it applied to Morgan, especially in my own voice. It had a vague, strangely incestuous connotation.

Morgan ignored me and continued to nuzzle my neck, bringing her hand further up my leg to rest casually on my groin. "Do you really want me to stop this?" she said.

"Yes," I lied.

"That's what you say. You twitched. You always twitch when you lie. Besides, my little friend down here says differently." She gripped me and I gasped. When I managed to steal a look at her, she was watching my face, closely. I could see the pleasure she was gaining from her mastery of me.

"If you don't stop that, your little friend is going to erupt and he won't be of any use to you when we....if we get to the motel."

She sighed and moved her hand away, but she continued to tease me with her mouth, gently biting my ear lobe and whispering what she planned to do to me if I ever got us to Detroit. My heart was throbbing so heavily, that for a moment I thought that I could feel my coat moving with it in unison.

I closed my eyes, for no more than a second or two, visualizing quite vividly the portrait she was painting with her words. When I opened them, there was a human shadow moving directly in front of the car, running through the thick whiteness like a dark ghost. I pulled the wheel quickly to my right, swerving off the road and into the embankment, where mounds of snow left from the plows brought the car to an abrupt halt.

"Who was that? Did you see that guy?"

The headlights revealed nothing but the distant darkness and sweeping snow. The windshield wipers beat laboriously back and forth. "He looked like he was in trouble. He was waving his arms around," Morgan said. The colors of passion were gone from her cheeks, replaced by the wan discoloration of fear. "You didn't hit him, did you?"

"No, I'm sure I didn't." I felt a vague panic set in. But whether it was caused by my concern for the shadowy figure or the prospect of being stranded in a blizzard, I wasn't sure. I sat for a moment, gripping the wheel, trying to consider what to do next. "I'd better get out and see if I can push us backward out of the bank and back onto the highway. You take the wheel."

Within a few minutes I managed, with a good deal of tire spinning and backbreaking effort, to get us back on the road. I fell into the deep snow twice when the car lurched back into position on the interstate. I returned to the car half-frozen.

When I finally quit shivering and caught my breath, Morgan suggested that we should try to back up and see if we could find the man who had jumped in front of us. "He might be stranded," she said. "Maybe his wife and kids are sitting in a car a few yards behind us. We'd never have seen them in this snow. We have to go back."

The eroticism of the previous few minutes still gripped me. Cold as I was in every other respect, I was not enthusiastic to delay our honeymoon any further, but I knew she was right. I could see no headlights except my own, either behind us, in front, or on the other side of the interstate. There was only the dark and the swirling snow.

I shifted to reverse and backed up cautiously, attempting to stay on the swiftly disappearing expressway and still avoid any traffic that might be coming, though no cars had passed us in the twenty minutes that we'd been stopped. In the headlights, I could see the tire tracks, rapidly filling, where I had swerved to avoid the man. He should have been somewhere nearby, and I kept asking Morgan if she saw anything. Her responses were continually negative, though she was peering intently into the wild night.

"He can't have gone far," I said. "We're a good fifty yards in front of the place where we began to go off the road. Where could he have gone? He just disappeared."

"Where could he have come from?" Morgan asked. She looked distressed and anxious. "Pull over to the right," she said. Her brow was furrowed and I knew there was no point in arguing. "We'll have to get out and look."

"Morg, listen...."

"We can't just leave, Ben. I don't think the guy even had a coat on. He looked like he was older, maybe thirty-five or forty. He won't last very long out here."

I sighed, I think, or it would have been like me to do so. I lifted the door handle, then felt her hand pulling at my jacket. "Wait a minute," she said.

"What?"

"I don't know. I just felt...something. I don't think you're supposed to go out there."

"Are you okay? What's the matter?"

She looked pale, too pale for the cold. "I think you should drive on. We'll stop at the first place where we see a light and call the state police. They can search better than we can. Okay?"

"Okay. You all right?"

"Yes."

"What was it?"

"A feeling.... I don't know. It was strange."

We pulled back onto what I hoped was the interstate. We couldn't see any tire tracks, either where we had gone into the snow bank or where we had backed up.

We were considerably sobered and Morgan sat on her side of the car, staring out at the storm. "Where could he have come from?" she said, more to herself than to me. "There're no cars

43

anywhere. Why would someone be outside in this storm, without a coat, in the middle of the night, wandering around on the interstate?"

My nose was almost touching the steering wheel as I strained to see where I was going. "I don't know," was all I could manage.

We crawled along at fifteen miles an hour for twenty minutes or so until we finally discovered a gas station just off the expressway at the end of an exit ramp. I called the state police who assured us that they would investigate immediately. I was able to give them the exact location because I had counted the miles on the odometer. I explained that we were heading to Detroit on our honeymoon and gave them the name of the motel where we would be staying if they had any more questions. I filled the tank and inched back onto the interstate. Morgan didn't mention the incident again. The phone call seemed to have erased her concern. It took another two hours to travel the last forty miles to our exit. We heaved a collective sigh of relief when we saw the bright sign in front of the motel. There was a large swan swimming in the lights below the neon lettering which read: "Leda's Haven."

After checking in at the desk, we drove to our room that—like most motel rooms in the sixties—had an exterior entrance. Once inside, Morgan called her mother to let her know that we'd arrived safely and asked her to call my parents. It was five o'clock in the morning. I heard Morgan explaining about the man on the interstate and the storm, as I went back outside to retrieve our luggage from the trunk of the car. As I left, Morgan whispered "hurry," and licked her lips in such a lascivious fashion that she left me no doubt as to the reason for the urgency.

Outside, I tried to open the trunk. The lock wouldn't respond to the key, which I bent in my shivering frustration. The wind blew the wet snow against my face, stinging me like dozens of hornets. I went back inside, willing to forget the luggage for the night, but Morgan had purchased special lingerie for her honeymoon and had no intention of allowing the frozen lock to thwart her plans. This night had to be subservient to her imagination and, therefore, so did I. I went back outside and, with a brick I worked loose from the wall that surrounded the obsolete swimming pool, I hammered the key straight. I returned to the car, pulled out my Zippo lighter and, cupping it carefully in my red and frozen hands, I assaulted the recalcitrant lock with its flame. After consuming all of the lighter fluid, I forced the key in, and gave it one, last turn. Mercifully, the trunk popped open.

Back inside, I set the suitcases down and removed my sodden coat. Morgan was just saying good-bye to her mother. She replaced the phone in its cradle. She rose from the bed, pulled back the covers, and told me to undress as she fetched one suitcase and headed for the bathroom. "Try not to think about me," she snickered as she closed the door. I took off my wet clothes and slipped between the warm sheets

Following her advice, I picked up the Gideon Bible and opened it. My father had once told me that when you open the Scriptures, God always directs you to the right passage. I wasn't sure I needed guidance that moment, but I certainly required distraction. It opened to Proverbs. "There be three things which are too wonderful for me, yea, four, which I know not: The way of an eagle in the air; the way of a serpent upon a rock; the way of a ship in the midst of the sea; and the way of a man with a maid."

When I looked up, Morgan was standing at the foot of the bed, and I knew my father had been right.

Chapter Six

Oz

A man's life of any worth is a continual allegory.
    —John Keats, in a letter to Benjamin Bailey,
    November 22, 1817

We were allowed three weeks of halcyon days before the United States Government decided that my life could be better spent serving its interests. The letter from the Selective Service System struck like a tornado, uprooting my reality and spinning me away from home. I told them I was a student. I told them I was married. The draft board replied that they didn't recognize student status unless it was full time, nor did they see any validity in a marriage without children. In their view, my life was worth the risk.

I was ordered to report to the Wayne County Armory in Detroit for a physical exam. I passed. It was the only time in my life that I regretted good health. On the test to determine one's psychological profile, I tried to answer every question absurdly and included an additional essay about the family history of manic depression and its tendency to genetic inheritance. I failed to understand that they wanted killers, and that my bizarre profile would only make me more desirable.

When I realized that there'd be no escape from military service, I enlisted in the Air Force. I had two reasons. First, although enlisting would mean four years' active duty instead of the two that draftees served in the army, the air seemed safer than the ground. Perhaps, the recruiter told me, I would never have to leave the States. Secondly, it would delay departure for basic training by three months, allowing Morgan and me to spend the summer together.

Time collapsed on us. We saw it, for the first time in our young lives, as the Enemy. Every tick of the clock signaled the coming separation and created a terrible strain. Neither of us could bear the thought of it. We clung to each other at night, as if by doing so, we could become a single person and avoid the inevitable. We saw a program on TV about Siamese twins. Morgan said she wished we could be like that, joined physically. We never watched the newscasts. All they did was report death.

I was scheduled to leave for basic training in Texas on September first, a Monday. On Saturday morning, we lay in bed in our tiny, one-bedroom, rented house. I'd taken a military leave of absence from my job on the assembly line. I'd finished my night classes at school. We were both awake, but silent. Morgan's head rested naturally in the crook of my arm. She was born to fit there. "I don't want you to go," she said.

"I don't want to go. I don't have a choice."

"We could go to Canada."

I rolled on my side to look at her. I could see the effect of the moonlight in her eyes. "You really think you'd want to do that?"

"We'd be together."

"We'd never see our families again."

"You have to understand, Ben, in the deepest sense. I can't lose you. I can't. We're connected. I can't explain, I just...I just..." She began to cry. She seemed so weak and confused, vulnerable. With a grim smile of resolution, she erased the rivulets of fear that wetted her cheeks and she kissed me. In moments, we were naked, physically joined, if only temporarily.

My bus left at 6:30 on Monday morning. I was taken to Detroit Metro Airport and flown to Texas. Morgan and I were separated for the next eight weeks, dead lions but living dogs. Basic training was grueling heat, scorpions, dust, and as much humiliation as the troglodytic drill instructors could dispense. Amarillo was as close to hell as I ever wanted to go. Surprisingly, I could not be touched by it all. I'd left the sensitive "awareness" part of me with Morgan. Drill Sargent Anderson, a very short man, was frustrated by his tall recruit, whom he could not reach. I was stone. I could not be made to cry or complain or grimace or become angry. Anderson wrote in his evaluation that I would make an excellent soldier. He didn't understand that he was only observing a man without a soul.

In early October, I "graduated" from basic training. I was promoted and assigned to Turner Air Base in Albany, Georgia. The government, in its infinite wisdom, decided that I would make a good cartographer, so I began the process of learning how to make maps with the 1370th Photo-Mapping Squadron. I guess it was as good a job as any for a man who felt totally lost.

Morgan was allowed to join me. I rented a little duplex apartment on a road of red clay lined with Georgia pines. These housing units were specifically designed for military personnel. They were close to the base—actually at the end of the flight line, so that everything rattled constantly as the planes took off and landed. The duplexes were made of red brick. I think someone must have thought this would provide its tenants with a homier atmosphere. Each Spartan unit had a kitchen, a bedroom, a bathroom and a living room. Nothing was carpeted. All the floors were covered in dull gray linoleum. The walls were whitewashed. A laundromat was located at the end of the clay road, undoubtedly owned by the same person who had built the duplexes without space or hook-up for a washer or dryer. The sign in the front window proclaimed: NO COLOREDS. Harlan would have been pleased.

The duplex was the only living quarters I could find within walking distance of the base. I didn't own a car. Morgan flew down from Michigan just before Christmas. When I saw her emerge from the umbilical that attached the plane to the terminal, I felt reborn. I became animated again. The smile on my own face seemed unnatural. For the last eight weeks I'd been a dumb beast. The sight and feel of her brought me back—the path home.

We hired a taxi to get to the duplex. I remember the wry

smile of the driver, who probably observed such reunions with regularity. He tolerated the gushy endearments and heavy breathing with admirable aplomb.

When we stepped inside our new home, I turned on the lights. She frowned. "It's nice," she lied.

"It's all I could find for the money." I plugged in the lights on the Christmas tree, hoping this would alleviate the starkness of the flat. She laughed. "Oh Bennie," she giggled, "that's the saddest-looking tree I've ever seen."

"My intentions were good," I argued.

"Hell is paid with good intentions," she answered. I didn't correct her.

Later, I would always think of that tree when I watched *A Charlie Brown Christmas* with our children. She joked about it for years, telling family and friends how pitiful it was. My children still tell the story, when the holiday rolls around. I never again bought a tree like it. I think it'd been symbolic of my mood. I remember it better than any other since.

She'd brought with her a box tied with a red bow. It was the only thing we carried in from the cab that wasn't luggage. She made me open it right away. It was a portable television, a tiny black and white with an antenna that broke off less than a month later. The screen was small enough so that we had to sit within a few feet of it to watch. It only allowed us two channels.

"It's a gift from my mom and dad. They didn't want me to go without the comforts of home. They knew you'd fail to provide for me properly. Judging from that tree, I can see they were right." She grinned and put her arms around my neck. She always had to stand on her toes to do it, since I was six-three. I loved her smile, which was so much a part of her eyes. It was natural for her to smile, but her father had told her that her full and sensuous mouth reminded him of "nigger lips." She knew that I loved her full lips and she didn't see them as bad, but she spread them as widely as she could when she smiled, reducing their fullness, so that her father didn't have to suffer this "defect." It was an artifice that would always be a part of her naturalness.

Making love that December night in Georgia was an escape to another dimension. It was dark and warm and musky, like a winter burrow in the earth—the softness of her, the wonder of entry and union, something beyond vows or law, or time. It was the same merging of the fish that breathes water or the tree that draws from the soil—necessary to life. Morgan and I would wither without it.

Three months later, my father returned to Ypsilanti, unable to deny what God had told him to do. My mother despaired. She had to deal with Ella and Tommy-Jeff by herself most of the time. Ruth did what she could, but she had another baby and her time was spent attending to the very task for which she felt such guilt. Mom wrote to our congressman, trying to get me home on a hardship discharge, but the government didn't really believe in hardship and I think they knew that I didn't want to go back to Michigan. Anyway, I was already home.

Shortly after the holidays, I learned that Turner Air Base was to be closed and the 1370th would be moved to Forbes Air Base in Topeka, Kansas. Morgan's only comment was that perhaps there would be fewer cockroaches in the drier climate. She thought she was being pragmatic. I thought she was being romantic.

We found an apartment next to an Atlantic and Pacific Food Store in downtown Topeka. It was a huge, old house, chopped into four apartments. The broad porch in front that looked out on Harrison Street was for all the tenants' use, but Morgan and I were really the only ones to ever sit there, because the foyer leading to our apartment opened onto it. The other tenants could only access it from the outside. I could lean over the side of the porch and touch the wall of the A and P. It made for a lousy southerly view, but convenient shopping. We bought a car, an old Ford, since the base was several miles away. Morgan got a job as a teller in a bank, only a few blocks away, across from Macy's Department Store. She

50

walked to work.

There was a college in Topeka called Washburn University. It'd been badly damaged by a tornado a year earlier. Several buildings were in ruins. I registered there for classes and began, in earnest, to pursue a degree, taking one night class a semester.

After a year, we'd settled into a routine. Dad had returned home again, unable to bear the martyrdom that his situation required. I'd received two letters from him during his year's sabbatical. Tommy-Jeff was going to school without being escorted every day. Like Dad, he was beginning to understand that when you choose not to be forced, you become free. This was as democratic as life got, but I sympathized. We always got a much more interesting education at home.

They had winter in Kansas. Morgan and I would walk a few blocks down to the state capitol building on cold, snowy nights, enjoying the old-fashioned lights. Converted from gas to electricity, they lined the walkways leading to the capitol steps. Across the street was an old Episcopalian church, which was open twenty-four hours a day. We would duck in there when the weather became too fierce and warm ourselves for the trek home. We sat in the back pew, talking and kissing and worshipping God in our own way. No one ever bothered us. It was a sanctuary in the truest sense of the word.

Then, and always, we never tired of each other. We went to work each day, only in order to make the money necessary to keep us together. We hurried through time so that we could get home to our real lives. When I went to class, she often went with me, at least in reasonable weather. She would walk around the commons at dusk, waiting for me to take my break. She would always be waiting in the car when I was finished for the evening. We lived in each other's pockets—a fine, warm place to be.

One Sunday afternoon in early summer we took a picnic lunch to Gage Park. It was a lovely place. It contained a zoo and several acres of lush lawn and picnic tables abutting the Kansas

River. We laid a blanket out on the grass and just lay there watching the clouds, not much interested in food, really. A few feet away, the river rolled west. The sun broke from behind a cloud, forcing me to sit up to shield my eyes. I saw a swan on the river, which initially, since it didn't move, I mistook for an inflatable water toy. It was simply allowing itself to be carried along by the current. "Morgan, look!" I said.

She rose up, her eyes following my finger that traced the brilliant light of the sky to the shadowy darkness of the river. "It's beautiful," she said, rising and moving to the river's ridge to get a better look. I followed.

"Such immaculate whiteness," she said.

"Chaste nudity," I joked. But she nodded her head slowly in agreement, her eyes never wandering from the stoic splendor of the bird.

"Is it male or female?"

I told her I didn't know.

"I'll bet it's female," she said. "It's too beautiful to be male."

"In the animal kingdom, my dear, the males are generally the most attractive, particularly among birds."

"Maybe," she said, ignoring my cavalier presumption, "but this creature doesn't belong to any kingdom. It's alone." There was a shadowy discomfort in what she said, something that struck a part of me that I didn't yet know. The river carried the swan along. None of the other picnickers farther downriver took any notice.

"They mate for life. Its love must be gone." Morgan stood there for a few minutes more, watching the sad and stoic bird drift into another place, another memory.

I turned back to our blanket and discovered a little dog trying valiantly to break into the basket which held our sandwiches. As I approached, he didn't retreat, but took an aggressive stance, prepared to defend his dinner to the last. He wasn't much bigger than my foot and he must have believed that that part of my anatomy was his opponent, because he growled and snarled at my shoe as if it were not attached to the rest of me. His noisy protests brought Morgan running. He retreated when we collapsed on the blanket, but didn't move very far away. "Scat," I yelled.

"Don't," Morgan upbraided, "you'll scare him."

"That's the idea."

"Well, don't, or I'll bite you myself."

"Would you, please?"

"Stop."

She took some ham from one of the sandwiches and extended the morsel toward him. He crept closer, eyeing me to make sure that I didn't interfere with her generosity. He knew he had won her over. In a few minutes he was in Morgan's lap, happily chewing on more ham. My own hunger was left unsated. I swear, even now, that the little imp smiled and winked at me.

"Look!" Morgan said, fingering his collar. "There's an address on his tag. I don't think this street is very far away. Ben, why don't we take him in the car and see if we can get him back to his owner?"

"Is there a name on it?"

"A. Landon."

"Okay. But we'll stop and buy a mess of cheeseburgers on the way home."

"Deal."

Being strangers in a strange land, we carried a map of the city in the car. It wasn't too difficult to find the street that was, indeed, only a few blocks from the park.

"Pretty swanky neighborhood," I observed, as we moved slowly along the avenue, surrounded by magnificent homes. The smell of old money was everywhere. At the end of a line of giant cedars, a brick column held a brass plate that contained the matching numbers on the dog's collar. We turned onto the drive and were unexpectedly confronted with a colonial mansion of red brick and white pillars that more properly belonged in

Williamsburg. The house and surrounding acreage had to be worth millions, but there was no gate, no security. Anyone could wander in, as we were proving. The name "Landon" had seemed familiar to me when Morgan had read the little dog's tag but strangely, the only image that came to mind was "Little Joe" on *Bonanza*. Now I remembered Alf Landon, the former governor of Kansas. He lost the presidency to FDR in the thirties, the worst defeat in the history of presidential elections to that time. Could he live here?

A distinguished-looking old man, dressed in a gray coat and baggy black pants, rose from his rocking chair between the pillars on the veranda and approached us, hearing the little dog barking hysterically down the winding approach. He was Alf Landon. After a joyful reunion with "Joe" (apparently the governor had watched the Cartwrights a few times too), he invited us to sit on the porch and instructed a servant to bring iced tea. I assailed him with a million questions about his career, his place in history. He wasn't at all reticent. I found him to be open and sincere. That did more toward explaining his loss in the election than anything else.

After an hour or more, Morgan finally pulled at my arm, indicating that we had caused Mr. Landon enough suffering for one afternoon. He offered a reward. We declined. He didn't press. Years later, I read about his death. He was very old. It affected me more than John Kennedy's. I hadn't believed in Camelot.

* * *

Doctor Kim Dong-Ho
Notes on the Second Interview with Ebenezer Riveridge
September 10, 2000 Ypsilanti State Hospital
The patient appeared less belligerent today. He still persisted in his delusions concerning Mrs. Hall, but seemed receptive to alternative interpretations of her role in his life. Strangely, Mrs. Hall had applied for a visitors' pass to see Mr. Riveridge in spite of the fact that she had previously obtained a restraining order

against him, which would seem to indicate her fear of him. I've scheduled an interview with Mrs. Hall in an attempt to discover her motivation for this unusual request. The patient is unaware of all of this and I've chosen to keep it from him for the present.

The patient's son and daughter and their spouses have visited him twice in his short tenure here. They were also by his side, I understand, throughout the legal proceedings. They appear to be devoted to him, and both have asked me not to dismiss what he believes without careful investigation. They love and respect him, I think, more than the average adult offspring, who are often too busy to bother with a widowed father. They don't believe he's delusional, and both have appealed the court's decision to have him incarcerated here, though it's only for a brief time. He has not been committed.

The patient also has a brother and sister who have, between them, visited three times. His sister, Ruth, is a kind woman who obviously loves her brother very much. Though nearing sixty, she looks much younger, There is an aura of indulgence about her that, mixed with a fierce loyalty, would make her the best of sisters, I should suspect. Thomas Jefferson Riveridge, like his brother, is highly intelligent and well-read, with a romantic nature that is present, but not nearly as pronounced, as that observed in his older sibling.

The only other visitor has been the custodian at the high school where the patient teaches. He was granted a pass on assurance from the family that he is Mr. Riveridge's close friend. I asked the patient about this man, whose name is Jack Csinos (pronounced Chee-nosh), since their occupations seemed so incongruous with their relationship. The patient described Mr. Csinos as "the most educated man in the school," though the latter's formal learning does not extend beyond high school. They were brought together, Mr. Riveridge told me, because of their mutual addictions to books and tobacco. They both smoke cigarettes and, since smoking, by state law, isn't allowed anywhere on school grounds, they drive next door to the parking lot of a bowling alley on breaks and at lunch to smoke and discuss literature. They socialize a bit outside of school and seem to know each other's families. Jack appears to be the patient's only close friend. Riveridge seems to have many people who care about him (he's been bombarded with letters from students and acquaintances), but these relationships are peripheral. I think he's experienced little intimacy with anyone beyond those people previously mentioned.

The session went fairly well. I pointed out to him his constant use of the word "hand" during this interview. As can be noted from listening to the recorded transcript, his conversation with me this time included such words and phrases as: "handy," "handsome," "high-handed," "hand-in-hand," "handshake," 'beforehand," "hands off," "the laying on of hands," and a Biblical allusion to Matthew 5:30; "If thy right hand offend thee..." When I pointed this out to him, he told me that he had intended to "tip his hand." He was, I'm sure, testing my powers of observation.

I told him that my name means "hands of the clock." His wry smile suggested that either he knew already (in which case he was constantly punning at my expense), or he simply accepted it as part of what he refers to as his "life's motif." I suspect the former explanation to be the most likely, given his apparent antipathy to doctors—or Vietnamese.

He told me about a song that he particularly admired called *The Hands of Time*. It was, he said, the theme to the motion picture *Brian's Song*. He said he listened to it continually after the sudden death of his wife, Morgan, three or four years ago. I purchased a recording of it in an effort to understand its significance to him. Several lines follow:

If the hands of time were hands that I could hold
I'd keep them warm and in my hands they'd not turn cold.
Hand-in-hand we choose, the moments that should last
The lovely moments that should have no future and no past.

At first, I believed that he was simply mocking me again, but then he began to expound on something he referred to as "Edenic Time," a concept which is not original with him, but one he has adopted, and the song's metaphors appear to promote. He defined it as a pre-historical or non-temporal existence, a point before or beyond time. It is, he said, another dimension, co-existing with society, but not really contained within human consciousness. He told me that we are aware of it only through the supernatural, archetypes, dreams, metaphors. It is a place of static innocence—motionless, arrested, suspended, soporific. It's possible, he believes, to move to this dimension, then return to "reality" through a kind of non-physical reincarnation (as paradoxical as those terms seem), still conscious, but only subliminally, of one's previous temporal existence. He believes that both of us (indeed, most of us), have returned from Edenic Time on several occasions. We discover the reasons for our interaction through metaphor. All of literature, he says, is devoted to discovering or, more properly, uncovering, where we have been and who we have been connected to.

He said that we don't ever live in the present completely, but in a past or future removed from historical, linear time—our own Eden, where moral criteria are absent and we live without guilt or judgment.

I confess that I was fascinated by his discourse and, though he was clearly animated, he did not appear at all irrational. We won't be able to keep him long.

He has connected this philosophy, in some way, with Mrs. Hall, who pressed charges against him for stalking her. He defied the restraining order, which led to his arrest and his temporary incarceration here (ninety days), for observation. The patient will not discuss Mrs. Hall, though she seems to be the focal point on which his philosophy centers.

Chapter Seven

Sparrows

That willing suspension of disbelief for the moment, which constitutes poetic faith.
—Samuel Taylor Coleridge, *Biographica Literaria*

It had never occurred to me that I was actually training for a reason. Cartography seemed like something to do while I waited out my enlistment and took literature courses at Washburn University. The Air Force, understandably, looked upon it as my avocation. They could be imaginative, too.

The reason manifested itself in the summer of 1968 when I received orders to be transferred to temporary duty at Tuy Hoa Air Force Base in the Republic of Vietnam. Good cartographers were in demand to draw directions so that the bombers wouldn't get lost on their way to the killing fields.

I went to my commanding officer and asked him why I'd been chosen from among the forty-six other men in my unit who had gone through the identical training. Many were single, I pointed out, and several even wanted to go. I gave him names. It didn't matter. I'd been dumb enough to finish first in my class. That was all that mattered. Strange, that later on it should matter so little. The captain told me that I had ten days to get ready.

Morgan was distraught. "I can't stand to think about it!" She was crying and pacing across the living room. It was the first time I'd seen her without courage. "You enlisted to avoid this. Oh, no, no! You could be...you could never...oh no!"

"I'll come back, Morg. I will. We aren't supposed to end this way."

"And how do you know that! Huh? Your father tell you?" She stopped. "Oh Bennie, I'm sorry. I didn't mean that. I'm just helpless and I know that you are, too. You can't keep your promise. You can't stop death."

"I just know." And I did know. "You're afraid, that's all." I tried to soothe her with a poor imitation of FDR: "Remember," I said, with my best Hudson Valley accent, "we have nothing to fear but fear itself."

"Bullshit!" she shouted. "Don't try to comfort me with some tired impression. Roosevelt didn't have to go to Europe or the Pacific and die. He might as well have said *we have nothing to die for but death itself.* Do you really think a killer with sharp teeth is any less dangerous to a swimmer if we call it a shark? Death has its own name. It's real."

"Okay."

"Fear's enough. It's not inconsequential because some politician minimizes it to comfort the masses."

"I know."

"I'm not stupid, Ben."

"No."

"Then don't try to comfort me, okay? You're going over there and I don't know if I'll ever see you again."

"Okay."

I wanted her to go back to Michigan and stay with her parents while I was gone. She refused. She wouldn't give up the apartment. Housing was at a premium. "Besides," she argued, "this is our home. If I keep it going, I...I'll feel like you have a better chance of coming back. Death might decide that since you have a place...I don't know. I'm babbling. But I won't leave. You're going to have this same place to come home to. I'm afraid, Ben. I'm really afraid. I can't live my life without you. You know. You know!" She put her arms around my neck and clung to me, sobbing. I decided then that I hated the war. Both of us had pretty much been oblivious to all the protest. I didn't care about borders or ideology. It just seemed unnatural to dictate to people what they must die for.

The night before my departure, Morgan packed my clean

uniforms and made my favorite meal, but neither of us ate much. We spent the last week ignoring the inevitable. Because lust originates in the mind, preoccupation took the eroticism out of our lovemaking that night. Sex was an afterthought, subservient to love—and fear.

At dawn, we got in the old Ford for the short trip to the flight line. We could already hear the whining engines of the C-130 as we entered the base and the AP on duty waved us through. Airmen, a row of khaki and duffel bags, were lined up at the ladder to board the big bird. I parked at the edge of the tarmac where a little slope of grass surrounded a visitors' parking area. I got out without looking at Morgan and pulled my duffel from the back seat. Morgan came around the car and kissed me, fiercely. It tasted of desperation. The newscaster on the car radio announced, through the open window, that a swan had been found, shot by some gunlover, where the Kansas River exited Gage Park. The city council was offering a reward for the capture of the assassin. I looked at Morgan and knew that she'd heard. Turning toward the rising sun, I waded through Aurora's tears on the grass, and ran to the plane. I could not have done it otherwise.

We must always live in our imaginations. I believe that if we saw only what was "real," we couldn't tolerate life. There has to be a constant vision of what will come. It's how we anticipate reunion and dread death. It's our only comfort and our only real terror. We live in a dialectic of dreams. I think all humanity lives this way, but only a few admit it. Those few are poets or madmen, occasionally enshrined for their courage. The rest would rather not think about it, and operate like all other living things on this planet that only gather wealth and reproduce by instinct alone. But the existence of love, art, religion, literature, music, theatre, war verify the romantic nature of man. In war, the imagination must work overtime.

My plane stopped twice to interrupt the twenty-three hours of airtime—once in Anchorage, Alaska, to refuel, and again, in

Tachikawa, Japan—before landing at Tuy Hoa Air Base, named for a nearby village, and situated about a hundred and fifty miles north of Saigon. The base was right on the edge of the South China Sea, surrounded by thick jungle and majestic mountains. I didn't have to graduate from West Point to understand its value as a natural fortress.

When the side of the C-130 slid open, the tropical air immediately curled around our throats. Breathing in Vietnam was like trying to inhale ragged sheets of wet paper toweling. The heat was surreal, outside the experience of any North American. Even the boys from Mississippi and Florida complained. I was instantly saturated with my own sweat as I disembarked, and would remain in that condition, day and night, until my departure.

The cartographic unit, with its adjacent photo lab, was located right on the edge of the flight line, so I was directed there, splitting off from the other dozens of travelers I had shared the C-130 with for two days. After orientation, as evening approached, the new arrivals were reunited and loaded onto a flatbed truck to be taken to their respective quarters.

The barracks were merely cement slabs, about a hundred feet long, with a corrugated tin roof over them. The "walls" were made of dark screening with a door at each end to provide maximum ventilation and keep the billions of jungle insects at bay. Each unit contained ten double bunks on both sides so that forty GIs could occupy a building. For every four barracks, there was a roofless, cement block structure, which was the shower room and latrine. At the end of every barracks, bomb shelters stood ominously ready. These were cement rooms, two thirds subterranean, with sandbags piled on the "roof." The whole base was located on a wide beach, so that GIs were constantly slogging through sand if they didn't stick to the paved roads. There were four or five large mess halls, a Base Exchange (which was stocked primarily with alcohol, tobacco, snack foods, toiletries, stationery, and men's magazines). There was a small chapel, a barbershop, an outdoor movie theater, the commander's headquarters, a small library, the USO Club, a radio shack, a post office, and the armory. The perimeter was lined with barbed wire, a minefield, and guard stations about every fifty feet, stretching from the shore of the South China Sea in a wide half-moon along the jungle's edge, and rejoining the sea at the other end. The only access to the base— other than a single road through the jungle that ended at the heavily guarded entrance—was by water or air.

Concrete roads crisscrossed throughout the base to prevent vehicles from becoming mired in the sand. Jeeps and trucks of every description, all painted in rough camouflage, mixed the sounds of their grinding engines with the high-pitched whistle of the planes taxiing on the flight line. I remember thinking how clearly these green, olive and khaki machines must show up against the almost white sand. Mine pulled in front of a row of barracks and I spotted the number I had been assigned at orientation, painted in rough characters over the entrance to one of them. It felt good to stand up on the flatbed and stretch my legs which, it seemed to me, had seen too little use since my departure from Morgan. I threw my duffel to the sand and had barely followed it before the flatbed pulled away.

A tiny man, clearly Vietnamese, instantly emerged from the barracks and greeted me with a yellow smile. His height was that of a prepubescent teen, but his wrinkled skin and thinning hair indicated greater age. He moved on spindly legs issuing from khaki shorts that were far too large for him and were secured about his skinny waist with a length of rope. He wore a fatigue shirt, GI issue, that was obviously someone's castoff. He swam in it. Since the buttons had long since disappeared, he wore it open, exposing his sunken chest and protruding ribs. I was to discover, this was all too common among his people. His feet were shod in children's shower clogs. They were bright yellow and lime green and adorned with the happy face of Disney's famous rodent. I later learned that he was forty-five, had a wife and five children, and was referred to by the other GIs as, simply, "Papa-san." He was always smiling, exposing teeth that had never seen a brush or a dentist, and wrinkling the leathery skin that was already drawn too tightly over his gaunt face.

In the weeks that followed, I was surprised to discover the large number of Vietnamese who worked on the base, especially after learning that one of the native barbers had turned out to be VC and had slit the throat of the commander's aide-de-camp while giving him a shave. As if to dismiss my doubts, the little man before me said, in his best pidgin: "Papa-san numbah wan. Pwezdem Yahnsan numbah wan. Pwezdem Ky numbah wan. Ho Chi Minh numbah tan. God bress Mehicah." I learned very quickly that the Vietnamese "domestics" expressed their preferences numerically; one being the superlative and ten, its opposite.

Having established, in his mind, at least, his loyalty to the United States, Papa-san hoisted my duffel bag over his diminutive frame and struggled with it toward the barracks. I followed, feeling somewhat guilty that a man half my size and twice my age should be carrying my bag.

He seemed to know exactly where to go, and turned into the cubicle whose number matched the one I had been given. There was a double bunk, two footlockers, and a small desk with a chair. The bunk occupied the one interior wall; the other was papered with Playmates of the Month, as was the ceiling above the top bunk. My roommate was not in attendance. In fact, there were no other airmen in the structure that I could see, probably because they were still on duty.

Papa-san set to work opening my duffel and carefully placing the contents into the empty footlocker. I was tempted to object, but there was nothing to hide and the man appeared to understand where everything should go. When I attempted to rearrange some of my toiletries, Papa-san interrupted me and shook his head disapprovingly. "Spection," he said, waving his finger at me, and put everything back the way it had been.

Having done so, he continued to unpack. He placed the 5x7 framed photograph of Morgan on the desk, admiring it as he did so. Once the contents of the duffel bag had been emptied, he folded it neatly and slipped it under the lower mattress. He closed the footlocker, handed me the key, then grabbed a nearby broom and began sweeping the cement floor, which was gritty with sand. There was always sand on the floor, either tracked in or sifted through the screen "walls." We slept with it, ate it, drank it, and shook it out of our clothing. I noticed as I glanced through the screening, that I could only see the lower legs of passersby. The eaves of the roof extended very low, I would later learn they acted as a buffer against the monsoons.

Within a few minutes, Papa-san had swept up the sand and replaced the broom against the wall. He took up a position adjacent to it and merely stood there smiling, exposing again his rotting teeth. He attempted no further conversation, but with his work accomplished, he seemed content just to lean against the wall and, like the broom, fade to unobtrusiveness. I assumed he was waiting to be paid for his efforts, so I reached into my pocket and withdrew some coins. "How much?" I said.

The little man's expression immediately changed to a frown and his gestures clearly indicated that he didn't want the money.

"I don't think you should do that." My eyes moved in the direction of the voice and rested on a tall GI who had appeared in the center aisle. The owner of the voice was my equal in height, but he had an aesthetic frame, his skeletal features hidden from the world only by the baggy fatigues he wore. His cheekbones rested high on his face and made the sunken hollows beneath more pronounced by their prominence. As he removed his sweat-stained hat, his deep tan was contrasted by wispy, blond hair that was far too scarce for his face, which was youthful, in spite of its thinness. He had a crooked smile, as if half of his mouth was frozen with novocaine. His voice, like his blue eyes, was soft and unaggressive.

"I just thought I'd give him a little something for helping me out," I responded.

64

"He wouldn't take it."

"Why?"

"Because it's his job. Every GI in this barracks pays him a dollar a week. That's buku money by Vietnamese standards."

"Buku?"

"Vietnamese for big. So he gets paid. Besides, you'd be treating him like a coolie by tipping him—a big insult."

I looked back at Papa-san who was shaking his head in agreement even though I was relatively certain that he didn't understand most of what was being said.

The airman stepped forward and extended his hand. "Name's Billy. Billy Borden." I shook his hand with a firm grip, having been instructed by my father at an early age that the more damage one could do to another man's hand when greeting him, the more he would convince the stranger of his warmth and the sincerity of his masculinity. Borden winced, then pointed at the blue nametag above my shirt pocket. "You're Riveridge."

"Ben is fine. Hey, thanks for straightening me out. With the Vietnamese guy, I mean." I nodded toward the spot where Papa-san had been standing, but he'd disappeared during our conversation. "They don't tell you this stuff at orientation."

"Mind if I sit?" Borden didn't wait for an answer as he planted himself in the solitary chair and picked up the photo of Morgan. "Your girlfriend?"

"My wife. Make yourself comfortable."

"She's beautiful."

"Thanks. She's a remarkable person, in many ways." I felt a tightening in my chest at the thought of her and a fluttering, as if a small bird were trapped between my sternum and my skin. My hand went instinctively to my heart.

"You okay, man?"

I felt like a child caught snooping around Christmas presents. "Yeah, fine."

"How long you been married?"

"Eighteen months."

Borden reached in the pocket under his name and extracted a pack of cigarettes. He spent a good deal of time removing one, then began searching for a lighter. I would discover that Billy spent much of his life looking for a light. I dug in my own pockets, pulled out my zippo, and offered it. Billy thanked me, lit his Winston, and put my lighter in his pocket. "That's mine," I protested.

"Sorry," Billy said, swiftly returning it. "I do that all the time. Got a collection of about thirty or so in my footlocker. I'd return them, but I don't know who they belong to anymore." He took a long drag, exhaled a cloud of smoke, then sat in silence, apparently content to concentrate on smoking. I decided to light one too, then sprawled on the lower bunk.

Billy broke the silence. "Where you from? Originally, I mean. What state?"

"Michigan. You?"

"Colorado. That's the latest one, anyway. I'm an Air Force brat. My old man's a colonel, career officer, so we've moved all over the country."

"You were born in the South?"

"No. I never even lived there. I've been in California, Colorado, Oregon, Alaska, Nebraska, Illinois. I was born in Nebraska. Why would you think I lived in the South?"

"I thought I detected an accent."

"Don't think so."

I realized then that Billy's slowness of speech wasn't a drawl. He just spoke slowly, as if his thoughts were either very far behind or very far ahead of his ability to verbalize them. His speech was laced with pauses too, as if he were trying not to stutter. "How long you been here?"

He reflected and rubbed his chin as if to weigh some ponderous philosophical problem. "Six months, I think."

"Where were you stationed stateside?"

"Forbes Air Base."

"In Kansas?"

"Yeah. You ever been there?"

"That's where I came from."

"No shit?"

"No shit."

"I'm with the 1373rd Recon."

"1370th Photo-Mapping."

Billy stood up and grinned his novocaine grin. He looked around for an ashtray, shrugged, and put his cigarette out on the cement floor. I noticed that a crucifix was attached to the chain around his neck that also held his dog tags. Both contrasted significantly with his dark skin.

"I'm surprised that I never saw you on base. What barracks were you in?"

I pointed at the picture of Morgan. "I'm married, remember? We live in an apartment off base."

"Yeah, that's probably why."

Again, there was a prolonged period of silence as Billy studied the picture of Morgan. He kept looking back at me too, as if he were trying to picture us together.

Morgan forced the next question from me. "Have you seen any action here?" Billy knew the question and its import. His eyes shifted from Morgan's visage to my hopeful face.

"Hell no. It's safer here than in Kansas. The biggest crisis I've seen was when a poisonous snake got in the barracks next door and our papa-san killed it with some guy's copy of The Uniform Code of Military Justice. Oh yeah. Sargent Garcia got stung by a jellyfish. Never heard of anybody getting shot. Stay out of the water and the jungle and you'll get home to your wife." He got up and moved toward the opening of the cubicle. "I'm right across the aisle here. You ever want to shoot the bull, just stop over. I'm gonna go get some chow."

I got up and followed him. "Mind if I tag along? I don't know where the chow hall is and I haven't eaten for a long time."

Billy looked pleased. "Sure. Hey, you got a light?" he said as we left the barracks and joined the river of khaki outside rushing toward the aroma of food.

On our way back from the mess hall, Billy suggested that we head down to the beach and watch the sun set. He assured me that the view was far superior to the food and worth the trouble of wading through the hot sand and postponing my shower for another few minutes.

Though I was exhausted from the long journey, and anxious to get some sleep, I acquiesced. On some intuitive level, I sensed that Billy and I were becoming good friends.

As we struggled toward the water, Billy talked about the Vietnam experience. It was not, he said, a struggle for democracy or hellish aggression or the establishment of an Asian buffer or a means of protest against tyrannical imperialism. It was, simply, a very hot waiting room, where people would not admit that they were only pausing to exercise hope and test its wings. We were like sea turtle hatchlings, knowing where life really was and having to scramble across the open sand and avoid predation to get back to it—back to the sea, to home; that place that spawned us, nurtured us, loved us.

Morgan.

I noticed that all of the Vietnamese who worked on the base were hopping onto the same kind of flatbed trucks that had brought me in from the flightline. They were huddled together like convict crews, heads down, waiting patiently to return to their villages or farms for the night. No Vietnamese, except those in the regular army of South Vietnam, were allowed to remain on the base after dark.

We stopped for a moment for Billy to bum a light. I had to remind him, again, that the zippo was mine. "Old Papa-san is a good man," he continued, turning once more toward the sea. "He lives in Tuy Hoa. A few months ago, the Cong destroyed his house, probably for collaborating with us, but he doesn't take any shit.

Didn't stop him from coming back to work the next day. He and his wife and kids just lived in a hut of cane and palm thrushes anyway. We convinced the commander to let us have some lumber and the guys from our barracks went into the village and built him a new place out of 2x4s and plywood. It's only three rooms, but it's the best house in the village now. I really think Papa-san would become an American if he could. It's not fawning. He really likes us, wants us to win."

"That the way most of them feel?"

"Hell, no. Ninety-five percent would just as soon see us die. They only work with us because they're spies for the Cong or they're starving—and feeding their families, for the moment, is more important than political considerations. I wouldn't trust old one-eye, for example, to clean my dirty shorts."

"Old one-eye?"

"Yeah. He's the papa-san in the barracks next to ours. Suspicious little prick. He's always creeping around, watching, noting. I think he reports to the VC every night. He's got a sunken cavity where his left eye used to be. Not sure how he lost it, but I think he holds us responsible. I told you about the poisonous snake. The damn thing was found in a guy's boot! They suspected one-eye, but nobody could prove it, and he's real good at being a lackey. The colonel believed him. Our papa-san's got no use for him. Says he's a 'number ten,' but nobody listens. Watch out for one-eye."

I looked up for the first time since we'd left the cement road. I'd been concentrating on what Billy said and trying to keep my balance as we labored through the deep sand. The pounding surf drew my attention at first, and then the sky. The horizon was on fire! Surrounding the dying sun, which now appeared to sink into the purple water, were slashes of rose and blood and orange and mauve. It looked as if God had set up an easel in the western sky and found combinations of color unknown to any artist. I remembered reading somewhere that one of Monet's contemporaries had said that the old impressionist was not an artist—he was an eye— "but what an eye!" This was God's eye. Morgan was here, somewhere.

Billy stopped and sat down in the sand. It had cooled enough in the gloaming to tolerate it. I joined him. He kept staring at the sky. It seemed more an act of worship than observation. There was an expression of euphoria on his face. "Why, do you suppose, things like this appeal to humanity?"

I wasn't sure what he meant. "You mean nature? Because it's beautiful, I guess."

"But why is it beautiful?"

"I don't think it is to everyone. If it were, there'd be more than just the two of us watching it."

Billy shook his head. "No. I think beauty is an intrinsic thing. It has its own value, beyond man. That's why art is eternal. As a species, we recognize it, but most individuals don't. That doesn't change anything, of course. It's not dependent at all on our perception. I think Keats was onto it, but I don't understand everything he wrote. You ever read Keats?"

"Some."

"You think I'm queer because I talk this way?"

"No."

"Most of the guys in the barracks think I'm a fag because I talk about things like this. I'm not, though. I wanted you to know that up front."

"Beauty is Truth, Truth, Beauty. In this world that is all ye know and all ye need to know."

Billy looked at me with the expression of a trapped miner, deep in a dark tunnel, who has just seen light. "We're going to be good friends, I think," he said, brushing his thin, blonde hair from his forehead and rising to his feet. The sun was deep in the water now, transferring the color from sky to sea, where it would drown in darkness.

"Yes," I agreed, "I think we will."

We turned and headed back to the barracks in the half-light that evening allowed. Giant insects whirred and buzzed above our heads. We didn't converse. When we reached the building, it was noisy and fully occupied. As we went in, I had to duck to avoid being struck by a tennis ball someone had launched from the other end. GIs were walking and lolling around in various stages of undress. Some were trying to sleep in the glare of the bare light bulbs, but most were talking or playing cards. Everyone carried a can of beer, and the humid air was dense with cigarette smoke. I said goodnight to Billy and turned into my cubicle. My bunkmate was still absent. I undressed and lay down on the bed, exhausted. After deciding to shower in the morning, I soon drifted off and, in my mind, went home to Morgan.

Like Odysseus, the voices of sirens came to me from a far shore, mixed with the whispering curses of men fumbling in the dark. There was a sudden brightness through which I could, as I opened my eyes, make out wraith-like shadows—then darkness again. There were explosions, the staccato of automatic weapons fire. My heart shuddered, an omen to my mind, as it slowly returned from the remnants of a dream.

Helicopters stuttered overhead, dropping flares to enlighten all below. None paid heed. More bright flashes. Panicked voices. One voice of authority: "Get into the bunker. All noncombatants, into the bunker, now!"

I scrambled from my bunk and reached for my clothes. I thought how ridiculous it would be to die in my underwear, like some old lecher in a whorehouse. I'd been dreaming of Morgan. She'd been watching me swim in a river. I was in full view. She'd looked past me, as if I were transparent. She'd seemed frightened, sad, alone—then the sirens, from the river's ridge.

After successfully maneuvering my uncooperative pants over my legs, I pulled on my boots, not bothering to lace them. I couldn't find my shirt, so I pulled a tee shirt over my head and stepped into the aisle to join the other men who were being herded by an MP toward the rear door of the barracks. Once I was outside, the sloping eaves no longer obstructed my view and I could see the sky, filled with choppers. In the distance, in the direction of the flightline, I could see huge fires. The ground shook with continual explosions. Someone grabbed my arm. In the temporary illumination from the flares I could see the face of Billy Borden. "Mortar fire," he shouted. "They're after the planes."

"Move, damn it!" someone yelled behind us. I could see the men ahead of us ducking their heads as they descended single file into the bunker. Billy and I followed. We were forced against one of the sandbag walls and then ordered by someone to sit and hold our legs tightly against ourselves so that our chins rested uncomfortably on our knees. I realized that we had been among the last to enter the bunker. There were many men huddled inside already. Billy and I were close to the entrance. Shortly after we sat down, the river of refugees stopped. Strangely, two military police, not air police, stood at the entrance with M-16s. I supposed that it was their responsibility to defend the bunker, since they were the only ones with weapons. It didn't make us feel very secure. They stepped aside for a moment, allowing some late arrivals into the shelter. Three of them were women. I later learned that one was a nurse, while the other two were part of a USO troupe. They looked like frightened mice taking shelter from a hawk in the den of a rattlesnake.

"Safer than Kansas, huh?" I whispered to Billy.

"First time it's happened since I've been here," he said. "I swear. You're just lucky, I guess."

One of the MPs turned around. "Shut up back there," he growled. The mumbling stopped immediately. People afraid of dying don't question authority. All eyes turned to the flashes of light at the entrance to the bunker and all ears tuned in to the sounds of war. A heavy thud shook the ground beneath us. Sand sifted down the sides of the bunker and clods of dirt fell on our heads.

I didn't consider my own death or capture then. I just kept thinking about Morgan. I trembled at the threat of broken promises. The sirens kept up their piercing wail, like banshees on the wind. More explosions shook the ground. Guns rattled like snakes, spewing venomous bullets into the night air, searching for prey.

One of the MPs ventured outside to determine the severity of the perimeter breach in the light of the flares. When he returned, he told his companion: "I can't tell what's happening. There's a shitload of people running around, but I can't tell if they're theirs or ours. We'll have to wait. We'll either get the 'all clear,' or the gooks'll come visiting. Looks like the whole damn flightline is on fire. How many clips you got?"

"Ten," the other responded.

He looked around the huddled group. All eyes were on him. "Anybody else in here armed?"

Silence.

"Okay, we wait."

Morgan told me later, that on that same night, as she was preparing to go to bed, the doorbell rang. She was badly frightened when she saw two men in uniform on the porch, waiting for her to answer their summons. They were police officers. She could scarcely catch her breath, she said, as they explained that our car, which had been parked in the store lot next door, had apparently been left in neutral, slid down a little rise, and bumped into the stone wall of the A and P. She went with the officers to check the damage. The car had struck a drainpipe. That was the only real harm that had been done, except that the car had pinioned a sparrow's nest behind the pipe and the chicks in it had been crushed. She knew then, she said, that I would come home.

When the sirens stopped, and the *all-clear* was issued, Billy and I and the others emerged from the bunker to greet the half-light of dawn. We returned to the barracks where we were informed that most of the planes on the flightline had been destroyed and we wouldn't be able to work until replacements could be found. The Viet Cong had entered the base from the sea, twenty of them, and they had used mortar and plastic explosives to immolate every aircraft on the ground. They had all died in the process, martyrs to their cause. Three sentries, unlucky enough to draw the duty that night, were also dead. Twenty-three deaths for a few days' interruption in the process of making maps. When I considered it after a shower and some breakfast, I told Billy, who was stretched out on my roommate's bunk, that I didn't believe in any ideology enough to do that. What had they gained? The endless adoration of their countrymen? Their names would never be remembered, nor their sacrifice, except in a general way, and what price to their parents, their wives, their children?

"Get the hell off my bunk, Billy-boy," Sargent Knapp snapped as he entered the cubicle and slapped his wet towel over the piping that served as the frame for the cots. "It's been a long night." He was a small, somewhat stocky man of middle age, with cherubic, red cheeks, thinning auburn hair, and a golden handlebar mustache. One of his prominent front teeth was metal and it was often on display, since he almost never failed to be smiling, regardless of the emotion he might be feeling at the moment.

I stood up and proffered my hand. "Ben Riveridge. I just got in yesterday." I pointed at all the pin-ups. "Nice wallpaper."

He shook my hand weakly. "You picked a hell of a time to arrive. I was working on the flightline, nightshift, when the damn gooks attacked. Luckily, they didn't hit the labs, just interested in the birds, I guess." He crawled into the bunk that Billy Borden had just vacated and stretched out with a deep sigh. "Man, I'm worn out. Talk to you later." He turned his back and, within a few seconds, he was snoring.

"Man's got a remarkable gift for sleeping," Billy said. "He's rarely conscious. He told me once that he was going to sleep his hitch in 'Nam, then it'd go faster. I thought he was kidding, but if he's not on duty, he's usually zonked out."

As if he'd heard Billy, the sargent rolled over toward us and propped himself up on one elbow. "Hey," he mumbled groggily, "I almost forgot to tell you guys. The commander says you can call home if you want. Guess they made some kind of mistake in broadcasting last night's little party. Said the base had been taken by the VC. They're allowing everyone to make an extra call this month to let their families know they're okay."

He no sooner finished his sentence than he was snoring again, oblivious to the excitement he'd generated. "You mean I can talk to Morgan now? Sargent?" I looked at Billy.

"Let's go to the radio shack," he said. "I'll show you where it is." We rushed out into the searing heat of the Vietnamese afternoon, and began scuttling across the hot sand like a pair of crabs trying to avoid the gulls.

There was a long line, and we stood in the terrible, tropical sun for more than two hours before we finally approached the door of the shack. Billy had been in line before me, but he surrendered his position when our time came, knowing that I was burning as badly inside as out and another few minutes of waiting could result in spontaneous combustion.

Once inside the blessed shade of the hut, it took a little while for my eyes to adjust. I gave the radio operator the number and waited for the connection. The airman who ran the equipment motioned for me to put on the headphones and suddenly, through the static, I heard Morgan's voice say "Hello?"

"Morgan! It's me, I'm…"

The operator broke in. "Please wait until your party has completed the transmission. Both parties must end each communication with the word 'over' so that we know when to transmit. Is this clear?"

"Yes." Morgan and I answered in unison.

"Are you okay?" Morgan's voice was full of fear.

"Is that the end of your transmission, ma'am? If so, you must say 'over' before your party can respond."

"Are you okay, Ben? Over."

"Yeah, I'm all right Morg. Over."

"What happened?"

"I'm sorry, we can't transmit until you say 'over.'"

"What happened? Over."

"The base was attacked, but I wasn't involved at all. I'm okay. Don't have a scratch on me. A friend of mine here says it's the only attack in six months. It probably won't happen again. You okay? I miss you terribly." There was a long silence. "Over."

"I'm fine, but I was so scared. You can't know, Ben. After the broadcast...."

"You have thirty seconds before your time is up. Please finish your conversation."

"I love you so much, Ben." There was calm strength in her voice. "Over."

"You know, don't you, that I'm going to make it home. You know now. Over."

"Transmission ended. You may call again at your scheduled time."

I left the shack and was immediately blinded by the tropical sunlight. I told Billy later that my experience in the radio shack did more to make me hate the military than anything else except the killing. When he asked me why, I told him that it was a crime against intimacy.

* * *

Doctor Kim Dong-Ho
Notes on the Third Interview with Ebenezer Riveridge
September 18, 2000 Ypsilanti State Hospital

This session commenced shortly after 2:00 P.M. It was, at first anyway, nothing more than small talk, laced with the usual denigration. I decided to attempt to manipulate the patient into reflecting on his tour of duty in Vietnam, since I believed his experiences there might account, in some way, for his apparent belligerence.

The ploy seemed to work, at least initially. He told me that he was stationed at a place called Tuy Hoa. I was quite shaken to hear it, since I was born in that small village. That was where my family, with the exception of my older brother and myself, was slaughtered there by "patriots," for collaborating with the enemy. I was an infant, and escaped the fate of my sisters and parents only because my brother took me into the jungle. We hid there until it was over.

I didn't share this information with the patient because I feared that it would only contribute to his propensity to see his life as predestined, and such a coincidence would only fuel these misconceptions. My reaction, however, did not go unnoticed as he asked me why Tuy Hoa should be significant to me. I lied, and told him I had never heard of the place. He said: "Facial expressions, like the sign language of the hands, are the primordial heritage of humanity."

I ignored the statement. He didn't appear to be nervous at all in these interviews. Although he is a chain smoker, his general demeanor was calm and relaxed. He is a very big man, with pale blue eyes and thinning white hair. He always appears to have a secret.

I asked him to tell me the most humorous incident he'd observed while in Vietnam. The idea was to draw from him some pleasantry which would keep things light and allow for deeper probing, the way a parent will joke with his child while attempting to clean a wound.

He considered for a few seconds, then talked about how he had been assigned the graveyard shift of perimeter guard duty, something everyone on the base dreaded and attempted to avoid. He said he was very nervous about it, especially since the base had been attacked two weeks earlier and three perimeter guards had been killed by the Viet Cong. He said he remembered standing in the sentry box that stood a few feet above the sandbag and barbed-wire wall that served as the outer defensive network of the air base where he was stationed. He was especially worried because, he said, he was a terrible marksman. In basic training, his target on the firing range showed five hits out of fifty rounds fired. The targets on either side of his had more than sixty-five hits each. He seemed quite amused by his own ineptitude.

As the sun went down, he became increasingly agitated. Although there were manned sentry boxes on either side of him, they were too far away to be seen at night, and he felt completely alone. The noise from the jungle just beyond the perimeter did not reassure him.

Sometime in the middle of that night someone shot at him from the dense jungle, some fifty feet away.

The bullet splintered the wood just above his head. Mr. Riveridge laughed when he revealed this, as if almost-dying were funny, but I began to realize that he was anticipating the real humor. He was so afraid, he said, that he switched his M-16 to automatic and began firing in the general direction of the sound of the gunshot. When one 20-round clip was gone, he loaded another, and another. He laughed quite uncontrollably as he described how he'd riddled the plant life and cut down trees with his continual fire. He didn't stop firing until he'd emptied more than two hundred rounds into the defenseless foliage and awakened the entire base. He escaped death, he said, and a court martial, by the narrowest of margins, but had to suffer a written reprimand as part of his permanent service record.

When the patient had regained his composure, I tried probing a bit more, and asked him what he felt he had gained from his entire experience in Vietnam.

"The wisdom of Bisquick," he responded, without hesitation. I was certain, then, that I'd found the means by which I might extend his ninety-day internment here. "What's Bisquick?" I asked him.

"Billy Borden is Bisquick. My lifeline. You need to know him to understand. I was out of place in the military, but not like Billy. His father was a lifer, a full-bird colonel. Bill barely made buck sargent." His blue eyes were envisioning something—something far away.

"He was a friend?"

"Yes."

"Please, continue."

"In his four-year hitch, he received several Article Fifteens and was busted—twice."

"Which means?"

"He was severely reprimanded and demoted."

"Why?"

"Once, it was for what *The Uniform Code of Military Justice* calls 'dereliction of duty.' Another was for 'disrespect toward a superior officer.' The former was for oversleeping and reporting late, the latter for waving at the squadron commander instead of saluting. Bill had different definitions. He called them 'felonious bed-snuggling' and 'premeditated amity,' as I recall. He didn't consider either offense to be detrimental to the security of the United States."

I worked hard to contain my amusement. "He was there? At Tuy Hoa, I mean?"

"Yes. But he hated the war. He tried to learn Vietnamese because he thought he ought to try to open up communication. I often saw him reading something called *The Berlitz Vietnamese Phrasebook*. He said there were six tones in their language. I think it was...high and long, high and short, low and long, start low and end high, and...damn, can't remember."

"Level."

"Level, right. Figures that I wouldn't remember that."

"Anything else you can tell me about him?"

He thought for a moment, then lit another cigarette. "He could play the guitar—folk guitar. He had an old six-string Gibson and used a pencil and rubber band for a capo. I had a decent voice, so did he. We both loved Peter, Paul and Mary. We began to harmonize. His friendship helped me to survive without Morgan.

He was a bridge—a connection. He was always unintentionally stealing my lighter. What else do you want to know?"

"Have you seen him at all, since Vietnam?"

"Sure. He and I were both stationed in Topeka, Kansas. When we got stateside, he somehow found the apartment we were renting in town. Morgan connected with him, as I had, instantaneously. For about the next year and a half Billy spent more time at our place than his own room on base. Morgan always cooked for three, although Billy was often hours late. We formed a trio. Her voice blended with ours. She was almost as good as Mary Travers. She got it from her dad, I think."

"Did Billy have a girlfriend?"

"A few weeks before he was discharged, he met a farm girl who was also named Morgan—Morgan Streeter. He was in love with her. He didn't come around as often, but we all knew the connection would survive the disbanding of the trio. Morgan and I met his Morgan a couple of times. We approved. They appeared to have the same soul, something we knew about."

"When did you separate? Did you see each other after the Air Force?"

"Bill was discharged in July, I think, July of 1970. He went home to Colorado. He left Morgan Streeter behind. We said good-bye to him in front of our apartment. 'Big Red,' his crimsoned, rusted dinosaur of a station wagon, was crammed with the usual empty cans, burger wrappers, cigarette butts, confiscated lighters, guitar and duffel. My Morgan, pregnant with Michelle, our daughter (I think you've met her), cried when he embraced her. I did too. After he left, I took out a cigarette to relieve the emotional burden, but my lighter was already on its way to Colorado.

A month later, in August, I was discharged and Morgan and I returned to Michigan. Michelle was born shortly afterward. I went back to school and became a teacher. Our son, Tysen, was born. We became immersed in our children and our new life. We lost track of Billy."

My genuine curiosity was aroused. "Did you ever hear from him again?"

"After about ten years. The kids were both in school by then. Billy called to tell us that he'd gone to a concert in Denver where he'd kissed Mary Travers. He had also married a girl from Boulder in 1975. He had a B.A., but couldn't find a job in philosophy. He said he was changing the bulbs in traffic signal lights for the city of Boulder and that it was the most important job he'd ever had. People had to know when to stop. He missed us, he said. He told us that his wife wasn't a singer."

"Did you maintain contact after that?"

"I didn't really. I was too busy. But Morgan kept up a regular correspondence, writing him several times a year. Typically, Bill found the postcard to be an interesting 'medium of expression' because you could fit exactly a 'gross' (twelve dozen), words on it before it popped out of the typewriter. I read every word he sent, but it was Morgan who always wrote back. Billy became a father at age forty-seven. The child was a little boy. Bill tried, but couldn't find regular and reasonable employment. His wife was rich. She came from money and was, as he put it, a 'natural entrepreneur.' Bill became a house husband and full-time father. To him, it seemed logical; to her, it was grounds for divorce. Billy was discharged again, after twenty-one years of matriotic duty. She got custody of their son.

He wrote that he'd gone back to Topeka on a whim, one foot-loose weekend. He had, incredibly, encountered Morgan Streeter on the sidewalk downtown. She'd recently divorced as well. Her husband had been abusive. She was a nurse. She had two adult kids and cancer. She was constantly sick from the chemotherapy. She wore a wig to hide her baldness. Billy stayed, this time, and moved in with her. He became her nurse as well as her lover, confidante and healer."

He was smiling and seemed content in this memory. I tried to keep him focused. "When your wife passed away, did you continue the correspondence?"

There was a long silence, before the patient continued. "A postcard came about a month after Morgan's heart attack. Her death had been so sudden, he knew nothing about it. He explained that his Morgan's cancer was in remission and they were going to get married, as they should have twenty-six years ago. It was addressed to Morgan. I didn't care anymore about any of that. I'd quit singing. I quit listening. My daughter wrote to Billy and told him of Morgan's death. He cried bitterly, he wrote to me later. He continued to send me postcards. One of them touched something in me. I've read it so many times that I've memorized it. He wrote:

B orden
I nstitute for the
S tudy of
Q uestions
U nanswered
I n
C onventional
K nowledge

Dear Ben:

I don't know why we don't love everyone equally, why we love some people more than others. I think if we knew the answer to that question we would probably know how the fabric of the universe is woven. We must somehow be connected to those people that we love more than others. On the day your Morgan went away, mine came back. I saw a rainbow that night. I remember because we were in a ferris wheel bucket. I still talk to people who don't seem to be here anymore. Of course, you know this already.

Billy

It made me write back. Other than my nightly letters to Morgan (a journal I've kept in that form since Morgan died), it became my only correspondence. Billy's postcards eased my pain somehow. In November, Billy Borden and Morgan Streeter Borden pulled into my driveway. I tell you, Dr. Kim, I didn't know who they were at first. Bill walked with a limp and he was terribly thin. Like his wife, he'd lost all his hair, but hers would grow back. We didn't say much at first. It was polite conversation, laced with caesura. We had dinner together. Billy had quit cigarettes for years, but began again when the mother of his child had left him childless. We sat in the garage and smoked and talked about why death and divorce and wars and cancer happen. We talked well into the night. Then Billy got his guitar out of the car and he and Morgan sang some Peter, Paul and Mary tunes. I couldn't stop myself from humming along."

"This visit helped you with your grief?"

"I began to understand time better."

"How long did they stay?"

"They left for Kansas the next day, a Sunday, I think. Billy's limp was more pronounced and I asked him, as he got in the car, what had caused it. He fumbled for words, I remember, eventually explaining that he had been laying cement as a part of his latest 'menial laborer' position, and he'd stepped in the stuff by accident. It had overflowed into his shoes. He knew nothing of chemistry and hadn't cleaned the stuff off until much later. He lifted his pant leg and I could see that the skin around his ankles was blistered and raw. It looked hideous. I smiled. 'What is it?' he asked. I answered that one could expect to get burned if he stood too long in the concrete. He nodded and smiled.

I waved at them as they pulled out of my driveway, remembering and wondering if I would ever see them again. I spent the rest of that day looking for a light."

Addendum: I'm afraid the delusion I was looking for didn't appear, and I'm forced to concede that the ninety day "sentence" will have to remain in effect until I can find some psychological justification for an extension. I must admit that Mr. Riveridge has given me no indication that he's ill, but I've had enough experience in the field to know that this doesn't mean he's healthy. Still, he's given no indication of dementia or hallucinations and he certainly isn't dangerous, though he can be offensive. Time will tell.

Chapter Eight

Creating Lives

*Courage is more than endurance, it is the power to create
your own life in the face of all that men or God can inflict, so that
every day and every night is what you imagine it. Courage
makes us dreamers, courage makes us poets.*
—Penelope Fitzgerald, The Blue Flower

Our daughter was born in August, 1970, shortly after we left
Kansas and the Air Force and returned to Michigan.

She was tiny: five pounds, fifteen ounces. Setting a pattern
that would always be hers, she was premature. We named her
Michelle.

In the recovery room, I pushed little wisps of dark hair from
Morgan's pale face. They had curled from the sweat and effort of
birthing. She was exhausted, but ecstatic, and accepted my kisses
and gratitude with tenderness. She told me that the tiny thing was
a gift to both of us and that she had merely done the unwrapping.

Elyda Woodson was thrilled to be a grandmother and was
always hovering nearby, limping badly on her withered leg, but
never sitting for long. She was constantly attentive to Morgan and
Michelle. They were her treasures. I was merely a depositor.

My own mother was happy about the birth, but she already
had a grandchild and the novelty wasn't there. Besides, Jennie had
always been partial to boys. My father was lost in his dark depression, but did force a smile at the news. Harlan, as always, talked a
great deal, but had little to say.

I was in love again. I didn't think anyone could touch my
heart the way Morgan did, but Michelle proved to own the same
magic. When I first held her, her head and most of her torso fit
neatly into my hand and I marveled that such tiny delicacy could

have so much strength. I had no idea how much she would control my life, but I entered into my indenture without hesitation.

I stayed as late as the bellicose nurses would allow, that first night, watching Morgan nurse the baby. The scene reminded me of the real purpose of breasts and I would ever after look at my naked wife through different, but no less appreciative, eyes.

I rented a house for us, got my job back on the assembly line, enrolled in night classes at the college. I had to become something. I took literature and history courses mostly, impractical disciplines which limited my future to teaching. So it was, that secondary education became my career, although even after twenty-eight years, I still think of it, strangely, as temporary.

I received my B.A. in 1972. I did my student teaching at the same high school where Morgan and I had met. I still remembered her locker number and walked by it on occasion. A boy was its tenant then. He seemed lost and entirely alone. I was glad when my tenure at Arthur Hill was finished. Its reality disrupted what was real.

My first teaching job was at a Catholic school. I signed on for an annual remuneration of $7,800, low even for those times, but it was the only position available in late August. The principal, Sister Mary-Margaret, warned me that since I was avowedly an adherent of the philosophy of the "Great Reformer," she was hiring me on the assumption that I wouldn't expound on religion in my litera-ture classes and would keep my "unorthodoxy" to myself. I assured her that I would never knowingly teach anything contrary to the religious principles upon which the school was founded. We shook on it. Her hand was ice.

Despite my meager salary, we thought it important for Michelle to have a full-time parent around. So, although Morgan wanted to work, she agreed not to look for a job until Michelle was in school all day.

The baby grew quickly into a toddler. She had blue eyes, strawberry-blond hair and white, almost translucent skin that became rosy at the mildest touch. Morgan's dark eyes and hair had become misplaced in the genetic transmission. I, as doting father, was reduced to a ridiculous cretin in Shelly's presence. I believed that there was nothing about her that wasn't cute. I wore her milky spittle on my shirt like a badge of honor. Her tiny farts were "tooters" and initiated little endearments like "Tooty Bird." My r's and l's became w's, my t's converted to d's when speaking to her. "Der's daddy's widdle Tooty shnooks," I would cry on entering the house after work. "Shelly pookums do do." Even Morgan, as accomplished a maudlin fawner as she was, couldn't help but be amused by my obsequious debasement.

Shelly's first word was "da-da." Though I was thrilled, it didn't seem fair. "Ma-ma" should really have been first, since Morgan did ninety-percent of the caretaking. If she thought it, she never said so.

By the time Shelly began to talk and quit soiling her diapers, Morgan was pregnant again. Tysen was born in October, 1974. With the advent of Lamaze, I was able to watch him come screaming into the world. The doctor didn't have to slap him or clear mucus from his mouth and nose in order to get him to breathe. He began to bellow as soon as his gray little head emerged. As we would learn, he despised restraint.

The nurse had brought him to us in the recovery room. I recall that she had announced, quite cheerfully, that Ty was a perfect little baby except.... It was that word that had set Morgan off. "Except." She began to cry. She shook uncontrollably. She told me later that she could hear the nurse finishing her sentence: "except that he's blind," "except for his cleft palette," "except for a chronically weak heart." She braced herself, but was still unprepared for what the startled nurse finally did say: "...except for his crooked little toes." Morgan's agony disappeared, turning to mollification, then amusement. She'd pulled the sheet up and wiggled her own, defective digits. "He gets them from me," she'd crowed, and had held her arms out to receive her son.

My father cried when Ty was born. He was at home and becalmed by lithium. He was attempting to finish out his last year at General Motors. He was constantly sad. Medication only contained the manic half of his affliction. He'd barely been aware of Shelly's existence, but Tysen would continue the Riveridge lineage, and this meant something. Amazingly, Dad said nothing about the dreaded Ebenezer name.

Ty, as a male, was more deeply prized by my family. Elyda, who had raised a single girl, would always favor Shelly. Harlan's favorite, of course, was Harlan. Morgan and I loved them equally, but I think Morgan was the better parent. She knew how to use the word "no," and exhibited a kind of bravery I never possessed.

The best example I have of this courage was Morgan's conquest of thunderstorms. I'd discovered her phobia of them shortly after our graduation from Arthur Hill in July, 1964. Lyndon Johnson was escalating the conflict in Vietnam. To us, that tempest was very distant in the blue life-sky of youth.

The thunderstorm caught us unawares as we ran from a restaurant to the relative safety of my '59 Chevy in the parking lot. Nature, perhaps displeased by my complaisance, rocked the car with disapproving blows. We were pummeled with elephant-tear raindrops, which turned to icy hail, pinging off the hood like marbles. Thunder reverberated through the cushioned seats, making our steel bunker seem oddly vulnerable. Morgan trembled. It wasn't a nervous shiver, but the violent shuddering of grand mal. She was seized with fear. From my hormonal perspective, the storm was a welcome opportunity, because her escape from it was to cling as tightly to me as she could. I always weathered such moments with ease and, associating nature's virulence with physical intimacy. I began to listen to meteorologists with greater interest.

In spite of her suffering, I enjoyed the harsher weather. Not only did it foster physical closeness, but it also nurtured a dependence, which I found exhilarating and aggrandizing.

When we married, the phobia persisted. Strangely, as I would discover on our wedding night, winter storms, even blizzards, didn't faze Morgan. It was the lightning that made her tremble, the thunder that caused her to cower. She loved to walk in falling snow, but detested the harsher heaviness of rain. There was great selectivity in her fear.

She often chastised herself for such unreasoning paranoia. Perhaps what bothered her most was its irrationalism. Her parents had never abandoned her in a storm. She'd never been struck by lightning. No childhood trauma, that she was aware of, could account for her illogical terror.

In most crises, Morgan had the heart of a lioness. I depended on her far more than she did on me, but she disguised this disparity well. Her natural intrepidity, therefore, made her timorousness in rainstorms all the greater an enigma. It was an impediment she was determined to conquer.

In Topeka, after a particularly bad conflagration, I came home to discover her in the broom closet, quaking and soaked with her own sweat. Once she'd regained her composure, she declared that this incident was "the needle that broke the camel's back," and that she was going to "nip this silliness in the butt." I applauded her resolution.

Still, try as she might, when the little "W" appeared in the upper corner of the television screen, Morgan would begin pacing, and glance nervously out the window at the creeping clouds.

She learned to control her phobia when Michelle was born. She'd suffered so long with her dread, that she was determined not to pass it on to our children. As soon as Michelle was old enough to be remotely aware of her surroundings, Morgan tackled the problem. As a storm clawed at our rented house with priapic force, raised the curtains with cold, damp breath, and rattled the chandelier, Morgan picked up the baby and ran out onto the porch to duel with her tormentor. While the wind howled at her, and lightning shredded the sky, she gave our child a gift.

I hear sometimes, when storms come—the barely controlled terror beneath the giggles and defiant laughter—as she tried to kill Satan with joy. "Whee! Ha ha ha! Mommy's baby wike da pwetty sky? O-o-o-o, see da big wights? Oh wisten to da big boomies. In't pwetty? So pwetty and wild!" Shelly squealed with delight.

To me, that was greater gallantry than any Spartan ever displayed at Thermopylae. They *wanted* to face death, after all. Her purpose was not to die honorably and be brought home on her shield, but to keep the damn Persians out of her house.

She succeeded. Both Michelle and Tysen grew up loving violent storms. I was concerned that our children might learn not to take the power of nature seriously. I was right to be worried.

Shelly loves the rain, but her child was once put in danger by a tornado. Consequently, although she still watches the "sky monsters" play, and nature's tantrums are associated with a happy childhood, she watches from a cautious distance. It's Tysen, now twenty-five, who seems to believe that nature will always spare him. He plays golf in lightning storms, swims in tumultuous oceans, fords swiftly-flooding rivers, without ever considering their lethal potential.

Morgan and I argued about it once.

"I know the risk is there, Bennie," she said, but there's risk everywhere." She put her small hand on my jaw, affectionately soothing. "I'd rather have risk than intimidation. I know both. Risk is better."

"For you, maybe," I said.

"For anyone."

I missed protecting her in that way. As she often did, she was reading my mind. Looking up at me with her indefinable eyes, she brought her other hand up and cradled my large, balding head, as if it were a precious icon. I felt like a child, though I was at least twice her size, vastly more educated, and old in the manly arts of war and teaching.

"I still need you," she whispered and kissed me.

"I know, but not for storms."

She smiled. "Don't you know how afraid I still am?"

I was going to say "no," but she would have read my dishonesty. I always twitched when I lied. She'd picked up on it the first time I told her that storms were nothing to be afraid of. I didn't mind that she knew. I didn't lie to her often, and never about hand or heart.

"Okay," I said, "but storms produce rainbows. That ought to count for something. You love them."

Her answer was quick and sharp. "The sun causes them."

"You need the rain to refract the light."

"Yes, but what causes color—light or water?"

"Light," I admitted.

"Then we're not at odds." She kissed me. "I do love rainbows. They signal an end to wrath, and what purpose is there to a storm other than God's rage? The rainbows, they're like a promise."

"What kind of promise?"

"Oh I don't mean the promise in the Bible, after the flood. There doesn't seem to be an ending to water and death. Maybe the rainbow just tells us that after one storm is finished, something will happen that will make it possible to face the next...sort of what we know and believe about each other."

Time is the image of eternity and metaphors are the conversion of time to purpose. Through the last night of Morgan's life, Michelle and Tysen and I sat with her, three adults, listening to the serpentine hiss of the respirator and watching the artificial rise and fall of her chest. I silently begged her to live. Outside, lightning tore bright wounds in the black heart of night and the thunderous firmament drowned out my pleas. Ty and Shelly watched in unintimidated awe as the virulent rain pelted the window, attempting to violate the peace of sleeping royalty. Like my kiss, it didn't wake her.

The next afternoon, the healers who couldn't heal testified that Morgan's life was over, as if people really possessed such omnipotence. I turned from the bed in agony. Our children clutched me. We sobbed through a thousand details and left her behind to be disconnected. We emerged into the late afternoon smell of wetness and storm-ending quiet. There was a strange, roiling luminescence in the sky, tinted by the dying sun. The kids saw the rainbow first, though they couldn't know its meaning. I remembered a promise.

The difference between poets and the rest of us is time. Poets learn earlier. Perhaps that's why they fear storms, live too quickly, and exist inside metaphors.

After that day, my facial twitching increased, although I mostly lied to myself. For four years, storms and rainbows, for me, vanished altogether. I heard only the sounds of steady weather in the dark, masculine, and discontented night.

Then, she returned.

Chapter Nine

Bridging

I also know that it is romantic to believe that human empathy is commonplace, since empathy demands connection, and connection demands that one take on the burden of another's life, another's suffering.
—Kenneth A. McClane Walls, *Essays 1985–1990*

In 1978, after six years there, I left the Catholic school. I had gotten myself in hot water by pointing out the existence of Jesus' brothers and sisters to children who had been raised to believe in Mary's life-long virginity. I didn't mean to step on Vatican toes but, as a Protestant, I was unfamiliar with this immaculate theory. When summoned into Sister Mary-Margaret's presence and thoroughly chastised, I apologized and explained that I had been unaware of Joseph's amazing self-control and understood better now, his canonization. This did nothing to eliminate her distaste for me, clearly inscribed on her forehead, just below her habit.

I wasn't out of work long. The Missouri Synod had just constructed a new high school in Saginaw. My heresy at St. Joe's was regarded as reforming spirit at Lutheran High and I was hired there with a significant raise in salary.

Tysen started kindergarten the next year. He and Shelly both attended the Lutheran elementary school, which was attached to our church. Our lives became a cyclonic circle of Lutheran grade school, Lutheran high school, and Lutheran church.

Dad retired from General Motors and waited for God to fetch him. Mom saw her friends, volunteered at the hospital, and spent a great deal of time on the phone with Ruth and Tommy. She knew that I didn't want to deal with all the pain with which she was forced to live.

To everyone's surprise, Ella got married. Her husband was an odd little duck, half her size, who worked for, of all things, a chemical company. He was a great admirer of Hitler, and I often suspected that his employment had something to do with the production of Zyklon B. He looked like Himmler. Once they were married, he became Ella's Fuehrer, although she thought of him as Rhett Butler. She was always afraid that he wouldn't give a damn, so she faithfully obeyed him and refused any further contact with the family that had nurtured and tolerated her for thirty-seven years. I never blamed her. She was only following orders.

Tommy-Jeff graduated from high school, hitchhiked across Europe, slept with innumerable women, got his B.A. in Criminal Justice, an M.A. in Political Science, and a second M.A. in Sociology. Finally, at forty, he became a husband and settled down to a career in substance abuse counseling.

Ruth had two daughters by this time. John, her quiet husband, went about the laborious task of acquiring wealth.

I didn't see my family very often. During Dad's last committal, he'd been so angry with me for my part in it, that he'd called me every vile name he could muster, accused me of being Oedipal, and threw a chair at me. I withdrew then. Not like Ella—not completely. I just kept my distance. I felt safer. The family Morgan and I had created was the focus of my attention.

If you asked our kids now what they loved most about their childhood, they would both tell you that it was our family camping trips by the Mackinac Bridge.

It's the longest suspension bridge in the world and connects the lower and upper peninsulas of Michigan by spanning the five-mile-wide strait where the waters of Lakes Huron and Michigan conjoin. On the northern side is the quaint village of St. Ignace, once a mission to the Huron Indians and founded by the Jesuit, Pere Marquette, who named the settlement after the originator of his order, Ignatius Loyola.

On the southern side of the strait is the little community of

Mackinaw City, originally a French settlement that extended outward from the log stockade known as Fort Michilimackinac. It's now a tourist attraction of fudge shops, gift shops and arcades. Boats of every description are moored in both harbors, the summer treasures of doctors, lawyers and CEOs from Detroit and Chicago.

Mackinac Island, one of the Midwest's greatest tourist attractions, sits serenely in the strait, almost equidistant from the two peninsulas. Ferries from Mackinaw City and St. Ignace run every half hour in summer to the island, bringing millions of vacationers. Its quaintness is its largest draw. No motorized vehicles are permitted and one must either walk, bicycle or take a horse-drawn carriage up to the Grand Hotel, a pillared monolith nestled in the hillside, which was the set for *Somewhere in Time*, a popular movie with Christopher Reeve and Jane Seymour. It was one of Morgan's favorites.

In 1978, quite by accident, Morgan and I discovered the idyllic campground in St. Ignace, where we would spend most of the next twenty summers with our children. Located right on the shore of the strait, it's called, appropriately, Straits State Park.

Campsite number twenty, mystically, became our "property." If someone else occupied it upon our arrival, we would take some other inferior site and wait until they left, then move. In order to change sites, one had to be among the first in line when the ranger station opened at 7:00 A.M. Consequently, to ensure success, I would set my folding lawn chair in front of the station door at midnight and wait through the dark night, listening to owls and watching bats hunt mosquitoes. Morgan would bring me coffee at first light, then hurry back to her slumbering babies.

In succeeding years, Shelly and her boyfriend, and Ty and his buddy would "camp" in front of the ranger station door, relieving me of that tedious duty. They'd play euchre all night and attempt to scare each other senseless with gross stories of murder and mutilation. We always got Site Twenty. No one else wanted it as badly.

This utopiac space was located only a few hundred yards from the base of the bridge and was the most remote site in the park. It was separated from the site next to it by a mass of cedar trees, and from the St. Ignace Cemetery on the other side by a chain-link fence that was mostly camouflaged by flora.

We had to have this site in this campground because it afforded the perfect view of the bridge, and Morgan would be satisfied with no other. In time, the "Mighty Mac" became Morgan's property as well. She always referred to it as her bridge. Although Site Twenty was ours, the Mackinac Bridge was *hers*.

We first came here to heal. Tysen had scared us to death. In the summer of his third year, he began complaining about his leg. We inspected, but nothing seemed amiss. He began to limp. Neither Morgan nor I were concerned at first. Little boys, especially active ones like Ty, were bound to twist an ankle or bruise a knee, but the pain persisted and the limp became more pronounced.

We took him to the pediatrician. He ordered x-rays. "Nothing," they told us, "perhaps a mild sprain." After three weeks, Ty could no longer stand and resorted to crawling. We took him to a specialist—again, nothing.

Morgan thought the worst. She saw leukemia, bone cancer. She couldn't sleep or eat. She worried incessantly as she watched the little guy, normally so active, forlornly curled on the sofa, his head in his caring sister's lap.

I honestly thought he had a deep bruise or, perhaps, a torn tendon that the radiologists had overlooked. I wouldn't allow anything worse.

We watched a National Geographic special one night that showed a male lion killing his own cubs. Morgan looked at me accusingly. We had to have an answer.

We went to see Doctor Goldman, a renowned orthopedist, in Detroit. He took x-rays and returned immediately with the verdict. "Your son has Legg-Perthes disease," he said.

Morgan's dark eyes filled with tears, though she sat upright and forced herself to listen. She looked at me as if to say: "Don't ever doubt me again."

"This isn't fatal or deforming or permanent," Goldman said, matter-of-factly.

"Don't cwy, mama," Ty said, his rounded baby-face wrinkled in concern. He looked so vulnerable and fragile in his little tee shirt and shorts. Sesame Street characters paraded across his chest. I plucked him off the papered table and held him in my lap, trying to protect him from the diagnosis.

"What is it?" I asked. "I've never heard of it."

"Few people have," Goldman answered. "It's quite rare. It's caused by a blow to the hip. The ball joint that fits in the hip socket begins to disintegrate. Nobody knows why."

Morgan wiped away her tears with disgusted violence. "Go on," she said. "Tell us."

Goldman was a big man whose face was a worn treadmill topped by a shock of unruly, thick, white hair. He was direct and unsympathetic. He didn't seem to notice Morgan's anguish or fear. Morgan would later say that he had no "bedside manners."

"The ball joint has decayed rapidly and it's slipping in and out of the socket. It'll grow back, but in order to keep it in place while it does, he'll have to wear a Toronto brace. He'll have to wear it all the time, probably for about two years or more. Until we can get it fitted, he'll have to keep all weight off his right leg."

A month later, little Ty, who had just learned how to walk so recently, emerged from the medical prosthetics center in Ann Arbor, wearing a contraption that made him seem bionic. It forced his legs wide apart. From a special harness that attached around his upper thighs, a steel pole extended from his groin to a rubber tip that rested on the ground. From the base of the pole, steel rods flanged out to connect to special shoes with thick, black, rubber soles, four inches thick on the outside and tapering toward the inside to compensate for the extreme angle at which he must move.

Hand crutches that clipped around his lower arms were provided for balance. In effect, Ty had to shuffle along while doing the splits.

I was horrified, Morgan was relieved—the difference in perception. She knew that her baby would live and, gratefully, she could face anything else. I saw a little boy who would be restricted in so many ways, who would cry because he would finish last in every race and be chosen last for every team. He would be called "cripple" or "freak" and would have to struggle just to climb a flight of stairs. Morgan saw an empty grave and a grown, healthy man.

She set about making it fun. She taught him how to put all his weight on the center pole and move his legs to rotate himself, like a top. In bed, the pole extended upward and drew the sheets up into a cone. She brought him a flashlight and books, knelt by the bed, and stuck her head under the "tent" to read to him. She made sure he was involved in everything and every kid in the neighborhood knew, that if he played with Ty, he could have his fill of chocolate chip cookies. I tried to get Ty to crawl across the white linoleum in the kitchen, or avoid it, because his orthopedic shoes left black scuffmarks that required hours of elbow grease with an abrasive paste, to remove. Morgan would have none of it. No one else in the house had to crawl, she said, and Ty wouldn't either. Four hours of every Saturday were devoted to cleaning the kitchen floor.

She made his burden a game and the two years went quickly for him. I'm not sure he knows yet what a gift his mother gave him, not only in her attentions, but also in her example of courage. The summer before he entered the first grade, he was back to normal, running free. That was our first summer on Site Twenty.

At the time, I wasn't sure why Morgan was so enamored with the bridge. To me, it was a suspended obstruction of the natural panorama of trees and sky and water. But for Morgan, camping *was* the bridge. I often suggested that we try another park, perhaps something more remote, a little closer to "real" nature and farther away from the masses of "fudgies" who swarmed over the area and from whom, by some trick of the mind, we disassociated ourselves. Morgan could not be swayed. Even a stay in the luxurious Grand Hotel (from whose pillared veranda the bridge could clearly be seen), would not satisfy her. It had to be Straits State Park, Site Twenty.

Eventually, I came to understand that it was the connectedness of the bridge that filled a gap, crossed a void. It was connection in the divisive wilderness of the world. One could not appreciate its defiance of disparity while sitting in civilized comfort, sipping crème de menthe and listening to dance music. You had to hear the waves, see the lights of the bridge reflecting off the water. You had to hold your children in your lap in front of a blazing campfire as a family of skunks meandered by, causing the marshmallows for the s'mores to burn to ash. You had to see the bridge wrestle a storm and listen to Morgan's laughing defiance to know that the bridge would stand—the peninsulas would remain conjoined. This knowledge could only be gained on Site Twenty.

When Morgan and I first connected, a gap began to open between me and my siblings. There were arguments over the wedding and who would be in it, disagreements over time spent with our aging parents, disputes over petty differences that seemed large then. But mostly, I just ran away. I couldn't be my father's father anymore, or a surrogate husband to my mother. Ruth and Tommy would have to bear it alone. Since Morgan was my abettor in this desertion, Morgan was blamed. Then, we went away to Oz.

After my discharge, I was polite to my sister and brother (Ella would never come back), but there was an accusing distance, a chasm. Holidays were shared. We were devoted to each other's children, but not to each other. We were connected to our parents individually, but to one another we remained, basically, unrelated.

Natural congeniality didn't begin to return until our parents died. Genetic bridges had been burned and my siblings recognized, long before me, that change exists only in the future, and the future's continual contraction diminishes opportunity. Ruth, my motherless sister, made overtures to Morgan, my motherless wife. They grew close. Tommy followed suit. I hesitated, avoided, denied.

Morgan pushed me toward a reconciliation I hadn't known I needed. It was the first time we'd ever come to Mackinaw without the kids, who were now grown and living away from us. We'd sold all our camping gear. Morgan's heart had been invaded by a catheter two weeks earlier and one of her arteries had been routed. We'd decided to come to the straits for the weekend to rest and heal. We'd taken a motel room near the beach with a more distant view of the bridge than what we were used to. We sat on the bed as we talked. The June breeze wafted through the screened window, bringing with it the aroma of timelessness and water.

"Ruth and Tom are connections to your mom and dad," she argued, "to your past, your childhood." Her dark eyes penetrated my apathy. She took my hands in hers and looked down at them, studying. She fingered my wedding band. "You can't uncouple them like a boxcar and hook them to a different train," she persisted. "You can't jump to a different track. You can only go on without them, and if you leave them behind, you won't be whole anymore."

This was all preparation I couldn't see. My estrangement had begun in her defense, I thought. This was betrayal. But I knew my accusations were no more valid than those of my brother and sister years ago. They probably stemmed from the same source. "They're connections all right," I said, "like a yoke is a connection for oxen. It attaches you to your burden."

"It gives you identity—and purpose."

I shook my head, knowing how much I had suffocated under the onus of duty.

"Your brother is a lot like your dad, you know," she observed. "In what way?"

"He's a connector. And Ruth is the embodiment of your mom. Don't lose them twice." She kissed my hands and let go. "I'm gonna take a shower, then we'll go out to eat, okay?"

"Okay."

When she closed the bathroom door, I went outside and walked down to the beach. I sat on a log and buried my bare feet in the warm sand. The bridge seemed very distant, but visible. I saw two swans bobbing in the waters of the marina and mistook them for an omen. I thought of all those wonderful days on Site Twenty and how sad I would be if Shelly and Ty were not close after we were gone.

I walked back to the room. Morgan was still in the bathroom, putting on her make-up. On my pillow was a piece of paper ripped from the motel TV Guide. There was scribbling on it. I picked it up and read it through my bifocals.

Dear Ben

I love you so much. I have all my life.

I folded it carefully and put it in my wallet. It is there still.

A month later, she was gone. My sister and brother stood by me through the funeral. We all knew that she hadn't been the cause of our estrangement, but would be the ending of it. They comforted the kids, held me up, and tried to help me bear the unbearable. At Bethlehem Cemetery, under a canopy whose flapping reminded me of a tent on Site Twenty, Ty, my grown son, held my left hand. Shelly held my right, while she cradled her ten-month-old son in her lap.

We sat in folding chairs in front of Morgan's flower-laden casket. I remember thinking that the green, turf-like carpeting laid out before us was much like the stuff we wiped our feet on before entering the tent. Ruth and Tom stood behind me, their supportive hands on my sagging shoulders.

Two months later, in late September, Ruth and Tom and Shelly and Ty drove with me to Straits State Park. After Labor Day, the campground had few tenants. We knew the park ranger would try to stop us, so we waited until 4:00 A.M., then entered the park by walking through the local cemetery. We circumvented the chain link fence by wading around it in the cold waters of the strait, and came ashore at Site Twenty. My children shared the burden of carrying the big lilac bush, Morgan's favorite flower, purchased hours before at a nursery in Indian River. As Shelly and Ty waded around the fence ahead of me, I pictured Morgan, twenty years ago, holding their hands and helping them maintain their balance in the rocky shallows. My brother shouldered a spade while I helped my sister, now nearing sixty, to wade ashore. The full moon and the Mackinac Bridge cast enough light to allow us to maneuver.

We moved among the cedars until we discovered an opening that would admit sunshine and, most significantly, afford a view of the bridge. We worked silently, each one taking a turn with the spade, more for ceremony than necessity. It didn't have to be a big hole.

Of the six hundred sites in the park, only a half-dozen were occupied and none of those were within a hundred yards of where we worked. The sites exposed to the cooling wind off the lake were coveted in the summer, but avoided in the chill days of autumn. Our greatest fear was that the park ranger might drive by and discover our subterfuge.

Within fifteen minutes, the excavation was judged adequate. Tysen placed the lilac reverently into the hole, like a novitiate at his first communion. Shelly filled a plastic cup from Seven-Eleven with water from the strait and baptized the bush. She made three trips before she was satisfied that the traumatized roots had enough moisture to begin the process of connection.

Ruth rested on a large boulder that the kids had played on years ago. I remember it being much farther from the water then. Her eyes glistened with dampness and the lights from the bridge. The only sounds, now that our labor was done, were the sonorous waves and the haunting bellow of a freighter, crawling slowly under the bridge, celebrating its disassociation from land.

"I hope it'll grow," my sister wished aloud, looking dolefully at the resettled bush. "I can just see some damned teenager hacking it up to throw on his campfire."

"If the roots are strong, it'll come back," my brother reassured her.

I felt suddenly miserable and, lighting a cigarette, sat on the sand, looking at the bridge I'd seen so often in the middle of the night while relieving my bladder in the dense cedars a few yards away. The lights of the bridge seemed different now, not so distant, yet intrusive.

Shelly, perhaps closer to her mother than anyone but me, sensed my mood and sat down next to me. A few feet away was the fire pit, emptied of refuse by the park service and looking unnatural without the blackened remnants of charred logs.

"The bridge is different now, isn't it, Dad?" she said. Her voice had grown so much older that it disturbed me. I always thought of her as a child, though she was twenty-six, a mother, and soon to be divorced. Her baby and the childish man she would leave, had matured her. Life—and death, had severed her innocence, though she still remembered what it was.

"Yes," I said, not willing to talk, yet wanting to listen.

My stoic son joined us, characteristically remaining quiet in the difficult moment. Tysen could talk for hours about his golf score or some methodology developed for his office, but when presented with the repugnance of emotion, his shields, Silence and Distance, protected him. Fortune, then, seemed not quite so outrageous. He hadn't talked of his mother since her death.

"I was just thinking about the year that we borrowed Uncle John's little camper," Shelly continued, staring across the dark water at the bridge. "Mom was so excited not to have to sleep on the hard ground or worry about saturated sleeping bags after a rain."

There was an uncomfortable quiet for a few moments, detached and palpable. Ruth and Tommy came closer, not wanting to intrude on this nuclear silence, but recognizing appeals that were both revealed and concealed.

"Are you talking about our old tow-low?" my sister asked. "Is that when it came off the hitch and rolled over on Interstate 75?"

I smiled, embarrassed at the recollection of wrecking my sister's camper.

"How'd it break loose, Dad?" Ty asked. He was staring at the newly planted bush, whose leaves sagged, temporarily, from the trauma of transplanting.

"I forgot to put the pin through," I explained. "The latch came loose, and the first bump we hit lifted her off the ball. Smashed it up beyond repair. It took me three years to pay your Uncle John back."

"I'm glad we got to use it before it was wrecked, Dad," Shelly said. "I remember you taking hours to park the camper on this site because Mom had to see her bridge from her bunk."

"Tell us about it," Ruth said.

Shelly's mind began to bridge the gap between age twenty-six and ten. "Mom would get out of the car and crank the roof of the camper up to its extended position. Then she'd get in the camper, which was still connected to the car, and convert the dining table into the bed where she slept. Then she'd crawl in, shut the camper door and raise the little window in the door. She'd yell to me, and I'd relay to Dad when to stop and when to angle until the bridge was perfectly framed in the window. All this so that whenever she awoke at night, she had a perfect view of her bridge!"

I drove across that bridge too, for a few moments, knowing it was the reason we were here, until pain drove me back to the other side, where Tysen waited.

"She's dead, Shelly!" he shouted. He was choking back a grief, which hadn't yet manifested itself in any form except silence. "Your stupid sentimentality won't change it, so why don't you just shut up!"

This sudden virulence startled everyone—not only because of its rancorous tone, but also its volume, which dispelled the sacred quiet of night and secrecy. His voice surged across the open water, dying halfway to the opposite shore, but the words aged much longer in his sister's mind, aged to putrefaction. Like her father, given to emotional evocation, she cried.

"What you call 'sentimentality,' Ty," I said, seeing the hurt in Shelly's face and not looking deeper than his, "some less indifferent souls might regard as attachment, a sentiment with which you seem unfamiliar."

"What do you mean?" His eyes narrowed, preparing for battle.

"I mean you don't seem to give a damn about people who love you. Your sister was describing a happy time with your mother and you bit her head off." A quite ludicrous image of a decapitated chicken suddenly flooded my mind. The severed head lay on the ground, wondering why the body continued to run aimlessly in circles when it must know that it was dead and should lie down. "It was insensitive at best, even cruel...a desecration of a very special moment. Your mother would have...."

"You don't know what mom would have wanted because she can't tell us. She's dead! Planting bushes and gushing about 'special moments' won't bring her back, so what's the point to all this shit!" He turned away, striding purposefully toward the cemetery fence, needing to be elsewhere.

His anger fed mine. What had begun as a poignant memorial had turned into a poison tree. The moment was ruined. I pursued him, intent on upbraiding him further for his meanness to his sister, but more for his detachment, his desire to cut off the past. He reminded me, only then, of my father-in-law, his grandfather, who had remarried four months after Elyda's death and never looked back. I'd always resented that way of thinking. It was a hurried uncoupling, disdaining reverence for what was. I saw it as a kind of cowardice and an admission of defeat.

As I started after Ty, my brother grabbed my arm. "The lights on the bridge have gone out," he said, and studied me with those blue eyes that once belonged to our father.

Ruth, her arm around Shelly, looked across the water. "Dawn's coming," she said.

Tysen stopped and turned around.

"Why don't you say what's really bothering you?" Tommy asked him. The tone was gentle, but there was a surety in his voice that came from experience.

"What?"

"I know you love your sister and your dad. You know your Aunt Ruth and I and your dad, didn't know each other for a long time." Tommy looked at both of us. "We found out that what appeared to be pulling us apart was actually not. So maybe that's what's going on here."

Tysen took another step toward us. "It's my fault."

It seemed too ingenuous a thing to merely request an answer and receive one. I'm good at questioning truth, but not at asking true questions.

My anger dissipated. I'd forgotten a rupture that had been healed, because I hadn't done anything to patch it. I'd set aside my own past. It was time to remember. "What's your fault?" I asked my son.

Shelly and Ruth had come to join us as the palest tinge of light joined earth and sky, day and night. We must have looked strange to the awakening gulls, a flock of humans huddled around an empty fire pit.

Tysen came closer. "Mom is gone because of me," he whispered. He didn't cry or tremble, demonstrations he regarded as unmanly, but looked fiercely at me as if I would suddenly strike him or sever all ties. Instead, I could only ask: "What're you talking about?"

"After Mom had her heart procedure, you told us not to argue with her, or stress her. I did it anyway, three days before she died. She didn't think I treated my girlfriend with enough respect and she said so. I blew up. I knew it was bad for her, but I didn't care. I'm sure she never told you about it, did she?"

"No."

"She knew you'd be angry. She swallowed it. I didn't talk to her again. She called to try and smooth things over. I wouldn't pick up. I hurried her death, I know, and there's nothing I can do about it." He turned to Shelly. "I'm sorry, Shel. I didn't intend to hurt you, but my memories are cruel."

I marveled at how handsome and strong he was. He had his mother's dark eyes and hair, his father's dark guilt. "Ty," I said, "I didn't kiss your mother good-night on the last night of her life. She'd been talking on the phone for over an hour and I was tired of waiting for her. I went to bed and she went to sleep later—forever. What should we do, Ty?" He saw my love for him, a connection of blood and water.

He hugged me, then moved away, to the melancholy bush that seemed to recuperate a bit now, in the rays of the rising sun. Tragedy had formed a connection. He looked at it tenderly. A single tear, hurriedly erased with the back of his hand, escaped one eye. "It's a good view," he said, looking out to the bridge.

The noise of an approaching engine gradually became audible as we all stood frozen for a few seconds.

"We'd better go," my sister cautioned. "That's gotta be the park ranger. He must've heard the shouting. If he finds us here, he'll make us dig up the bush."

We all waded into the water to go around the fence and return to the cemetery and our cars. For some reason, even though the frigid water was paralyzing our legs, we all stopped simultaneously and turned to look at the Mackinac Bridge. To me, it seemed like it'd grown now from the wilderness and was a part of it.

I counted five cars on its summit, early-morning vacationers, inching south across the span. Like us, they were going home.

* * *

Dr. Kim Dong-Ho
Notes on the Riveridge Case
October 1, 2000
I think it necessary to write my observations and opinions of the patient, both personal and professional, not only to aid in diagnosis and treatment, but because this case, this person, is so unique to my experience that a complete documentation may very well prove to benefit the general scope and erudition of behaviorism.

Ebenezer Riveridge is a big man. He stands well over six feet and carries around the better part of three hundred pounds, though he isn't obese. Perhaps twenty pounds or so don't belong; the rest is genetic, I think. He was just meant to be big. In spite of the difference in our stature (he could probably kill me with a single blow), I've never felt threatened or intimidated, at least not physically. I have spoken with the nurses on his floor and they have assured me that he is gentle, even docile, and always courteous.

In spite of his bulk, his most striking physical feature is his eyes. They are pale blue, almost gray and, as I have discovered, extremely sensitive to light. The classic texts on bi-polar manic depression maintain that his susceptibility is paradigmatic of the disorder. His father, George Washington Riveridge, suffered from manic depression most of his adult life and was committed to this same institution several times (I have reviewed his records). Still, I don't believe it fits Ben's profile. Indeed, I'm not certain he is ill in any way, by any definition. The district court turned him over to us for a ninety-day evaluation, thirty of which have gone by already, and I'm no closer to discovering what motivated the behavior that led to his incarceration.

His eyes pierce you through. They're intimidating. It isn't the eyes really, so much as it is his use of them. He stares at me during our sessions, but I don't think it's intentional. He's not trying to intimidate. In fact, I'm guessing that he's generally unaware of my discomfort. Oddly, I've seen him stare at his children and his grandson in much the same manner, and they seem to take no notice of his raptor-like concentration on them. They bask in the attentiveness, which they appear to regard as warm benevolence—but then, what nestling ever feared his own parent?

In keeping with this eagle comparison, he is balding and, what little hair he has left, is entirely white. I would say that he looks prematurely old for his age (fifty-four), but that isn't true either. He has a boyish face and walks in a swaggering manner that suggests the confidence of youth.

He's a heavy smoker. I have to air my office for hours after our sessions and I've requisitioned a purifier in a desperate attempt to save my own lungs and keep my laundry bill at a reasonable level. I tried to tell him that my office was off limits for smoking and he retaliated by refusing to come. The habit has taken its toll, somewhat. He has a dry cough which, he has proven on more than one occasion, can be at least temporarily eliminated by smoking another cigarette.

He's quite fastidious about his personal appearance, although not obsessively so. He sports a neatly trimmed, full mustache (also white). Otherwise, he's clean-shaven.

He insists on very little. Outside of his cigarettes, he has a penchant for chocolates and books. These are his only demands. The subject matter of his reading, in keeping with his disdain for rationalism, is generally literary fiction. His favorites, I've noticed in brief visits to his quarters, are Milan Kundera, Ian McEwan, Mark Helprin, Jim Harrison, and the eighteenth-century romantic poets. Non-fiction books tend to Jungian psychology, the theories of James Hillman, Joseph Campbell's books on myths and myth-making, and the Bible. I've never seen him read a newspaper or magazine and, although his room is supplied with a television, the nurse informs me that he never turns it on. He appears to have little interest in current events.

He's told me that he remembers visiting his father here as a young man, but he doesn't say much about the hospital beyond that.

During our sessions, he's cooperative and answers each question succinctly, but rarely elaborates or offers any information beyond that requested. He'll talk about anything or anyone, except Mrs. Hall. It's she, of course, who called the police and pressed charges against him. As far as I know, he feels no enmity toward her, but he won't answer any questions regarding her, or the "incident." Although he smokes continually during our talks, he appears calm and seems to enjoy the tobacco rather than to be dependent on it. There is no wringing of hands or nervous fidgeting. He generally slumps in his chair and, as I previously alluded, studies as much (or more), than he is studied.

He's devoted to his children. His daughter, Michelle, is a beautiful woman, petite and gregarious, but terribly distraught over her father's "misfortune," as she calls it. She's thirty, and recently married for the second time. The son, Tysen, if I may be so trite, is tall, dark and handsome. He's in his late twenties and already an executive with an insurance firm in Detroit. He's quick to anger, and I feel his belligerence whenever we meet. I'm sure he holds me responsible for his father's incarceration. I wouldn't want to have him for an enemy. Mr. Riveridge is proud of them both, it's readily apparent, and dotes especially on his four-year-old grandson, Christopher, Michelle's son, whom he refers to as "The Bean." "The face of a child," he once told me, "is God's best work."

His brother, Thomas, is a Director of Social Services for the western half of the state of Michigan. He lives with his wife and daughter in Traverse City. His sister, Ruth, lives in Saginaw. Although there is great disparity in their ages, (Ruth is sixty and Thomas is forty-four), the three of them are very close. I understand that there is another sister, but she hasn't contacted any of the others for more than a decade.

Ben Riveridge has few friends. As I've already mentioned, his closest association is with the custodian, Jack Csinos, which, he tells me, is a Hungarian word meaning "smart."

I think he's a popular teacher. He's received dozens of letters from students and several have attempted to obtain visitor passes, although the court forbids non-related minors to enter the hospital. He doesn't speak of them.

He has only one friend with whom he has been associated throughout most of his adult life, a man named Billy Borden. He met Borden in Vietnam, and although he's seen him only once since 1970, they communicate regularly and seem to share a special bond that distance doesn't appear to affect. I don't think Mr. Borden is yet aware of Ben Riveridge's confinement here.

Ben's favorite subject is his wife, Morgan, who died suddenly about four years ago. It's evident that he was devoted to her and she to him. He talks about their marriage of thirty years in hushed tones, as if he were in a church, and often produces tears when describing their relationship. It's obvious that his grief was, and is, monumental. I asked him once to describe what it was like to be alone now. He said: "Being alone isn't as bad as feeling alone." When I asked him what he meant, he said that he felt most alone when surrounded by people at social functions. He said that all the couples "stamp my singularity on my heart and remind me that I'm half-gone."

Today I asked him to define seemingly unrelated words in a further attempt to evaluate his lucidity. Although his answers were unorthodox, I found them to be, on close examination, almost aphoristic, and certainly not demented. He played the word-association game well.

I asked him first to define the word "house" for me. He answered: "Nature, wearing make-up."

"How about the word 'life'?" I offered.

He responded: "A game of connect-the-dots."

"And what is *love*?"

"A self-abnegating habit of which the practitioner is unaware."

"Good. Define 'hall' please."

His blue-gray eyes widened. His jaw clenched. I could almost see talons. "I told you," he warned, "I won't talk about her."

"I'm not asking you to," I tried to reassure him, although he knew I was lying. "Can't you just define the word?"

He hesitated a moment, then smiled. "A passage." He lit a cigarette and sighed. His hands were steady. He was calm. The jaw relaxed.

"Thank you," I said. "Can you define *hope*?"

"The façade of eternity."

"How about truth?"

"An amalgam of perceptions. Dr. Kim, may I tell you a parable?"

"You're bored with the definitions?"

"Yes."

"All right, certainly. Go ahead."

"One day, I went into a video rental store and picked out a movie. I got in line to check out. It was a long line because it was a Friday night in January and everyone was looking for something to occupy time. There was a teen-ager, a girl, in the front of the line of impatient and fidgeting people. The man behind the counter told her that it would cost her two dollars and fifty cents. She fumbled in her purse for quite some time, finally extracting several coins, which she counted out, appropriately, on the counter. The woman in front of me rolled her eyes, stepped from one foot to the other, and sighed. Two other people coughed vociferously. 'I'm afraid you only have two dollars and ten cents,' the clerk said. 'Oh dear,' she replied, 'it's all I have. Can't you give me some kind of charge on the account? I'm a regular customer. I'll bring it in next time. I'm going to meet some friends. They'll kill me if I don't get this movie. Please.' 'I'm sorry, Miss,' the clerk said, 'but company policy...' 'Oh for God's sake,' the man behind the teen-ager yelled. 'Here. Here's forty cents. Check her out and let's get on with it!' He slammed the coins down on the counter. 'Oh, thanks, Mister,' the girl gushed. The clerk typed her membership number into the computer. The people in line began to crowd against one another in anticipation. 'Our records show, Miss, that you owe ten dollars in late charges,' he announced fearfully, while surveying the ugly mob. 'What?' she said. A child further up the line from me began to cry. My heavy jacket was turning moist inside. A huge black man stepped forward. 'Here,' he yelled, and threw the money at the clerk. 'Get her the hell outta here!' The clerk grabbed the bills off the floor. The girl bounced out the door. The line began to move. I was the last person. 'Sorry it took so long, Mister,' the clerk apologized, 'but that girl was a real airhead. I thought I was going to get lynched. That'll be two-fifty.' 'I'm curious,' I said, as I handed him the money. 'What movie was she renting?' 'Huh? Oh. Same as the one she had late charges on; *Dumb and Dumber*.'"

Mr. Riveridge leaned back in his chair, folded one leg over the other, and was silent.

"That's it?"

"That's it."

"What lesson is it supposed to teach? Parables have morals don't they?"

The patient lit another cigarette. "What do you think, Dr. Kim?"

I confessed that I didn't know. I told him that it could illustrate that money isn't as important as time; that it might be representative of a grudging kind of modern Samaritanism; that it could be construed as a criticism of the interrogations he'd just been subjected to and he wanted to show me how dumb he thought I was. I wasn't sure.

He told me that we all interpret what goes on around us and we apply it to our lives. That's what I must do with it. That's what we all must do. There's no universal message, only metaphorical application on a personal level. "That's why I'm in here," he said, "and you, too." He paused for a moment and a wry grin spread across his broad countenance. "Then again, it could have simply been a ploy to redirect the questioning, put it in my hands. One never knows."

After a long silence, he asked me if I had been born in Vietnam. I told him I had. "As chance would have it," I told him, "in the village of Tuy Hoa, where you were stationed, I believe."

I waited to see the intended affect. He remained unperturbed. "No, Dr. Kim," he whispered, "not by chance."

He snubbed out his cigarette, looked at his watch, and rose from his chair. "Sixty more days," he said, and quietly slipped from the room.

Chapter Ten

Monsters in the Sanctuary

"GET ME OUT OF HERE!" the Prince of Peace said to Joseph.
And what is Joseph if not a man who does what he's told.
—John Irving, *A Prayer for Owen Meany*

After thirteen years, my second teaching position ended, like the first, on the issue of virginity. Although the Lutheran church did not expect abstinence from Mary and Joseph, they did expect it from their teen-agers.

In my second month at Lutheran High, a girl from one of my literature classes went to the school's pastor, and told him, in confidence, that she was pregnant. Her boyfriend (such a ludicrous description), was from another school. Pastor Edwards, whose name befitted a man who saw us all dangling from the hands of an angry god, promptly informed the principal. His primary concern was the tuition that would be lost if the "decent" families should withdraw their children from the school to avoid associating their children with such a Jezebel. The girl was expelled. I didn't see why she had to leave. Her child wasn't due until the end of June. She was a senior. She could complete her education, then have the baby. I tried to convince them that this was the time that she needed God the most.

Although Roman Catholics taught about degrees of sin, it was the Lutherans, I would discover, who really believed it—and sex was the most cardinal of them all. Students could lie, swear, defy authority, even steal, and still suffer little more than a study-hall detention on Saturday, but sex was always grounds for expulsion. Our little Hester Prynne was duly removed.

Most of the students learned three moral lessons from this incident. One: You should never trust a clergyman. Two: Although

God may forgive, the church (and in the Lutheran educational system the school was regarded as an arm of the church), does not. Three: Always lie about what you have done wrong.

It's difficult to always be placed in harm's way. I could never understand why humans were made to have such an uncontrollable itch at age fifteen or sixteen, and not be allowed to scratch it until they were mature enough to resist. Human society has forgotten how to be compatible with nature.

Over the next dozen years, I became an unofficial counselor and champion of the "fallen," though it wasn't a role I had chosen— or relished. I attended numerous school board meetings to plead the case of one sinner or another. Because they learned that I wouldn't betray them, kids in trouble often came to me, clandestinely, and confided. Room 106 became a kind of crisis center.

A girl who'd given in to her paramour needed to assuage her guilt, fostered and nurtured by Pastor Edwards in daily chapel messages. Another boy talked to me about his addiction to masturbation and his certainty that the *Playboys* under his bed were a ticket to hell. Although I was rigidly opposed to it, several girls confessed that they'd had abortions. It was the only alternative, they said, if they were to continue their education. They were all looking for absolution.

Morgan knew of all this, of course. I wouldn't keep it from her. But she worried about the subterfuge, and hated the hypocrisy. She believed that my liberalism would eventually land me in trouble, as, of course, it did. But I couldn't turn away from troubled kids whose parents would never believe them capable of such evil and whose church would offer them no redemption. Someone had to listen, someone had to care. God is only implicit through forgiveness.

I remember reading to my literature class, a quotation of Mary Shelley's, taken from the preface to her *Frankenstein*: "No man chooses evil because it is evil; he only mistakes it for happiness, the good he seeks." Reasons can be found in the darkest, mildewed corners of human experience.

The gradgrindian pharisees of Lutheran education were never willing to accept this truth. It's always easier to deny our own inadequacies by affirming those of others. The weight of self-righteousness feels good in the hand. It's a hard thing to drop that stone once you've picked it up.

A student named Joseph Swann was a frequent target. I didn't meet him until he was a senior (since I taught only that group), though I'd seen him in the halls many times. You couldn't miss him. He was small and delicate, stereotypically effeminate to almost comic proportions. His hair was always perfectly coifed, his clothes always immaculate and overtly conservative, but he never wore anything frilly or lacey or pink. He didn't have to.

Most human beings have forgotten what it's like to live in a claw-and-fang world and die as prey, to be torn apart, swallowed as food. Joseph was relearning. He lived in a universe of unbridled cruelty.

He hung on courageously, through three and a half years of abuse from his fellow students. But Joseph could be loveless fodder for the strong only to a point, and then he began to question the meaning of his existence.

He'd turned in an essay on *Frankenstein* for my class. He wrote about the desolate emptiness of his depression, stark and white as Mary Shelley's arctic landscape, where monsters learn about their creators—and die.

He wrote: "I exist in a world where reason has died and being is all there is. I exist, but I am not, reasonably, alive. I am a Bedlamite, caged and sprayed with a hose for the amusement and occasional enlightenment of the crowd. For me, as with all monsters, life has become all too unreasonable."

It was an alarming piece, a frightening, horrific window into his pain. What had sparked this angst, I discovered later, was a Biblical lesson by Pastor Edwards, in his religion class, on God's condemnation of homosexuality in First Corinthians. Joseph had managed to struggle through an unhappy and confused puberty, bolstered purely by a sure faith that God loved him even if no one else did. The pastor's homily had taken that comfort away. Joseph had learned that he was an "abomination." He wanted to die.

I asked Joseph to see me after school. I didn't think he would, but he came through the door and sat down. He'd decided that he wouldn't be alive tomorrow, and his decision had given him the strength and courage of apathy.

In twenty minutes, he shared the most intimate details of his life. Joseph had a tiny, stunted penis and no testicles. At thirteen, he'd begun to grow breasts, which he bound each day to conceal them. Every month, he suffered cramps. He'd been in love with several boys, but kept it secret. His father had been disgusted with him since birth. He'd never been kissed by anyone but his mother.

Last year, she took him to a clinic in Chicago while his dad was on a business trip in Oregon. They'd done hormonal tests. They told Joseph that he was a female in every regard except one. They recommended a sex-change operation.

"I'm a mistake," he'd told his mother.

"Nonsense," she'd replied. "God doesn't make mistakes."

So Joseph was destined to be a woman trapped in a man's body.

I told him he really didn't have a man's body or a woman's. I told him the myth of Hermes and Aphrodite and the result of their liaison, Hermaphroditus. It served to comfort him, he said, even if it wasn't true, if for no other reason than there must have been a real half-man, half-woman in order for the myth to originate as explanation. It meant he wasn't alone. I assured him this was true.

"But God hates...."

"God hates no one," I interrupted. "Man has done his level-best to simplify the divine, but God isn't that direct. Metaphor is God's language and it's heard in the imagination. You spend your time listening to what everyone tells you about God instead of hearing Him for yourself. You'll graduate soon. Then you can get a job, go to school, change into the person you want to be, and no one can stop you. The great sin would be to throw that all away."

He didn't come back to see me again, but he held on. I watched him, tiny and frightened in his cap and gown at graduation. He waved at me, then disappeared.

In the summer of 1989, blood appeared in my dad's urine. The lithium he'd taken for twenty years to keep "balanced" was destroying his kidneys. The doctor ordered him to quit taking it. Within a month, he had to be admitted to White Pine Psychiatric Unit. He was given a choice, or rather the family was, since he'd been judged incompetent—stay alive in confusion or die lucid. I made the decision.

His faculties slowly returned with the deadly lithium. By October, he was sane enough to understand what had transpired. He confirmed my decision. His kidneys deteriorated very swiftly. By Thanksgiving, he could only urinate through a catheter. Mom wasn't physically able to care for him.

In December of 1989, Dad, like his mother before him, entered a nursing home, something he'd always dreaded—the final irony of his existence. Some would look at his life, I suppose, and see the cluttered chaos of tragedy. He thought of it differently. Days before the end, he told me: "I was lucky enough, Ben, to love the same woman for fifty years. I've seen the miracles of my children's lives. I experienced baseball, lakes, good food, sensuality and God. In my trials, Ben, I learned compassion and in my delusions, I touched what was real."

Ruth, Tommy and I kept a fifty-six hour vigil over him as he slipped into a coma. In the early dawn of a Monday in late March, we decided to go home to shower and get some fresh clothes. That, of course, is when he slipped away. Still, he wasn't alone.

A pretty, young nurse, soon to be married, had held his hand. She'd been his special friend during his last weeks in that place. She'd known suffering and delusion too and knew how to comfort him. Her name was Josie Swann.

Almost a year later, in February of 1991, Tysen Riveridge, who was then a sophomore at Lutheran High, went to Pastor Edwards and confessed that his girlfriend was pregnant.

He didn't have the luxury of coming to me for counseling. I was his father. It really wouldn't have mattered who he told, since the girl was a student at the same school and she'd already informed too many friends. I was wounded by being the last to know.

I knew, as Ty did not, that there would be three targets for the Pharisees. He and the girl would be expelled and this would be the perfect excuse to get rid of the "liberal element" on the staff, i.e. myself. They'd never fire me. You can't fire a person who's been called by God, as they believed all teachers and pastors to be. However, they could hold me up as an example of the man who "troubleth his own house."

Ty was given a hearing before the school board. He was contrite and repentant. Morgan and I sat with him and hoped for clemency, but they were determined to root out heresy. I remember listening to one particularly vociferous board member pontificate on the dangers of "bad apples spoiling the barrel." The previous year, his daughter had told me of her abortion, an event of which he was still blissfully unaware. I suppressed the temptation to reveal it only because Morgan squeezed my hand and held me back. She knew that I couldn't stand to be one of them.

The vote was twelve to zero in favor of expulsion—same with the girl. She transferred to the public high school, Arthur Hill. Morgan and I home-schooled Ty through the rest of his sophomore year, but it was Morgan who saw Ty through this second great crisis of his life. As with the first, she kept him too busy to feel self-pity. I did the educating, she did the teaching. His lessons with me were at night and on the weekends, since we both worked. She wouldn't allow him to sit around alone during the day and arranged for him to volunteer at the hospital in the morning and bag groceries at a supermarket in the afternoon. Somehow, we got through until summer, though it was painful for me to see his empty chair in my study hall every afternoon. In July, we all went to Straits State Park, Site Twenty.

Morgan had always been opposed to change, now she insisted on it. Ty needed to start over, somewhere else. We needed new jobs, new schools, a new house in a new town. I began sending out my resume.

I got several offers, but decided on a public school in a small town called Swan's End, on the other side of the state, near Grand Rapids. It didn't offer the best money, but it had the best name. Shelly was a freshman at Saginaw Valley State University, but was still living at home. She transferred to Grand Valley State in order to stay with us.

We sold the house. I wrote a letter of resignation to the school board. I informed them that there had been many more cases of sexual misconduct than they imagined and that perhaps they ought to consider forgiveness as a policy in the future, since condemnation limited God's hand in things. I didn't mention any names. They didn't ask.

Ty didn't see the mother of his child anymore, as per her parents' wishes. As he began his junior year at Swan's End High School, we heard that she'd given birth to a boy. She named him Joseph to make him real, then gave him up for adoption. His new parents were from Wisconsin and they took him there. Ty never saw his son. We never saw our first grandchild. He must be almost ten now.

Morgan and I spoke of it seldom, Ty; not at all. He played football and basketball, became a member of the National Honor Society, went to proms and dated regularly.

We became immersed in work. Morgan got a position in the kitchen at the high school. Like the other women who labored there, she attained the exalted status of "lunch lady." The students adored her. Every kid who had forgotten his lunch money could depend on Morgan to bail him out.

At Swan's End, there were many pregnant girls. The absence of religion didn't promote it, but the administrators merely recognized its inevitability and dealt with it humanely. Virginity, like sin, wasn't an issue. I don't think we had any more pregnancies than at Lutheran High and I'm sure there were fewer abortions. Pregnant girls at Swan's End were still allowed to learn. The verb "to know" was decidedly unbiblical here.

In 1993, Ty graduated from Swan's End High. Morgan cried through it all. I guessed that she was thinking of how far Ty had come in two years, but she confided to me later that she'd been remembering our own graduation twenty-eight years earlier, and how we were closer to the end than the beginning.

Ty went to work for an insurance company the next month and began to take college courses at night in the fall. He would continue his education on a part-time basis for the next seven years, all the while advancing up the company ladder until the degree he was finally awarded was only garnish on the Barmicidal feast of promotion.

Shelly met Tony Dombrazo at Grand Valley State in her first semester there. He was good-looking, a great singer, and a better liar. He drank way too much. Morgan disliked him instantly. She was good at forecasting storms and, as with the storms, she feared what Tony might do to her child—but she put up a good front.

Shelly and Tony were married in 1993 and moved to Grand Rapids where Tony was employed in a factory. Christopher was born the following year. Shelly's visits to us began to increase after that. Tony was often unaccounted for. She talked of divorce. Morgan wouldn't hear of it. She told me that we were lucky enough to have been attached by the heart, but Shelly would have to live with whatever attachments she could. She'd taken an oath.

When Morgan began to suffer chest pains, I thought they might be little panic attacks over the unhappiness that Shelly was suffering, but I was wrong. After her surgery, her artery open again, the pain went away. But then, the fluttering began, irregular heartbeats that caused her to pale and clutch her chest. They told us it was nothing. Her pulse was normal, Dr. Singh assured me and, though he believed everything was all right, he scheduled a stress EKG. Her appointment was a week away, the soonest they could fit her in. They gave her nitroglycerine tablets to take if she felt any intense pain. Each of those days, she slept until noon, did a few minor chores, then took a two- or three-hour nap. She couldn't get enough rest. On the afternoon of July 30th, we'd just finished lunch and were sitting at the kitchen table together.

"Maybe we should head back up to Mackinac for a few days after your test tomorrow, Morg," I said. "It'd do you good to see your bridge."

She laughed. "We just got back," she answered. Her smile looked weak. "I just need to rest, Honey." She put her finger on my mouth and moved it lovingly along my lower lip. "You have to get ready," she whispered.

"For what?"

She took my hand and held it to her breast. No other words were wasted.

Chapter Eleven

The Incredible Lightness of Bean

He was a glance from God.
—Zora Neale Hurston, *Their Eyes Were Watching God*

After Morgan's funeral, Ty and Shelly stayed with me for a few days. Shelly cleaned, Ty cut the lawn. They both fixed meals and took turns not leaving me alone. We removed Morgan's clothes and shoes from the closet and packed them in boxes. We emptied her purses, applied for her life insurance benefits, contacted social security, cancelled her credit cards—but mostly, we just grieved. Christopher cooed in his playpen, happily unaware of the tragedy around him. Ten months of life is not enough time to learn weight.

In Morgan's dresser drawer we found the accoutrements of two lifetimes—memorabilia of her children. There were cards with "Happy Mother's Day" printed in macaroni, snips of hair and baby teeth, honor roll pins and newspaper clippings, programs from banquets and sporting events and school plays. Our life together was kept in another drawer—high school graduation, wedding announcements, little notes to each other, obituaries of grandparents and parents and Alf Landon, postcards from Billy Borden and other such weighty paraphernalia that pushed me nearer the earth.

My children saw me sob for the first time, an uncontrollable child-like demonstration of pain. I couldn't help it. Morgan and I had been the pillars that kept them from falling. Now, the strongest was torn down and the other teetered precariously. I decided to be stone after that, to keep the roof of reality from crashing down on all our heads.

After a few days, Ty had to leave. He had an apartment in Grand Rapids, a job, a girlfriend and school, all of which required his attention, too. Still, I had to force him to go, with assurances that I'd be fine and that he was only half an hour away.

Shelly stayed an additional week. She hadn't contacted Tony since the funeral and vice-versa, but he finally called and told her he'd taken some vacation time and wanted to take her and Christopher camping to "sort things out." I encouraged her to go. She needed to save her own family. I helped her to pack and get Christopher buckled in his car seat. As they waved to me and disappeared down the road, I felt a heavy dread of loneliness so overwhelming that I had to resist a terrible urge to fall to the ground and let it crush me.

Once inside, I sat in the same kitchen chair where, ten days before, Morgan had told me to "get ready." I thought, "Her fingerprints are still on this table. Her voice is still on the answering machine." I began to address, for the first time, the critical question of Being.

Ontological metaphysicians, from primordial shamans to Aristotleian classicists to Hegelian existentialists have pondered the mysterious question.

As a boy and a young man, this enigma failed to incite my curiosity. The question was not factually relevant to me. It was merely intellectual exercise. I existed, those I loved existed, and that was sufficient. Non-being was for the abstract "dead" and the unborn. I didn't yet realize that I could function as a living entity without Being.

For a theatre class in college, I read Sartre's *No Exit*. It heightened my interest in existentialism. That curiosity matured as those I loved gradually passed into non-Being; my grandparents, my mother-in-law, my parents.

I began reading Kierkegaard. I couldn't accept his universalist ethic which embraced cosmic law and duty above individual circumstances. When I explained his ideas to Morgan (she'd never read Kierkegaard herself), she said that she thought the Dane was "impersonally selfish." I had to agree, but his suggestions led to further reading.

When Morgan passed to non-Being, if Being is essential completeness, so did I. Orphaned, widowed, alone in a house designed for several, I felt lost—no longer a human being, but only a man. As a Christian, I believed in eternal life, but was not entirely convinced that life and Being were synonymous.

Heidegger contends, in his *Sein und Zeit*, that man grasps Being only through his constant dread of impending death. Our comprehension of Being is directly correlative, he argues, to our understanding of time and the finite. We know, he reasoned, unlike other living creatures, that time is our enemy and we, and those we love, in time, will die. This insight into non-Being, Heidegger insists, is the avenue by which we comprehend Being. It's a kind of ontological experience, where being sick is the only way by which we can know health, where happiness is measured by misery. This seemed a reasonable idea, but the presupposition of death-dread, in my grief, didn't apply. I *wanted* to die. I would later understand that Heidegger's error was in measuring time only as future. The past, I would eventually discover, is infinite and contains only beginnings.

Ty called every day. His job was going well. He thought he was in love, and might get married the next summer. He got an "A" on his exam in Statistical Analysis. Shelly never missed a day, either. The camping trip had been okay, and special fun for Christopher, but she didn't love Tony anymore, if she ever had. She said there were two incidences she couldn't erase from her mind: one of these was Tony refusing to drive her to Grand Rapids when Morgan was dying because, he said, he couldn't miss work. The other was the confusion of searching for Tony at the funeral service. As her son-in-law, Tony was one of the pallbearers for Morgan, and wasn't in attendance when the casket had to be carried from the church to the hearse. Shelly found him outside smoking a cigarette and joking with friends. She told me that it was these recurring images, not the lying or the drunkenness, that murdered her love. She wanted to come home. Remembering

Morgan, and believing my assent would only be selfish, I urged her to give it more time. She reluctantly acquiesced.

I went back to work in September, teaching without thought, moving without purpose, living without being. One night in October, I took a dusty copy of *L'Etre et le Neant*, (Being and Nothingness), from the shelf and sat down to read. It was late—after midnight. A single light illuminated the text. As I paused to digest a paragraph, I looked down at my hands. They seemed different. Arthritis and age spots were taking their toll. These couldn't be the hands, I thought, that touched her breast or slipped a wedding band on her finger. My band was still there, imprisoned by a swollen knuckle that refused to budge from the door it guarded. Her ring too, would still be where I had placed it, encircling now only a memory of flesh. "I want her back! You hear me?" My voice echoed off the walls and I cried. How pathetic to scream at nothingness. I wanted to travel backwards because she still existed there. Where was mercy? I remembered, but I couldn't get to the place before memory.

My rage collapsed into grief again—and silence. I listened to the metronomic cardiorhythm of the clock on the mantle. It was a beautiful thing, gold-plated, with a kind of pendulum extending down from the bottom that twisted several gold balls first one way, then the next. The whole thing was encased in a glass dome. It chimed every hour. Etched on a metal plate at its base was the inscription:

> *Happy 25th Mom and Dad*
> *We love you always*
> *Shelly and Tysen*

Mankind, Sartre said, is horrifyingly free, responsible for the choices he makes, completely culpable in his own misery. I began to see Sartre's "Being" as a terrible vision of man as "useless passion," having no meaning or purpose in existence except for the paltry goals he sets for himself. No wonder the existentialist's aesthetic characters tended toward self-destruction. That "hour upon the stage," they came to believe, was the futility of Being that had no exit, except in death.

The room seemed to grow larger shadows. The clock slowed its memorial cacaphony. Divine Being appeared too distant to imagine and I did not then, as I had suspected, possess human Being. So, for the time being (in the Hegelian sense), I accepted Sartre's nothingness and embraced it as my own. Like Morgan's heart, the clock fell silent. I waited to die.

I *became* time, ticking away, going through the motions of each hour. I was fifty-one. The last time I'd lived without her, I was seventeen. My future had always included Morgan, even before I knew her. Without her, Being was no longer a puzzle. I devolved into animal oblivion, going about the mundane tasks of existence and storing fat for a hibernation from which I didn't care to awaken.

I didn't think about life anymore. My children were grown. I knew that the best I could do for them now was not to become their burden and, perhaps, leave a large enough cache to help them survive a winter or two. Grief had hammered away at my heart and mind long enough to dull their edges. It was the triumph of concrete realism over metaphorical, conceptual, essence.

It was then, as I wandered in shadow, that Shelly, wearied by sorrow and a defeated imagination, decided to come home. Christopher came with her.

He was over a year now, only ten months when his "gamma" ceased to be. Morgan had coached Shelly through the birth while Tony slept. On that day, however, there had been nothing but gaiety and effervescence. The little guy enkindled an insouciance that mollified the world's dis-ease.

As births went in my family, he was light, weighing in at only six pounds. Both of my sisters were ten pounds, something, and Tommy-Jeff was eleven-two. I was the runt of the litter at nine pounds, six. My mother carried us all past term. Ella was the longest, at ten months, four days. Tommy said that this clearly foreshadowed Jennie Riveridge's reluctance to release us from her grip as adults.

Shelly had named her boy Christopher George—the first name because she liked it, the second out of admiration for her grandfather. Like his mother, Christopher was blond and light-complexioned, but his eyes were dark. Morgan had adored him. She couldn't pass the infant-wear or toy sections of any store without filling the cart. We made continual trips to Grand Rapids to see him.

She bought a video camera. The old Kodak was retrieved from a drawer and pressed into frenetic service. She cooed and giggled at him over the phone. He was "gamma's baby." Morgan carried a hundred photos of him in her purse and would assail both friends and casual acquaintances with the icons. There was always the veiled threat of a tongue lashing if anyone dared to reveal insufficient appreciation.

I loved him equally, but my devotion was less fawning, not as facile. I was a secondary element in an overwhelming demonstration of devotion. I was allowed to dote only by "gamma's" tender mercies. Then, she was gone.

Shelly and Christopher came home on a sunny day in mid-October. No longer an infant, the little boy tottered unsteadily across the carpet and put his baby hand on my knee. I patted it mechanically, as automatons do.

I got up to help Shelly unload her car. "I can get it, Dad," she said. "Could you just hold him for a few minutes until I get the playpen in?"

I picked him up, amazed by his lightness. He squirmed and bent backwards until I was forced to set him down. He stumbled off, hands flapping like an ungainly chicken, eager to explore the forgotten territory of my living room. I was amazed at how much he had grown in a few weeks, though I'd thought that I wasn't paying attention. He appeared to have no qualms about being alone with me. A slant of light cut into the dusty room. It had been cloudy earlier, masking the autumn dawn. The sunshine seemed foreign. I had been, I suddenly realized, unaware of the weather for quite some time.

The door slammed with authority. Shelly quickly assembled the playpen and threw her jacket into a chair. Christopher was busy pulling books from a shelf. "No, no, Sweetie," Shelly warned.

Cheerful perseverance earned him incarceration in the playpen and he protested vociferously.

"Sorry," she said, shrugging her shoulders. She kissed me on the forehead. "How are you, Dad?"

"Okay," I lied. "Glad you're here."

"Me too."

A pacifier worked its wonders and the room was silent again. "You and Tony?"

"Finished. I'm filing for divorce. We'll need to stay here for a while, until I can get a job. That okay?"

"Of course. As long as you're sure this is best."

"It is." Shelly looked at the mantle. "What's the matter with the anniversary clock?"

"What do you mean?"

"It's the wrong time. It's not working."

"I guess I hadn't noticed. Battery's probably dead."

She sighed. It was the patient suffering of all mothers. "I'll get one. Double A?"

"I think so."

"Keep an eye on the Bean for a minute, will you?"

She was gone before I could respond. I heard her rummaging in a drawer in the kitchen. She quickly returned and began fumbling with the anniversary clock. I saw Christopher staring at me. His pacifier dropped, revealing two tiny teeth in an otherwise gummy grin. I felt the edges of my mouth curve, but I gained control.

"What did you call him?" I asked Shelly as she put the clock down and began to open boxes.

"What?"

"His name is Christopher. You didn't call him that."

"Oh." She laughed and I remembered another just like it. "I called him Bean."

"Being?"

"No. No 'G.' As in Jelly, Lima, Boston Baked."

"Bean?"

"Yeah."

"Where did you get that?"

"I don't know, Dad. It's like 'Tooty Bird.' You know?"

She was hauling a suitcase down the hall toward what would now be her bedroom. I was confused. "Bean" stared at me from his roofless cell, a new grin ejecting the pacifier once again.

"Tooty Bird" seemed to make more sense than "Bean," although I couldn't remember why.

In the weeks that followed his arrival, I became "Buppa" to Christopher because "grandfather" was both too difficult for him and too stiff. When I came home from work, he ran to me as Shelly and Ty had both done. He "helped" me change my shoes. I took him for walks by the pond at twilight to show him swimming gold in the decreasing autumn light.

I read Dr. Seuss to him, and books about animal babies. We watched videos of *Peter Pan* and *Lady and the Tramp*. I thought of my mother for the first time since her death, without the pain of grief or guilt. The magic returned.

As the snow flew and I talked to him about Santa Claus, imagination crept, imperceptibly, back into my heart. The blithe spirit who came to live with me, gradually gave me the courage to rebelieve what I now know to be true. I learned to go on by going back.

I was afraid. I still am. Yet the fear subsides when he roosts in my lap, points at the picture of his "gamma" and asks: "Zat?"

I explain who she was. I can't explain what she meant.

One morning, many months after the divorce was final, I walked through the living room, spotless except for the careless vivacity of Beanie's toys, and I heard the clock on the mantle chime. The sun reflected off the golden balls that spun around inside its glass case and made it tick. It was only a thought, but I wondered if Sartre had ever had a grandson.

Chapter Twelve

The Transport to Avalon

I wake to sleep and take my waking slow.
I feel my fate in what I cannot fear.
I learn by going where I have to go.
                    —Theodore Roethke, *The Waking*

Ty would often surprise us and drop by. Like me, he adored Beanie and would allow him, dressed in Batman pajamas, to use his stomach for a springboard by which means he would swan dive into the sofa to capture "bad guys." In quieter moments, I would catch my son studying his nephew, perhaps wondering about his own child. Characteristically, he said nothing. He did marry the girl he thought he loved, but I think he was trying to fill a void that nothing could ever really occupy again. He didn't understand yet, that vacuity can't be repaired. He divorced her a year later and dated a succession of leggy, buxom playmates, mistaking stimulation for emotion. Sometimes he brought them to meet me, more often, he didn't. None of them ever interfered with him coming home for Thanksgiving or Christmas, or birthdays.

He got his B.A. with a dual major in business and criminal justice. His former boss, now working in Ohio, recommended him for a position with a larger company in Detroit, two hours away from Swan's End. He took it. At twenty-six, he was earning more money than I was. His ambition, he said, was to be the youngest CEO the company had ever had. He visited every month and called several times each week. His job consumed him. He began to speak of another position that would open soon in Chicago.

Shelly and Christopher lived with me for two and a half years after she left Tony. She went back to school, enrolling at Michigan State University in the fall of 1997. From Swan's End, MSU was about an hour's commute, but it was the closest school to offer a decent theatre program. She took night classes, Saturday classes, summer classes, so that I would be able to care for the Bean.

Every spare moment I had was devoted to him. I relearned how to change diapers, treat rashes, use an anal thermometer, spoon baby food and test the warmth of formula. I saw him through colds, the flu, scraped knees and chicken pox. As he grew, I read to him each night, helped him recite his prayers, and let him win at Hungry Hungry Hippo. He helped me cut the lawn with his plastic mower that spurted bubbles. We raked leaves, shoveled snow, fed the fish in the pond. We went to the zoo in Grand Rapids, the park, the beach. He strained my patience and, like a metaphor, converted time to purpose. He filled up the present. I believe I would have died without him.

Shelly did well in school. She'd decided that education was no longer an accouterment, but a necessity. She was always speaking of the future as I always looked to the past. Living with a grieving father was no life for any young, beautiful woman. She grew steadily more discontented and restless. She was eager to have a place of her own. I dreaded the day.

It was my own fault when it came. I introduced her to the man who would take her away. He was a young colleague of mine at Swan's End High School. He was two years her senior, a history teacher, who had the remarkable gift of making the Gilded Age interesting. He was popular with the kids and staff alike and devoted to his profession. His fiancée had just broken off their relationship and he was in the doldrums. I told him to give Shelly a call. He did. They connected right away. His name was Charley Rose and, despite Gertrude Stein's admonitions, Shelly adorned him with connotations. Charley lavished gifts, attention being the greatest. He immediately accepted Christopher as his own.

Shelly graduated from MSU in December of 1998, and Charley bought her a diamond. That winter, I saw her and the Bean less and less. They often spent weekends with Charley, including several trips to visit his parents in northern Michigan.

Charley's dad owned a string of gift shops and bookstores in several of the little resort towns around the Mackinac Bridge, including St. Ignace and Mackinaw City. But he and his wife lived in Wawatam, a "channel town," as the locals called it, a short distance inland from Lake Huron and riddled with channels and rivers and inlets that were ideal for storing the ferries and sailing vessels that required dry-docking during the savage winter months. Charley had been adopted through an agency downstate and brought to Wawatam as an infant, where he watched his father get rich from tourists and shrewd investments in valuable lakeshore property.

Charley was their only child, and the Roses were growing impatient for their thirty-year-old son to settle down and give them grandchildren. Under such circumstances, it wasn't surprising that they instantly fell in love with Shelly and Bean, embracing their son's ready-made family with rich enthusiasm.

Charley's dad used his many connections in the community to finagle a teaching position for his son at the high school in Wawatam, then offered to buy the kids an expensive home on the beach. I knew that he was purchasing proximity and I would lose if I entered the bidding. When Shelly saw the place, she couldn't resist.

She was extremely animated as she described it to me. Her cheeks were flushed with excitement. The three of them had come over for dinner to tell me about it. Christopher couldn't be made to eat. He kept looking out the window, happily enthralled with the violent thunderstorm that had rolled in with them. Charley was trying valiantly to make him sit down, but Beanie was having too much fun laughing at the lightning, a behavior that puzzled his father-to-be. Charley winced at every peal of thunder.

"You can see the bridge from our backyard," Shelly said. The use of the possessive convinced me that my approval was only adjunctive. "All I can think of is that Mom would have wanted me to live there. You believe so much in symbols, Dad, don't you think this goes beyond coincidence?"

"Yes, of course, Honey," I answered. "But Wawatam's a four-hour drive. That's a long trip for a weekend. The winters are pretty harsh. You'll need to work, too."

"Oh," she said, "I didn't tell you. Dad Rose thinks he can get me in at a radio station there, maybe even do some broadcasting." It was the first time she'd ever used that word to refer to anyone but me.

She got up, came around the table and hugged me. "We'll see each other a lot. I promise. At least once a month."

Charley was spooning peas into Christopher's reluctant mouth and whispering the age-old parental wisdom about the importance of vegetables.

I knew it was right for them. My concerns were selfish. But it wasn't either of these things, or Shelly's reference to the bridge that convinced me. It was Charley, spooning peas. Shelly watched him lovingly, through rose-colored glasses.

They moved the following week. A group of Charley's friends and students, along with Ty and myself, helped them load the rented U-Haul. Beanie, no longer a baby, proudly carried toys and pillows and light boxes up the ramp of the truck and handed them to me. "Here Bupps," he said. "Be careful, de're hebby." Tears formed in my eyes as he marched back to the house for another load. I felt a creeping fear. My lifeline was breaking.

Shelly was right. The place was perfect for her. She and Charley and the Bean could sit on the deck that opened off the living room and look out at the Mackinac Bridge, though it required a keen eye and a clear day. It was the kind of home Morgan and I had dreamed of all our lives.

The next morning, Ty left for his apartment in Detroit and I for the house at Swan's End. It was a difficult parting for Shelly, who embraced me, then her brother, then me again, as if trying to retain the past. Morning mist concealed the bridge.

"You going to be okay, Dad?" Shelly's voice quivered as she fussed with the zipper on my jacket.

"Yes," I whispered and kissed her forehead. "I'll be home by noon." A place to grow old and die.

"C'mere Beanie!" Shelly was shouting in the direction of the beach, and the sound carried over the morning water. Christopher was poking a dead fish with a stick. "Buppa and Uncle Ty are leaving. Come and give them hugs and kisses." I could tell that the carrion was much more interesting to him, but he dutifully came running. I picked him up.

"I love you, Buddy," I told him. He squirmed, eager to be off.

"Big hug," Shelly ordered. He obeyed in manly fashion, trying to twist my head off. He did the same to Ty, then hurried back to shoo the gulls off his prize. We shook hands with Charley. "You're welcome here any time," he said. I know he meant it.

I followed Ty for about fifty miles, then he had to continue on Interstate 75 to Detroit, while I veered off on West 27. As I waved to him and watched his car disappear in southbound traffic, I knew I'd never felt so alone.

The return to the house where Morgan had died and Beanie had kept me alive, suddenly seemed like a tomb. I could hear the clock on the mantle again and I knew its batteries were running low. My children and grandchild, I began to realize, would now be only an interruption in the terrible routine of lonely grief. Stark reality, deadly acceptance, black rationalism, fluttered over me like starving vultures, anxious to feast and clear the land of one more corpse, for corpses only provide a cradle for maggots, and spread disease.

I didn't sleep all night. It'd turned very hot that July, and though I had central air, I didn't turn it on. I don't think I even opened a window. When dawn finally came, I got back in the car and drove east. I wasn't sure that I had any intention, or destination, but two hours later, I arrived in Saginaw. I drove by my sister's house. Ruth and John were probably at their cabin with their daughters and grandchildren. I didn't stop to check.

I went by the ancient house where I'd grown up. There were children playing on the huge swing set my father had built for us a half-century ago. The steps where my mother had so often read to me were gone, replaced by a wooden deck that was far too modern, an odd incongruity. I looked up at the bedroom window on the second floor where I'd once watched with such great anticipation to see Santa Claus glide across the sky. I wondered if my sister, Ella, was still alive.

I drove on, meandering through a city I was beginning not to recognize. I stopped when I reached the house that we had vacated less than a decade ago, when Morgan was alive, when we were all together. The house was painted a different color now, and the lawn was unkempt, otherwise it looked the same. The pine tree I'd planted in the front yard now extended a dozen feet toward the summer sky. Soon it would be entangled in the utility wires that ran from the pole on the corner.

Morgan and I stole the tree from Mackinac Island. I dug it out of the island's interior where it would have perished because of the aggressive growth of its gigantic neighbors. These leviathans monopolized the sunshine and in their desire to live, they blotted out the life-giving light, leaving their unfortunate offspring to fend for themselves in a world of shadow and half-light. It was the brutality of Nature, Morgan said, to reward greed. She insisted that it was our duty to save at least one of the less aggressive.

It was only a few inches tall, but had a root ball the size of my fist. Morgan said that it indicated that the poor thing was reaching for the only world open to it. I slipped the dirt-encased roots into a clear, plastic bag we had used to bring sandwiches, then I poured water into it from a nearby brook.

When we arrived at the dock to take the ferry back to the mainland, I slipped it inside my jeans for concealment, since state law forbade such piracy. Halfway across the strait, the plastic bag ruptured. The moisture soaked the front of my jeans. Shelly, then nine, noticed first, then Tysen. They laughed so hard at my apparent incontinence, that they immediately drew the attention of the other passengers whose expressions indicated their discomfiture with a man who, apparently, possessed less bodily discipline than his children.

Morgan snickered. "It's all right, Darling," she said as loudly as she could. "We all have accidents now and then." Then she leaned over to whisper. "It's nature's revenge." I still remember her broad, lip-thinning laugh, as her dark hair whipped about and caught in her white teeth. She brushed it away with a delicate finger. The bridge stood solidly behind her, rising from the lake, holding two worlds together.

The little pine survived the three-hour-long trip home. Ty helped me to plant it and eagerly pounded in the fertilizer stakes around it with thoughtful aplomb. It'd grown slowly at first. It was so small that I had to put a wire fence around it to keep from running over it with the lawn mower. But then the fertilizer had done its job and in the following summer, it grew two feet. By the time we moved, it was too big to transplant. When Morgan had said good-bye to it, she'd clipped a little snippet from one bough. I remember Shelly asking me, when she was going through her mother's things after the funeral, why there was a tiny, brown piece of pine among the memorabilia. I'd told her then, that I didn't know. I knew now, and felt ashamed at having lost a memory.

I sat in the car for several hours. The sun had gone down behind the old oak tree across the street and it would be dark before long. My heart was empty, my mind overflowing with images from a past now removed from existence: Shelly jumping rope in the driveway; Ty struggling across the lawn in his braces, balancing with crutches; a Christmas tree twinkling in the picture window; Morgan waving from the kitchen, calling us to supper. The pine, evergreen and immortal, rooted the past here, and struggled toward the sky. It stood as absolute reality, an axis on which revolved two different worlds. A flaming sword had driven us away. All I could think to say was: "Kyrie Eleison," which I whispered now, as a plea.

I turned the key in the ignition, grinding the silence, and pulled away from the curb, Morgan's voice still calling. I was a beast, slouching toward the place where Morgan waited.

Unconscious driving brought me onto the gravel road that ran under the wrought-iron sign: BETHLEHEM LUTHERAN CEMETERY. I parked, got out, walked to her grave. Weeds sprouted around the stone. There was white bird dung on the rose marble.

Elyda Woodson was buried nearby. Like Morgan's stone, it carried the name of her husband too. Death awaited Harlan and me. It only needed to record the appropriate day, month and year.

I knelt by the rose stone that bore the rings and the "One Hand, One Heart" inscriptions. I felt the agony of my isolation overwhelm me then, the onerous, galling grief rising inside like nausea to disgorge itself in a queasy expulsion of wrenching lamentation. I threw myself over her grave, sobbing in convulsive, heaving pain. I pulled at the grass and dug in the dirt, as if I might dig my way back to her. A wild animal shrieked somewhere in the dark night of my unconscious and I knew that its name was Ebenezer.

The sexton woke me at sunrise. I was still sprawled on the ground over Morgan's grave. He was an old man whose facial wrinkles were made deeper by his frowning concern. He knew I'd been there all night. I was dirty, unshaven and damp with dew. I gave my excuses and thanked him for his kindness. He asked me if there was anyone he could call for me. I told him no.

I made my escape. By noon, I was back in Swan's End. A week later, on the third anniversary of her death, I tried to sleep through the day, but Shelly and Ty both called, understanding the significance of the day and offering as much comfort as voices can give. I was walking through the kitchen later that day, not really thinking much about anything, when the sorrow and rage inside me took control. I struck my fists against the kitchen counter until they were purple and wet with blood. I yelled every obscenity I knew, over and over again, working to expel the blasphemous grief, but I knew that the attempt was inanity. It wasn't possible. The leaden cruelty clung to my heart like a noxious tumor, a demoniacal malignancy that gleefully celebrated the triumph of anguish over hope.

I watched a movie on television that night called *Patch Adams*, while I immersed my swollen hands in a bowl of ice. It was playing only to keep silence away. When Robin Williams yelled at God and was ready to throw himself off a cliff, he got his answer in the form of a butterfly on his medical bag. I wasn't moved. He would learn. A butterfly is a butterfly is a butterfly. I hated life for its pain. I hated death for killing the romantic in me. I hated love for taking away the hope I'd found. I hated music and magic and metaphor. I hated and hated. I concentrated on what was real—despair.

I settled into the gray existence of waiting, of killing time, of denying purpose—Sartre, and the slow homicide of the imagination. Shelly and Ty couldn't erase it. Beanie still made me smile, but his visits were fast and illusory, like a half-remembered dream. I'd finish each weekend as it had begun—alone. Pain could only be drowned in liquid apathy.

On a snow-filled night in December, I sat in my chair, staring vacantly at the television. *A Christmas Carol* was playing for the thousandth time. I'd watched it often lately, but only to the point where Scrooge falls upon his own tombstone. I didn't like to see him abasing himself before Death. One Ebenezer watching another, canceling reclamation. I felt empathy with the old recluse, the bitter miser, not the gleeful philanthropist of Christmas morning. I didn't wish to see beyond that, and kept hoping that the hooded specter would just take him, before conversion turned him into a giggling goose.

It was some commercial that made me think of the bear.

Years ago, when the children were small (I seem to remember Morgan carrying Tysen in a baby blanket as I held Shelly's tiny frame in the crook of my arm), we were wandering the aisles of a department store. It was Christmastime, and Yuletide music emanated from the store's public address system. The place was crowded with shoppers.

Shelly was adding new ideas to her already substantial "Santa List" and I was preoccupied with explaining that even good children didn't get everything they asked for, when I became aware that Morgan had stopped behind us somewhere. I turned to see her several yards away, examining some toy.

As I drew closer, I could see that it was a stuffed teddy bear, dressed in a Santa hat. It was nearly the size of the infant Tysen, whom she cradled in her other arm.

At first, I thought she wanted me to buy it for one of the kids, but it was she who was enamored. She showed me that if you pressed its paw, it played "God Rest Ye Merry Gentlemen." She looked at it wistfully for a few minutes, pressing the paw several times before putting it back. I told her to get it if she liked it. She told me it was silly and too expensive. We couldn't afford frivolity.

I went back the next day, after work, and bought it for her, believing then that frivolity was all we could afford. She was thrilled. She kissed me and chattered happily, as she pressed the paw and it began to play its ditty. "Look," she'd said, and pointed at a light that was flashing on the bear's fuzzy chest. It was a plastic heart, through which a tiny, red light beat in unison with the music. Only then did I understand the connection and her fascination. Press the hand to start the heart.

Every Christmas, she pulled it out of the box where it had been lovingly stored the previous year and placed it on the back of the sofa where it reigned throughout the season. The kids never understood its significance and, even now, tell stories about "Mom's toy," because it was, to them, an enigma—a child's plaything that children were never allowed to touch.

Ebenezer Scrooge had come to his grave and looked in. It was time to lie down and sleep. I turned the TV off and headed for my empty bed.

It was so muffled, that at first I didn't really hear it. I sensed it, in the same way that my father had once described to me the voice of God.

It was music, the chiming of spiritual knowledge. It was coming from somewhere beneath me. I opened the basement door. The volume immediately increased. The light switch was at the bottom of the stairs. I descended into the sounding darkness.

I recognized the tinny strains of "God Rest Ye Merry Gentlemen" and in the darkness, saw the flashing heart/light as it synchronized with the tune.

My own heart outraced the beat, pounding in measured time between the rhythm of bliss and the cadence of suffering. "Morgan?" My voice was foreign or, more accurately, counterfeit—like the impersonating mimicry of a tape recorder.

I switched on the light. The little bear lay on its side on the floor, the Santa hat drooping comically over its glass eyes. The box that was its normal home, lay next to it. It had, apparently, fallen from one of the shelves behind. Collision had forced the box top open, and the Santa Bear had tumbled onto the concrete, the impact, apparently, triggering the music. Such would always be the explanation of rational men. But what caused the box to fall? An animal? I had no pets. No mouse or rat or squirrel was ever discovered there. Why did the music continue to play? And why that box and why that moment? Who pressed the hand to bring the heart to life? Theodore Roethke once wrote:

"All lovers live by longing, and endure:
Summon a vision and declare it pure."

I learned that night to listen again to God's language. He allowed Morgan to speak to me. I would find her. I could not be dismayed.

Chapter Thirteen

Reclamation

*Any metaphor between us and a river is that we can't help
ourselves one bit.*

—Jim Harrison, *Sundog*

Shortly after Shelly married Charley Rose, I sold the house. The kids thought it was a good idea—too many memories, they said, but I didn't sell it for that reason. I didn't want to escape the past. I wanted to pull it forward, merge it with the present and the future. I sold the house because there was something else waiting. I was guided.

It sold quickly, but finding another was a tedious and frustrating affair for my real estate agent, to whom I could give very few guidelines. I gave him a price range, but that was all. He showed me dozens of appropriate houses. But at each showing I said no—even when he managed to get the owners to reduce their prices to well below market value.

By the spring of 2000, conditions were desperate. According to the closing agreement, I had less than thirty days to vacate my house, and my agent warned me that unless I wanted to put everything I owned in storage and rent an apartment for an extended time, I'd better settle for something soon.

My agent, Quentin Pern, was a surly old man, a good fifteen years my senior, whose dour disposition didn't jibe with his profession. It seemed to me that his grumpy and disdainful personality was more appropriate to, say, a gravedigger, than someone who depended for his success on the positive impression he might leave with his customers.

Nevertheless, "Q" was the most reliable real estate man in the county, with a reputation for honesty and a strong, almost maniacal obsession to get his client a "deal." He'd wheedled ten thousand dollars more out of my house than it was worth, and was now determined to do as well with the purchase of a new house.

It was a Saturday morning and the sky was finally beginning to clear after days of torrential rain. Q picked me up in his Jeep and headed away from town, passing into the pleasant farmland that surrounded Swan's End.

He was taking me to look at a place that he said was over-priced, too old, and had too much room for a widower, but he'd shown me everything else. This house had been on the market for over a year and the seller, now out of state, had refused all offers below what, Q assured me, was an exorbitant price. Though the owner was losing money each day that it sat empty, he refused to budge.

We turned north onto a two-lane, passing Lucas Jasper's dairy farm, and continued in silence for another few minutes until we turned again, this time onto a dirt road. It was badly pock-marked with watery holes and I remember thinking that if the ride was this rough in Q's jeep, what would it be like in my Cavalier? Q, I was certain, was just waiting for me to comment so that he could once again admonish me for all the bargains I'd declined. I kept quiet.

The pastures turned to light brush, then thickening forest. The road dead-ended in a circular, gravel drive, and through the dense trees, I could make out the structure of an old farmhouse. Behind it, a rainbow arched across the clearing sky.

We climbed the steps to the porch, a section of which was overrun with creeping grapevines. Q used a skeleton key to let us in the door.

The house was very old, perhaps a century or more. It smelled musty and deserted. The ceilings towered above us at ten feet before the floor of the second story began. The hardwood floors slanted to the right. Our footsteps echoed in the vast empti-ness of the place.

"Piece of junk, if ya ask me," Q said. "Not nearly as nice as what ya had, Ben, and almost as much money." He wiped the sweat from his balding head, hopelessly snarling what little wisps of white hair remained. The expression of disgust on his red, oval face as he glanced around, indicated his unwillingness to waste his Saturday on such an obvious white elephant. "Seen enough?" he said.

There really was nothing extraordinary about the place, except for its endurance, but I told him I wanted to look it over, although I didn't know why—perhaps the rainbow. With the uplifted eyes of the patient martyr, he sighed and lit a cheap cigar, the odor of it dispelling the dry, dusty emptiness. We walked through the massive living room and up the stairs. On the second floor were three large bedrooms and a bathroom. There was no shower, and the tub looked like it'd been there during the Civil War, clinging to the tiled floor with iron claws that defied modernization. The ceilings in the bedrooms, like those on the first floor, were very high, probably to accommodate the tall windows, most of which would likely cost the price of a slipped disc to open.

It was a glance out one of those back windows that really aroused my interest. "Is that a river out back?" I asked.

Q was standing behind me, dumping ashes from his cigar into his cupped, chubby hand. "More like a creek," he answered. "I hear the fishing's lousy."

"Let's get a closer look." We went back downstairs and into the kitchen, a huge, open area, with paint-chipped cupboards all around, obviously designed for baking bread and frying chicken for a family of a dozen or more hearty appetites. To the left of the kitchen proper was a pantry, the size of a bedroom, with shelves on every wall. The only door to the backyard was through this vacant room. The access had probably been created for delivering large bags of flour or bushels of fruit from horse-drawn wagons. I imagined the shelves stocked with canned peaches and gunnysacks of sugar, perhaps glass jars of pickles and strings of smoked fish. I wondered again at the richness of imagination—how concrete

objects could create abstract images. What we call the "imagination" is our true vision. The objects that people call "reality" are
only the tools that trigger larger truth, like the words to a poem,
and for some reason, modern humanity has decided that the tool is
superior to the product. We have ridiculed romance, a high and
lovely thing, and relegated it to books on supermarket shelves that
assure us that it is merely the penetration of a vagina.

Williams was wrong. Very little depends on that red wheel-
barrow. We have named all things and are responsible for all the
connotations. Nothing is real until it is named, but naming and
being are such different things. Coincidence is the only thing that
should not be named, because it doesn't exist. A heart is a blood
pump, but it's also courage, love, sympathy and sorrow. All those
things are named and attached to another name. What it is, what
they are, is not really understood, yet we move through life as if all
could be explained by nomenclature. We only operate by magic, by
trusting how the words combine with what we see: a hand, a heart,
a bridge, a rainbow—the things that insist on recurring to impel us
to our destinies. That's why I bought the house. Purpose.
Converted time.

I pulled open the back door with some difficulty and found
myself on what must be described as a small landing, rather than a
porch. The dilapidated steps groaned as I descended to the yard
and hurried toward the water through a field of dandelions.

What intrigued me more than anything else, was the sound
of the water. It was the splashing, cascading reverberation of a
cataract, not the gentle sound of a river nor the gurgling of a brook.
As I drew closer, I understood why. I skirted a gigantic weeping
willow, whose sagging boughs touched the earth, and I saw the
waterfall. Q was right at my elbow explaining that the state or
county government had, at one time, dammed up the creek to form
a lake as part of some entrepreneurial scheme to develop more
"vacation" property. They'd constructed a solid, concrete dam
between two hills that contained the proposed reservoir, or "lake."

"Folks around here were plenty upset," Q said, " 'cause the creek dried up and a lot of the farmers used it for irrigation and watering their livestock in their pastures, including Lucas Jasper. The protesters won out, and rather than remove the dam entirely like they should've, the moneymen behind this fiasco settled for jackhammering away enough of the top and center of the dam to allow the water to flow again."

So the county had created an artificial waterfall, instead of a lake. It tumbled into the creek bed that had, for a brief time, been a dry ditch. "This is why the owner of this place thinks he can get his price," I told Q.

"What? You mean the dam?"

"The water, the willow, the apple trees over there, wildflowers—and look at that old oak! It must be six feet around!"

"It's a mess, Ben, weeds and vines growing all over the place. I'm surprised those flowers could bloom. And the house! It's so old, you know the plumbing's gonna go anytime, and the wiring..."

"Who lives over there?" I interrupted his tirade and pointed to the other side of the creek. It was the only other house within sight.

"Art and Sophie Hall," Q responded. "Art's in the construction business, owns that lumberyard over on M-28 too, near Corinth. You know the place?"

"I think so, yeah."

"He built out here about four years ago, summer of '96, I think it was. Same year the old man who lived here moved out. I think that's why he left. He was somewhat of a hermit. Didn't want people around. I remember he appealed to the city council to cancel Art's building permit. Didn't do no good, though. Art's got a hayload of money. Everybody knows him. He was a star football player in high school. Around here, that's like being a movie star."

I'd heard the name, possibly even met him. I'd taught several kids named Hall. His house was magnificent, a two-story log cabin structure with picture windows and sprawling porches. A beautiful, large, well-kept lawn sloped down to the creek from its foundations. Rose gardens and newly planted birch trees dotted the fastidious landscape. They had cut the property out of the forest, which was still thick on both sides of the estate. A little wharf extended from their shore and cattails emerged from the water to surround an old rowboat secured there.

I watched the rainbow blend with the brightening sky and disappear.

"I want to buy this place, Quentin."

He spit out the stub of his cigar in disgust. "Well we can bid I suppose, for what it's worth, I mean, but he's not going to come down."

"Give him what he wants."

Q looked up at me as if I had just punched him. He shrugged his shoulders in resignation. "My old man always said that bein' educated ain't the same as bein' smart."

"That's true," I responded, laughing, "but the opposing insinuation of that maxim doesn't necessarily stand either."

The weekend before the thirty-day deadline, I moved to the house on Creekpath Road. My kids came to help me and to see the place. They told me they liked the house, but their surreptitious glances to one another betrayed their reticence. They saw me properly installed, then drove back to their own houses, grateful, I think, for their independence, so that they didn't have to live here. They had brought me a house-warming present. Beanie was the proud presenter and, like all children who had nothing to do with the thought or purchase of a gift, he claimed my gratitude with genuine pride. It was a copper sculpture depicting the wrist and hand of an adult man, extending from a base of onyx. A baby's hand clutched one of the fingers. It was, they said, representative of how they saw me as their father. My tears had been enough for them to see that I understood. I placed it on the fireplace mantle next to the anniversary clock, and as I walked by them each day, unpacking boxes and arranging my books in shelves, I knew that Morgan had been a part of that, too.

I only had a few weeks before school started. Strange that I had no idea I would never teach again.

Boxes needed unpacking. Painting, hanging curtains, yard work and myriad other chores awaited. I kept very busy and the labor, tiring though it was, was also strangely invigorating.

The cooler hours of late afternoon and evening were devoted to outside work, and while cutting the weedy lawn, or painting shutters, I would often become mesmerized by the hypnotic rhythm of the water or the slanting rays of golden sun that cast shadows through the orchard and created ghostly puppet figures on the side of the old storage shed.

I often looked across the creek at the sumptuous log home of my neighbors, but never saw any movement or signs of occupancy. At night, the place was always dark. I thought, perhaps, that the front of the house was where they spent their time, and wondered why they had built the place here if they never intended to take advantage of the eden in their back yard.

One evening I spotted a teen-aged boy mowing the sloping yard. I shouted to him, but the noise from the cascading water and the lawn mower engine prevented me from capturing his attention. I thought he looked over once, but the setting sun was in his eyes and I was convinced that he saw nothing.

On July 31st, the fourth anniversary of Morgan's death, I woke late, as was my custom on that difficult day. Strangely, unlike the three previous anniversaries, I didn't wish to linger in my bed. My mood was strangely anticipatory and light. The anniversary clock chimed nine times as I came down the stairs and passed through the living room into the kitchen.

I was dressed in shorts and a tee shirt. The day, promising to be hot, was already very humid. Old newspapers were spread across the kitchen counter to protect it from splattering while I painted the cupboard doors, only half done. I made a pot of coffee and slipped two pieces of bread in the toaster.

That's when I saw Morgan.

She was standing among the reeds and cattails at the edge of my side of the creek, about thirty feet away. Her back was to me, but I knew the familiar movement of the shoulders, the way the hand swatted at an insect. She wore the same tan shorts and sleeveless, white blouse that she'd been wearing the day before she went away. She was standing in the water and her delicate fingers moved across the tops of the cattails as if she were trying to adjust them again to the wonder of feeling, the restored sense of touch. Her body, although somehow smaller, perhaps thinner, was shaped the same—the broader hips of middle age—of a woman with adult offspring, but the still-supple legs of youth, and strong, yet feminine, arms—the product of a half century of productive labor.

Her hair was different now, close-cropped and casually feathered instead of the long, gently curled tresses. But the auburn tint, normally submerged in the thick, luxuriant darkness, was revealed, as always, by the unveiling rays of natural illumination.

I was, at once, exhilarated and terrified. I knew that such things were not possible. I also knew that "impossible" was a name humanity had given to limitation and defeat. Names. Only names.

I rushed from the house and ran toward her. "Morgan!" I startled her. She spun around to confront me. They were her eyes, dark and charged with knowledge, filled with authentic faith, the same eyes that had captivated me thirty years ago in a high school hallway—the eyes I'd refused to give away. I stopped.

It wasn't her. The lips were thinner, the cheekbones more pronounced, the neck longer. This was a lovely woman, perhaps a few years younger than I. Smaller. Not Morgan.

I must have frightened her badly. The dark eyes searched for escape. She stepped out of the water to steadier ground, perhaps anticipating the need for flight, in the event that this strange lunatic should advance further.

Her eyes wouldn't let me go and I stood, dumbly, allowing my silence to feed her fear.

151

"Who are you?" she said. Her voice was trembling, lower, not the same. Morgan would have known me. She would have recognized me in hell. I forced my eyes to the woman's bare feet. Her painted toes, though partially hidden in the grass, were crooked.

She said: "What is it? What's wrong?" She may have said it more than once. Her tone was evolving from fear to concern. "Are you all right?"

Her voice was familiarly strange, as the subtle variance of water dripping from a cavern roof—a distant provocation, rather than the accustomed comfort of a leaky faucet.

"I'm okay," I finally managed, still concentrating on her feet. I forced myself to look at her face again. She was smiling now, perfect white teeth exposed in a thin-lipped parody of Morgan, but there was no mistaking the black eyes. I'd never seen their like on anyone else.

She walked up the bank and stopped a few feet away, still wary, but much more relaxed.

"I mistook you for someone else," I said, avoiding the piercing examination of those eyes that might read a lie. I felt myself twitch.

"Are you looking at this property?" she asked. "It's been on the market for a long time."

"I bought it."

"Really? We're neighbors, then. I'm Sophie Hall. I live over there," she pointed at the log castle, "across the creek." She extended her hand and I took it. I felt a fluttering sensation in my chest and took a deep breath to help reestablish my heart's rhythm. "I'm sorry if I was trespassing, but no one's lived here for so long. Ever since we've been here. I was beginning to think of this property as my own."

"Why come over here?" My question sounded rude, uninviting, and resentful of her intrusion. I condemned myself for having been trained so well to reject advances over the last four years.

"Art loves landscaping, to make nature submit to his will. Our place is too manicured, too orderly. I like Nature the way it is—

messy. I frequently come over to pick the wildflowers in summer. Seems such a waste to let them bloom and die here with no one to enjoy them. I was going to get some when I heard a splashing sound on the bank and went to investigate. It was a fish, caught in the shallows. I'd just set it free as you came out."

She really was remarkably beautiful. "In the fall, I pick apples." She pointed at the unkempt orchard. "Guess I'll have to keep to my own side now. I really am very sorry."

"How did you get over here? You didn't swim. It's too deep to wade." I pointed at the opposite side. "Your boat's still moored at the wharf."

She laughed, then raised her eyebrows in a conspiratorial grin. "A secret passage. I came across the old dam."

I looked upstream. Some weathered boards had been laid across the gap in the concrete wall. Water from the upper level of the creek cascaded beneath them. "I keep the boards behind those saplings on the other side and lay them down when I want to cross. They bridge the gap nicely, really, as long as you keep your balance and don't tumble in. I did you know, once—fall in, I mean." She unconsciously rubbed one elbow. "Pretty stupid, really. I used to leave the boards there, where they are now, all the time. They were constantly wet and some kind of moss or algae formed on them. Made them very slippery. I hit my arm on the concrete on the way down. I had to wear a cast for three months—fractured my ulna. I keep the boards dry now, except when I want to cross. A pound of prevention, you know."

"An ounce."

"What?"

"An ounce of prevention—worth a pound of cure."

"Oh, right. I'm always butchering those expressions. Art says I'm going to kill myself someday and he'll find my dead body floating face down in the creek. He's not much of a romantic. Hasn't ever stepped foot on this side."

"He's your husband? Art, I mean."

"I didn't mention it before?"

"The one who likes manicured landscapes?"

"Yes."

I was staring at her and she knew it. Her cheeks flushed scarlet. "I'd better go," she said.

She turned toward the dam.

"Wait!" My voice was too loud, too edgy. I could see that I was making her nervous. "You can't leave yet."

"Why not?"

"Well...you haven't asked me my name yet."

She stood there, waiting. Perhaps she didn't need to ask.

"It's Ben. Ben Riveridge."

"Nice meeting you, Ben." She turned away again.

"Listen," I said. "You didn't get your flowers. Please, take some home. Maybe it'll compensate for my rudeness a bit. You're welcome to take them anytime, apples too. I don't plan on changing much outside. I like Nature the way it is, too." I gave her my warmest smile, and she appeared to slip into a kind of tentative relaxation.

"You sure?" she asked.

"Absolutely."

I followed her at a reassuring distance while she extracted a small jackknife from her pocket and began to harvest some of the flowers that grew wild near the rim of the forest. I sat in an old Adirondack chair that was badly weathered. Chips of gray paint lay on the ground all around it.

"You live alone?" she said, breaking the comforting silence. Her back was turned to me and I was startled by her voice. So intent was she on arranging the growing bouquet in her hand, I thought she'd forgotten that I was there.

"I'm a widower." Though I'd used that word often in the last four years, it still seemed oddly misapplied, especially now.

She stopped, stood erect from where she'd been kneeling and turned to face me. "I'm so sorry," she said. There was a hint of responsibility there. "How did it happen?"

"She died of a heart attack. Four years ago today, actually. Her name was Morgan."

She was watching me closely through a pained expression of sympathetic confusion. "Today?"

"Yes." There was something there, deep in the eyes, a dim recognition—perhaps just pity misread—I didn't know then. I do now.

"You have children." It wasn't a question.

"Yes. A son, Ty. He's twenty-six and lives in Detroit. My daughter, Shelly, is thirty. She just got married again. My grandchild, Beanie, lives with them."

"A little boy, huh?" She seemed, for a moment, disoriented.

"What?"

"He's a boy?"

"Yes. His real name's Christopher. They live in a little town called Wawatam, up near the Straits of Mackinac."

"Oh, I love that area," she said. I wasn't surprised.

"Art and I used to take the kids to the island when they were little. My daughter loved to watch them make fudge through the shop windows. She can't pass a shop today without buying some."

I remembered holding Shelly on my shoulders so she could see over the heads of the other "fudgies" as the confectioners poured the steaming chocolate from the copper kettles onto the cool, marble tables. "You have a daughter too, then?" I asked.

"And a son. Both grown up, like yours—and out of the nest." She looked sadly at the flowers. "No grandkids, though."

I had to know more about her, to test. "Are you from Swan's End, originally I mean?" She concentrated on the bouquet, or memory, or both. I'm not sure. Her expression was one of distance.

"I was born on a farm," she said finally, "on the other side of the state. You?"

"I'm from Saginaw, originally. You have a beautiful home there." I gestured toward the opposite bank.

"Thanks," she said, but there was little enthusiasm or pride in her tone. "Art does pretty well. He owns his own construction business. He did most of the work on it himself." She paused for a moment. "I don't mean to pry, but what do you do? For a living, I mean. It's the middle of the week, you know."

"I'm a teacher at the high school."

"Swan's End?"

"Yeah."

"I thought I recognized the name."

"That doesn't sound good."

"Oh no, nothing bad. Small town, that's all."

"Do you work?"

"No. I've wanted to get a job for some time, but Art's not big on the idea." Her expression became remote again. I didn't try to bring her back, but just enjoyed watching her. I fought back the urge to stand up and embrace her. She looked lost. She didn't know who she was—yet.

When she did return, she caught my admiration. I must have been gawking like a schoolboy. We both turned our eyes away, looking for some other place to safely anchor them. "I haven't seen any lights over there," I finally stammered.

"Art and I have been away—on vacation."

"Listen," I said, standing up. "Would you like some coffee? The place is a mess, I'm renovating, but you could see what it looks like. You ever been inside?"

She looked back across the creek, then at the back door that entered the pantry. "I have to admit, I'm curious. Maybe just for a few minutes."

She stayed for two hours. I took her on a guided tour of the place, then we just sat at the kitchen table, among the paint fumes, and began slowly to remove the black veil of estrangement. The conversation was trivial at first, but then we began to talk about film, theatre, literature. She was well-read, which surprised me for more than one reason.

The morning sun had brightly illuminated the kitchen, but it suddenly passed into shadow. "Oh my," she said, and stood up. "I've been here too long. I've taken up your whole morning."

"It's all right," I reassured her. "I've been enjoying our...."

"It's clouding over. There's rain coming again. I hate storms. I've got to get home." She headed for the pantry. "Thanks so much for your hospitality, Ben. You're really sweet." She turned and looked at me again with those eyes I'd only known twice.

"You're welcome to come back any time," was all I could think to say. Then, she was gone.

I watched her from the door as she balanced herself deftly across the dam and pulled the boards in behind her like a drawbridge. She was out of my vision for a moment, as she hid the lumber in the saplings. Then I saw her scurry up the slope, take one last look behind her, and disappear inside the castle.

When I returned to the kitchen, I saw the flowers lying on the table. My first instinct was to take them to her, but I wasn't yet certain of what I would, eventually, come to accept. I put the flowers in a vase and placed them near the window. The storm lasted the rest of the day.

* * *

Dr Kim Dong-Ho
Notes on the Riveridge Case
October 20, 2000

A major breakthrough! I arranged an interview with Mrs. Sophia Hall. She met with me today. She is fifty-one years old, but she looks much younger. There is no gray in her hair, which is dark (brown, I think, with perhaps a hint of red). Her eyes are almost black. She's quite fit and one can tell that she works hard to remain that way. If I may be allowed an unclinical observation, she is a striking woman, and I can see why the patient, Ben Riveridge, is so taken with her.

Shortly after Mr. Riveridge was admitted here, she applied for a pass to visit him, which of course was quickly denied by the court, since she was the woman who brought the stalking charges against him.

Riveridge knows nothing of this interview, nor of her desire to see him. Since he refuses to discuss her at all, I see no reason, for the moment at least, to tell him of our meeting.

Mrs. Hall appeared to be extremely agitated. Throughout the session, she would cross and recross her legs, shift in her chair, and look nervously about as if she were involved in some clandestine business and feared discovery.

As I would later understand, she had good reason. Her husband, to whom she has been married for thirty-two years, was not aware that she was meeting with me, and she had, as she told me, gone to great lengths to hide it from him. She'd driven more than a hundred miles from Swan's End, where she lives, to the hospital here in Ypsilanti and could only do so, she said, because her husband was out of town for at least two days on a construction job in northern Michigan.

She is obviously afraid of Arthur Hall, and I suspected immediately, from both her demeanor and her subservient posturing whenever his name was mentioned, that he has mentally and physically abused her. The interview eventually substantiated that supposition.

After formal introductions and an exchange of courteous pleasantries to help her relax and develop trust, I asked her why she'd applied to see Riveridge.

She frankly admitted that she was in love with him. I confess here that I was entirely surprised, but I continued writing on my tablet in an attempt to maintain my professional deportment.

I asked her why had she then obtained a restraining order against him and, when he violated it, brought formal charges against him. "Art insisted," she told me. Apparently she expected people to accept that reasoning as valid without further inquiry.

Certainly, as I have discovered, those who know Arthur Hall would do so.

"Do you always do what your husband insists upon?" I asked her.

"Yes."

"Why?"

"Because..." She swallowed hard. She was, I believe, summoning a dignified courage that had long ago been sacrificed at the altar of brutality. "Because he threatened me."

"Mr. Hall threatened you?"

"Yes."

"Did he strike you?"

"He punched me in the stomach. He knocked the wind out of me. I was afraid he would kill me."

"Has your husband struck you before?"

Tears formed in her eyes, and she appeared to be struggling for control. "Many times, but not often lately, not until I met Ben, that is." I offered her a box of tissues, which she gratefully accepted.

"So his reaction was jealousy?"

"Ownership. Art doesn't like people to toy with his possessions."

"And he regards you as a *possession*?"

"Yes."

"Do you feel that way?"

"Not with Ben." She took a deep breath and pushed herself erect in the chair, as if the stiffening of fortitude must first be preceded by a more corporal intractability. "Ben doesn't belong here, Dr. Kim, you must know that. I was a coward to allow this. He's a gentle, loving man. He wasn't stalking me. If anything, it was the other way around. He saved my life, really. You can't keep him here. He's not crazy." She wiped her eyes and pulled another tissue from the box.

"No, he's not."

She looked hard at me with Mesmer's eyes. There was a trace of a smile. "Then you'll release him?"

"Probably, yes. After the ninety days."

"But that's over a month yet. He told me once that the thing he feared most in life was for his children to have to see him in a mental hospital. He had to deal with his father, well...he said he'd rather be dead. Now I've done this to him. You have to get him out of here."

"That would take a special petition of writ, and it would require more time than he has left. I'm afraid he's here at least until the ninety days have expired. Besides..."

"What?"

"He won't talk about you. I can't get him to open up, and his relationship with you has to be dealt with before I'll feel comfortable in releasing him."

"He hates me now."

"No. I think he thinks he's protecting you."

"From what?"

"Your husband, perhaps? Social condemnation? Simple gossip? I don't know. He won't discuss it."

She sat there for a while, silently. Her frustration was evident.

"You said you love him. Ben, I mean."

"Yes."

"Do you think he loves you?"

"I did, yes."

"Did?"

"Before all this."

"I see. Mrs. Hall, was your relationship with Mr. Riveridge sexual?"

She appeared to be offended by the question, but responded without hesitation. "Yes."

"When Mr. Riveridge is released, do you plan to continue this relationship?"

"No."

"Why? Are you afraid of what your husband might do?"

"Not to me."

"To him, then? Mr. Riveridge?"

"That's part of it, yes."

"And the other part?"

There was a long silence again.

"I can't help him, Mrs. Hall, if you won't talk to me either."

"I'm not sure he loves *me*. I mean, Sophie Hall."

"I'm afraid I'm not following you. You think he loves someone else?"

"In a way, yes."

"Who?"

"Morgan, his wife."

"You mean that he's still in love with her? That he feels guilty about his affection for you?"

"No." She gathered herself and took a deep breath. "He thinks I *am* her."

"Are you saying he believes that you're a reincarnation of his dead wife?"

"No, not exactly. I don't understand it entirely, although he tried to explain it to me. It's something he calls 'edenic time.' Has he said anything to you about it?"

"Briefly, yes, but not in connection with you. How do you feel about all this?"

"I'm scared."

"Why? Do you think he's delusional?"

"No. I think he may be right."

Chapter Fourteen

Naboth's Vineyard

"Reason must sleep," said Christabel.
"The stories come before the meanings," I said.
"As I said, reason must sleep," she said.
—A. S.Byatt Possession, A Romance

I didn't talk to Sophia Hall again for ten days, although I saw her often across the creek, tending to the neat squares of rose gardens that she kept for Art's sake.

She waved to me once, after carefully scrutinizing the windows of her own house to be certain she wasn't being watched. It was my first insight into her husband's brutality. I waved back. Though I longed to speak to her, rushing water from the dam would have prevented her from hearing me.

I know now that she is Morgan, although I don't believe in reincarnation, or the transmigration of souls, and my faith in resurrection is limited to the one-dimensional flight of the soul to heaven. I don't see Sophie as either Morgan's ghost, or a victim of possession. She is simply an answer from the Divine Wisdom who shatters the barriers of time and place for love's sake. Morgan was removed from historical time to somewhere else, a non-temporal place of co-existence, before and beyond time; the motionless, arrested innocence of the past that is not behind us, but beside us. Somewhere along that border, Sophia Hall and Morgan Riveridge, responding to a cry of desperation, stepped over. Sophie's dream was the explanation.

That's how I see it. It's my only reason for what I know to be true. When Morgan wrote that little note to me in the motel at Mackinaw City: *I love you, Ben. I have all my life,* she meant all— before our meeting at Arthur Hill, to my meeting of Mrs. Arthur

Hall—all. I was driven here, to this place, to find her, and, if that's lunacy, then I'll embrace it and be content.

I watched her often from my kitchen window, where the wildflowers wilted in the vase on the table. I learned to watch her from the back yard as well, without being seen by her or her husband. The big willow tree provided the perfect camouflage. From Sophie's side of the creek, its leaf-laden limbs obscured the view of the pantry door, so that I could slip outside unnoticed and enter the dense, protective canopy formed by the drooping branches. I could see out. I knew she couldn't see in, although I think she sensed my presence.

Each day when I arose, I went to the kitchen window over the sink to search for her. The willow didn't hinder my view there. Throughout the day, as I went about my painting and unpacking, I'd return many times, hoping just to catch a glimpse of her.

Ten days after our first meeting, in mid-morning of a beautiful, August day, I'd just showered and had come to the kitchen for a refill on my coffee. I glanced routinely through the glass. As I saw nothing, I began to turn away, once again disappointed, when my eye caught the movement of water on the dam and something registered, unconsciously at first, as different. Then I realized that the boards of Sophie's bridge were in place!

I looked frantically about, leaning over the sink to see below the window and craning my neck for a better lateral view. Nothing. "She's fallen," I thought. I rushed out the pantry door and ran to the edge of the creek, searching the water for a sign of her. The creek was a good twenty-five feet across. Q had told me it was very deep and warned me not to swim alone. She could've drowned an hour ago. She could be lying in the murky depths among entangling weeds.

"I'm over here," she said softly. Her voice came from behind me. She was in the willow canopy. I could see the pastel blue of her shirt, barely, through the branches. I parted the boughs and entered. "I was afraid you might have fallen in the creek."

"I'm fine." She wore peach-colored shorts that both flattered her shapely tanned legs, and complimented the sky-blue of her blouse. She was leaning against the willow trunk, harvested wild-flowers in hand. "It's almost like a cave in here," she said. "You sit here a lot don't you?"

"Yes."

"Why?"

"It's cooler, out of the sun."

"Why? Really."

"To watch you."

"Am I so interesting?"

"Yes."

"I think you shouldn't."

"How come?"

"My husband is...well, he gets jealous easily. He can be violent."

"To you?"

The dark eyes examined me in silence. I thought about what it would be like to hold her, to press my lips against the hollow of her neck in the mottled half-light of the tree shadows.

She read something in my countenance and averted her eyes.

"Why did you come here again, then," I said.

She held up the wildflowers. "I forgot them last time."

"I know. They're still in a vase on my kitchen table."

"What did your wife look like?" The eyes penetrated, burning through the icy grief that had been my shield for years.

"Why?"

"I've thought a lot about what she must have been like. I don't know why. I think about it most often when I pass a mirror. I think I dreamed of her."

"That's because she looked very much like you. You have the same eyes—eyes that I've never seen on anyone else, male or female. Your hair is the same color. Your mannerisms are very similar."

"Is that why you watch me?"

My heart was thudding, my mouth turned dry. "Sophia..."

"Sophie, please."

"Sophie. What did you dream?"

She hesitated for a moment, then told me. "I've never remembered a dream so vividly, in such detail. I was walking in a forest. I came into an orchard of apple trees. The limbs were sagging with fruit. Beyond the orchard was a wall. It was made of heavy stone blocks, like the kind they used to make castles from; thick, carved from rock. Much of the wall was overgrown with vines, heavy with clusters of purple grapes. The wall was too high to see over the top. I began to walk along it. It was circular and I was certain that there was some gate or opening somewhere along its length. As I walked, I could hear a woman laughing, and the movement of water. The sounds were very distinctive, although there were other noises too.

Birds were chirping and the wind breathed in the tree branches. After circling for a long time, I realized that I'd gone all the way around. I knew this because I recognized things I'd already seen, not on the wall, but outside it. A rabbit was nibbling grapes. It hadn't stirred when first I passed it and still seemed to take no notice of me, though I stepped within inches of its fuzzy tail. A white bird with a long beak, I think it was a heron, was standing on its stilt-like legs in a puddle. Its eyes were dripping tears as it looked, fearfully, at the sky. I saw a honeycomb attached to a wooden log, from which amber syrup oozed to the ground. I saw each of these things at least twice, so I knew I had progressed around the entire circle of the wall. I continued on, driven by the strange laughter inside, until I found an opening that hadn't been there before. The woman's laughter drew me in. I saw her immediately. She was standing before a fountain, her feet on the ground outside the shallow pool. She was dressed in a brilliant white robe. It seemed to be made of light rather than cloth. She knew I was there long before she turned around. She showed no surprise or alarm at my presence. Her only expression was one of calm fulfillment. She looked so much like me, yet she wasn't me. Somewhere, beyond the scope of my vision, I heard a train whistle and felt a kind of unreasoning urgency. She felt it too. She stepped quickly toward me, embraced me, and then whispered something to me. I heard the words, but not her voice."

Sophie's dark eyes looked far away, still seeing in the mottled light, that vision that pierced the willow boughs, and took her somewhere beyond herself. My knees trembled, my hands shook. I could hear the water rushing off the dam and felt my own tears. She continued.

"Though I felt her arms around me, felt her breath in my ear, she passed through me, like a spirit. I turned to watch her as she vanished through the opening. It closed behind her and was a solid wall again. I remember not feeling trapped or deserted or afraid as I should have felt. I went to the fountain and put my hands in the water, careful to keep my feet on the ground. The fountain tickled. I woke up laughing."

She turned her eyes to me. "Art woke up too. He thought I'd been drinking. That was the night before last. I haven't been able to think about anything else, except to come here and tell you this. I don't know why. I think I'm tired. I've been burning my bridges at both ends." She looked out through the willow's veil at the creek. "You must think I'm crazy."

"No. I'm glad you came back."

The black eyes examined me with intensity and I saw there a kind of sophic ignorance, a depth of vision limited by object realism, a desire to sink deeper into this pool of secret glory that waited at the bottom where drowning was the price for knowledge.

"I'm glad you came back, for the flowers. You like them so much."

She looked absently at the bouquet drooping in her hand. "We should put them in water if I'm to stay...for a while." She looked up at me and smiled, coyly, as if the suggestion had been my own.

"Yes," I said, "let's go inside."

She followed me up the steps and through the pantry into the kitchen. Wordlessly, she threw out the flowers she had brought on her first visit. They had died and were dropping their petals on the kitchen table. She rinsed out the vase, put the new flowers in, and arranged them artfully. Then she sat down and looked nervously around as if unsure about what to do next.

I asked her if she wanted some coffee. She nodded, so I filled two steaming cups, then joined her at the table. Neither of us spoke immediately.

Her hands twisted the cup around and around between sips of coffee. The morning sun glinted off her engagement ring. "That's a beautiful diamond," I said.

She smiled. "It's a zircon. The diamond that my husband gave me came loose from the setting and got lost years ago. It wasn't insured. I didn't want to tell him. He would've been very angry. So, without telling him, I had the setting filled with this stone. He's never noticed. It looks real, doesn't it?"

"Yes. Reality is relative anyway."

She looked at my hand. "You still wear your wedding band."

"Yes."

I thought she might be disappointed, but she looked pleased, and made no further comment about it.

"What do you think my dream meant?"

"I don't know."

She laughed. "You twitched, just then. I think you're lying to me, Mr. Riveridge." The dark eyes twinkled impishly.

"You're right. I was."

"Why?"

"Because you'll think I'm crazy and I won't have the chance to explain all that's happened to make me believe what I believe."

"I don't understand."

"No, I'm sure you don't, but I think the dream is your attempt to help you."

She stood up, went to the sink, and gazed out the window toward the creek. She held her arms tightly as if she were cold, in spite of the sweltering heat developing outside. "My husband and I haven't been happy together for a long time," she said. She had her back to me. The words were barely decipherable. I stood up and she turned to face me. "Were you and Morgan always happy?"

"Yes."

"I think it was quite a coincidence that we met on the anniversary of her death, don't you?"

"I don't believe in coincidence."

"No?"

"No."

"What do you believe in then? Destiny? Fate?"

"I think we're all shown what we should do and how we should go. Those who ignore all this are called realists, although they're actually denying what's real. Those who follow it are romantics—artists, mental patients, there's a variety of names."

Skepticism was plowing furrows across her forehead. She frowned, darkly. "You think dreams are the medium through which we're 'shown' how to go, or what to do?"

"I think...I believe, we're guided by metaphor, specific comparisons. Dreams are metaphorical, but so are specific incidences in every life."

"Like?"

"Like you showing up on my doorstep on July 31st."

Her dark eyes pierced me, holding me to accountability. They said, "No games. We will not play games." Then they focused elsewhere, leaving a burning hole in my brain, like the path of a bullet.

"I'm hungry," she said. "Do you have something for a sandwich?"

"Sandwich material is something a solitary male always has. We don't cook much."

I extracted slices of turkey breast, lettuce leaf and tomato from the refrigerator while she laid out slices of bread. In a few moments we had prepared the sandwiches and I was about to transfer them to the table.

"Do you have a blanket?" she asked.

"I think so, why?"

"Let's have a picnic...in the shade of that old oak."

"What about your husband? Would he...."

"He won't be home until after dark. His driver called in sick and they have to deliver a big order of lumber to a construction site a hundred miles from here, after closing. Besides, we're not doing anything wrong, are we?"

"No." I got the blanket from the linen closet in the living room and by the time I got back, she'd prepared some iced tea and everything was neatly arranged on a tray for transporting.

Outside, I spread the blanket on the ground and we sat in silence for a few minutes, sipping tea. I took out a pack of cigarettes and held them toward her.

"No," she said, "but you go ahead. It doesn't bother me. I used to smoke, but I quit, about five years ago."

"Worried about cancer?"

"No. Art decided we shouldn't do it anymore."

"Oh."

I took one, long drag, and then turned to throw the rest away, when I saw them.

Two elegant, white swans, side by side, were paddling gracefully in the calmer water where it slowed, some fifty feet from the dam. They'd obviously been swimming upstream and had just come around a little bend to our right and into our field of vision. They'd seen the barrier of cascading water ahead of them and now swam in circles, unsure of what to do next.

I stood up and moved toward them slowly, careful not to frighten them. "Look," I whispered to Sophie.

She nodded. "They mate for life. There are dozens of pairs around here. Swan's End, you know."

The two moved in perfect synchronicity, gliding first one way, then the other, and finally, retracing their wake, they disappeared back beyond the bend. "Beautiful," was all I could manage, resuming my spot on the blanket. Sophie waved away some flies that were attempting to use the sandwiches for a landing pad. She covered our lunch with a paper napkin, and lay back on the blanket, looking up into the massive foliage of the oak.

"They mean something to you, don't they? The swans. It wasn't just their beauty that touched you."

"No. They're archetypal, you know. Symbols."

"Symbols of what?"

"A lot of things," I explained. "But mostly purity. In old Germanic legends, virgins were transformed into sacrificial swans with prophetic powers. They're used often in mythology and literature and music—as metaphors: *Leda and the Swan, The Wild Swans at Coole, Swan Lake, The Ugly Duckling*, and so on. They make this strange noise which is often seen as a cry for the satisfaction of their desire. Once granted, though, it brings about their own deaths."

"The swan song."

"Yes."

"But these were silent."

"Does that mean something?"

"I don't know."

We ate the sandwiches half-heartedly, swinging at the flies, whose numbers were becoming overwhelming. "Ouch!" Sophie slapped at a horsefly that had decided to lunch on her exposed leg in lieu of the protected sandwiches. "That's it," she said and stood up, gathering the remains of our repast. "Let's go back inside."

I shook the blanket and folded it, then followed her to the steps, where she'd stopped and placed the tray on the landing.

"What is it?"

She motioned for me to be quiet until I heard it, too. The indistinct and muffled mewling from the cavity beneath the steps of a small animal—a kitten, I guessed. Sophie knelt down and put her ear to the opening.

She shielded the sun from her eyes and peered into the blackness. "I can see its eyes," she said. Her voice echoed in the hollow. She reached in and pulled out the tiny kitten. It was an unusual color, a kind of rust-orange, with wide eyes and an extended snout, which made it appear more canine than feline. It mewed pathetically as Sophie cradled it tenderly. "Poor thing," she said, as she stood up and offered me a better view of the sad creature. I'd never seen a homelier orphan, though the abandoned waif did draw my sympathy. I thought back to another summer, another picnic, another lost pet.

"Where do you suppose its mother is?" Sophie caressed its nape and it began to purr in a soothing kind of mechanical half-growl. The purr was a pleasurable relief from the pitiable cries it had emitted when rescued from its dark hole.

"Run off, maybe, maybe dead. It looks thin enough to have been on its own for a while," I said.

"It doesn't have a collar or tag. We'll have to keep it. We can't just let it go. It'll starve or the coyotes will get it." She was cleaning cobwebs from its fur. "Ugly little thing."

She looked at me hopefully. "You live alone. She'd make a nice companion."

"I don't want a pet, especially a cat."

"Have you ever had one?"

"No, and I don't want one."

"I'd take it myself, but Art wouldn't stand for it. He'd drown the poor thing. Won't you think about it? It can stay outside for a while. If you can just feed it, maybe I can find another home for it before the cold weather sets in. What do you think? Just temporarily?"

"It stays outside."

"Yes. It'll hang around here, probably under the porch, if you feed it every day."

"I think I've got a can of tuna inside. Let's go look."

She was so pleased that it didn't matter anymore how I felt about it. She found the tuna and scraped it onto an old dish. Then set the dish and the cat on the porch. The little thing greedily consumed its treat as we stood watching through the screen door.

"I'll get some real cat food tomorrow," she said.

"I can do that," I told her.

She took my hand as I turned away, making me spin back. "I want to," she said. "It'll give me an excuse to come back."

There are moments where a single word or gesture can change everything, and those moments are most often approached without thought or reason, but only an intuitive trust. It's how we're all conceived, and how we die.

I leaned forward and kissed her softly. I felt a tense acceptance in her lips. Her hand, still in mine, squeezed hard. We broke it off as quickly as it had happened. I could see fear in her lovely face and something else—a flickering, befuddled, recognition. But no regret.

"I'm sorry," I whispered. "I had no right..."

She said nothing, but placed her free hand over my mouth and said: "I want to know." She studied my face with such intensity that I felt naked, exposed. She lowered her left hand from my face, then released her grip with her right, as she stepped back a few paces.

"What do you want to know?"

"About my dream. You understand it, don't you? I could see it in your eyes when I told it to you. I want you to tell me. I feel like my life is slipping away. I see time in blocks—an hour, a minute, a year. There are never enough blocks to build the time I need. The blocks in that wall, in the dream, are eternity. I try to build time, to wall away death. I have the blocks stacked in my head, and when the day is over, I'm missing more than I've built. The blocks have become so precious to me. Their value is measured by what I do with them—or who I spend them with. So I'm desperate and I want to know. What did it mean?"

"I don't understand all of it."

"Tell me what you do understand, then."

I took a deep breath. The cat mewed at the door. "Time, in this life, is very much as you say it is—built in blocks. But there's another time that exists, that has no limitations. It's circular, rather than linear, like the stone wall in your dream. It's Eden-like, perfect, free of judgment, static and immovable, devoid of death. It's the happiness of all we have experienced, but it isn't the past. It lives beside us, contained and uncontaminated. I think you went there in your dream."

"To this other dimension?"

"It's not a dimension. That would make it a part of this world. It's a different place entirely, within itself."

"What else?"

"You went there, but you didn't come back."

"What?"

"The wall closed and kept you there, you said. You're not really here anymore."

"Then how can I stand before you now?"

"You're not."

She laughed, but the unfamiliarity of it frightened her. "Well then, who is?"

"The woman in the white robe. You said she passed through you and left you sealed inside, but you didn't feel abandoned."

"But who is she? Who do you think I am?"

I hesitated because I knew my answer could drive away the returning joy—that the revelation of my deep desire could destroy its fulfillment. But I couldn't lie to her now. I never could. "Morgan. You're Morgan."

"Oh, Ben," she sighed. A terrible sympathy, a kind of horrific pity, shadowed her countenance. She put a hand to my face and caressed my cheek. "You can't bring her back."

"You think I'm crazy then," I said.

She was silent. The dark eyes pooled with moisture. "I think grief has overwhelmed you, made you see things that aren't there. I should go." She turned toward the door.

A train whistle sounded somewhere far in the distance. She heard it, too. I grabbed both her arms and turned her toward me again. I expected to see fear. Instead, I encountered confusion. She didn't struggle, but waited for my explanation. I could sense that she wanted to be convinced, that her doubt was Thomasine.

"What did Morgan...what did the lady whisper to you? Do you remember? What did she say!" I shook her, as if I could jolt the answer from her.

She responded quietly, in a voice devoid of inflection. "She whispered 'thank-you.' That's all. Just 'thank-you.'"

I felt myself coming apart. I choked back my tears, tried to slow my stampeding heart, fought to drive away a flooding darkness that threatened to engulf my mind and short it out. "Why? Why would she say that, Sophie?"

"I don't know. It was a dream, that's all, just a dream. I woke up laughing, remember? Still encircled by the wall. Art was next to me. Why didn't I wake in your bed, Ben, if I'm your wife?"

"I don't know. I don't care." I kissed her.

"No!" She pushed me away and stood by the screen door, but she didn't leave.

"Sophie, I..."

"How can you call me that if you believe what you say you believe?"

"Because you don't understand yet. Our lives are composed of metaphor. We shrug it away and call it coincidence, but the metaphors need to be learned, Sophie, for you to understand. On the day I met you, you were wearing the same clothes Morgan wore when she..."

"A pair of khaki shorts and a blouse? The most common outfit in the world on a hot day in summer."

"You have her black eyes, the auburn tint in her hair that can

174

only be seen in direct sunlight, her mannerisms. You have her crooked toes and fear of thunderstorms. You couldn't get a cliché right if your life depended on it and neither could she. We met on the anniversary of her death. There was a rainbow in the sky when she died and another when I bought this house, a house I was drawn to, even driven to, when I didn't know you existed. I met her in the hall of Arthur Hill High School. I met you, Mrs. Arthur Hall, on this hill. Someday I'll tell you about bridges and picnics and swans and hands and hearts. But it's there, and it's not coincidence!"

There was a long silence and, as my words echoed in the air, they mixed with the foggy atmosphere of incredulity—hers and mine.

"Oh Ben, you're only seeing what you want to see. People can deny the Holocaust, or that the world is round."

"Yes, but this isn't denial. It's affirmation, and there's a vast difference. The denial is yours, not mine."

"You're denying what's real."

"I've never denied anything that's happened to me. I've only interpreted. We all do that, Sophie, and because we do, there's no reason to believe in the indisputable fixity of things."

She looked at me. "It was a dream."

"Do I dream now then? Are you here? Did we kiss before I told you my belief? I know what you are to me—my life companion, my soul, my heart, returned to me. What you need to decide is who I am to you. I'm not Art Hall, the husband that you fear. Am I just a dalliance then? A possible adultery? Why are you here, Sophie? What drove you here to me!" I was shouting and, as I realized it, I backed away. I could see her fear as she turned to face me. It was accustomed dismay in anticipation of danger.

Still, she gathered her fortitude and stepped toward me. As she approached, her courage rose. Her own voice exploded in anger. "What drove me here? How about thirty years of living with a brutal man—a man who beat me up every time I disagreed with him or had an original thought? How about my children being gone and for the first time in thirty years I begin to look beyond the borders of my yard? I didn't come over here to see you. I didn't even know you lived here. But when I did meet you, was it so surprising that I should be attracted to a good-looking man—a gentle man, an intelligent and compassionate man? Why is it such a damn mystery that I should want to be loved!"

She rushed past me, pushing me aside, and hurried out the screen door. I followed her, caught her hand, and pulled her into the sheltering canopy of the willow. "It's not a mystery," I said. "It's an answer. It's the..."

She rushed forward suddenly, and flung her arms around my neck, smothering my reply with her mouth. I crushed her against me with such force that I could feel the breath wrenched from her lungs. I tasted the salt of her tears. So, so long I'd been alone, without the touch of human hand or heart, that I became absorbed, like a living sponge displaced in a puddle, soaking up every drop of affection in order to continue life, even on such risky terms, knowing the consequence would be to use the precious moisture far too quickly, my only source of sustenance.

She pushed me away, with the intent, I believed, to run away from what she saw as insanity. I knew that if she did so, at that moment, I'd never see her again. But she stood still, studying my face, her shoulders heaving from the excitement and the fear. Then, with slow purpose, she began to unbutton her blouse. She discarded it. There was no sensuality in the action. She didn't smile seductively or express wantonness in her disrobing. She removed each article of clothing with a kind of unhurried determination, her eyes never leaving mine. When she was entirely undressed, she took several steps back until she rested against the trunk of the willow. She held out her arms.

I went to her. We kissed again. The slow, cool embrace rose quickly to searing heat, like the summer sun outside. I probed rapaciously, relentlessly, with a savage concentration that was

mirrored by my ravening lover. I remember little—only the
sweating, clinging, carnality of it. It was more a kind of mutual
rape than love-making. It was the driven, primordial lust of
animals. It was necessary—an act of survival and perpetuation.

When it was finished, I leaned against her—spent, shriveled,
drying up, afraid that I'd taken too much from her, from myself.
But when she opened her dark eyes and looked at me, I saw satisfaction in their depths. Regret, if it existed, hid far beneath the
surface. She smiled, sadly, and ran her fingers along the outline of
my jaw, studying the foreigner who still clung to her naked form.

"I have to go," she said.

"I'm sorry for all this."

"Don't say that."

"I don't mean what happened. More like how it happened.
I was pretty self-absorbed."

She laughed. "So was I. When you're hungry you can be
polite, but not when you're starving."

We picked up our clothes from the ground and dressed
hurriedly, like two teen-agers caught in the glare of a policeman's
flashlight. On her face, there was no evidence of our fierce
encounter. Once dressed, her expression was serene.

"What happens now?" I asked her.

"I go home."

"No. I mean between us."

"I can't be someone else, Ben."

"I don't want you to."

"You want me to become Morgan."

"No. You already are. There's nothing to change."

She sighed heavily. "Except my name."

"That's how we make things real."

"How?"

"We name them."

"I'm Sophia Hall, Ben. That's who I am. That's my name. If
you ever want to see me again, don't call me Morgan."

"Okay. It doesn't matter."

The late afternoon sun was slanting through the apple orchard when we stepped outside the canopy. There was a cool breeze coming across the yard that was wonderfully invigorating. We sat on the landing by the pantry door for a few minutes. She picked up the little kitten, which had again begun its plaintive cacophony. Sophie's touch transposed it to the perfunctory purr. "You'll take care of him?"

"I'll keep him outside, yes. You'll have to bring the cat food tomorrow, remember?"

She nodded. "I said I would."

"Still want to come back?"

"Yes," she said. There was no hesitation.

"You don't think I'm crazy then?"

"Crazy? No. Misguided perhaps."

"In what sense?"

"In the sense that these metaphors, coincidences, parallels— whatever you call them—are not really guiding you or me, they're just things that happen." She placed the kitten on the landing and descended the steps to the yard, heading for the bridge that would take her to the other side.

"What should we call it?" I shouted after her and pointed to the cat, which now rubbed itself sensuously against the hairy pillars towering above it.

She turned and cupped her hands to her mouth in an attempt to make herself heard above the noise of the rushing water behind her. "It's the same, weird color of the alien-life-form puppet that used to star in its own comedy series. Remember? It has a nose like it too. Call it Alf!"

Then she was across the bridge and gone. "Just things that happen," I mumbled. I picked Alf up and went inside. The second vase of wildflowers was still on the table.

Later that afternoon, with Alf curled in my lap inside the house, I read a postcard that had just come in the mail from Billy Borden. He wrote:

Dear Ben,

The Umbrella Bearer's Union is just another one of my day-dreamy ideas. It's an "amalgamation" of concerned fellows who think it's important to give shelter to the people around them. It's a goal of this organization to assure that you be you. How is you being? I'm still busy swimming in my wordsea, paddling between the waves of ideas that wash over me every day. I think all humans feel this love of saying something right, of naming things to make them real. I think that is what a human being is, or am. My Morgan and I moved to Boulder to help my parents out for a little while. I met an artist here because my father said that she had painted a pastel of "my tree," an umbrella-shaped, gigantic willow, that sheltered me as a child and stands at the top of the hill, just south of Boulder. I had three chances to talk with her, very briefly. Morgan and I went up to the tree to take some pictures, and when I got back, I read in the morning paper that the artist had died. A car had struck her bicycle. In her obituary, they said there was a rainbow at her memorial service. It turned out she was from Saginaw, Michigan. Does the rainbow ring a bell for you?

B.

Chapter Fifteen

The Assumption of Shadow

Ar, that? Let's see. Used to say there was four women in
every man's heart. The Maid in the Meadow, the Demon Lover,
the Stouthearted Woman, the Tall and Quiet Woman. It was just
a thing he said. I don't know what it means.

—E. Annie Proulx, *The Shipping News*

I saw her husband that same evening, and I think he saw me.
Art Hall was inspecting his roses. I say "inspecting" because he
marched through the rows of flowers in much the same manner as
a West Point general would survey his troops. His demeanor
reflected pride, power, possession—as though the roses existed,
like soldiers, only to advance the ambitions of their commanders.
He reviewed them in groups, never once touching them. I don't
believe he ever noticed their individual beauty, only the orderly
rows of color.

When he looked across the creek, I waved, but he either
didn't see me (although I stood in the open) or, more likely, chose
to ignore me.

From what I could see, he was a big man, though not as tall
or heavy as I. I envied him his thick, black hair. He must have just
returned from work, since he still wore an empty tool belt, blue
jeans faded at the knees, workboots, and a denim shirt. He held
something in his hand. I think it was a can of beer.

I'd hoped that Sophie would join him, if only to catch
another glimpse of her, but he didn't stay long, and left the roses at
parade rest before marching in a direct line to the door of his headquarters.

I fixed a toasted cheese sandwich for supper and sat down at
the table. I looked at the wildflowers in the vase and out the

window across the creek, alternately, for half an hour. I dumped the uneaten sandwich and went outside again to sit within the canopy of the willow. I caressed the bark of the tree where her bare back had been.

I regretted my aggression with her. I thought I smelled her perfume, still lingering in the willow-chamber, and I sat down, replaying the joy of the day in my mind. Above the noise of the water, I heard my own distant voice say: "Thank-you."

I sat there until well after darkness had enveloped the canopy. I saw lights go on in the house across the creek. I listened to the archaic perseverance of the water, the primordial sibilation of the wind in the catkins of the willow, the scuttlebutt of gregarious insects, the husky, plaintive grousing of unsatiated frogs. I sensed a commonality.

I'd been waiting, afternoon and evening, for guilt to find me, to pierce my hands and heart with nails, to crucify me on a tree of knowledge. But a man can't commit adultery with his wife, just as a woman cannot betray a husband to whom she has returned. I could see it no other way. I heard a mosquito buzzing near my ear. I saw, by the light of the kitchen window, a conclave of them gather on my arms. I thought. "Let them have their blood." But even they would not punish me.

When I went inside, I discovered that Alf had vomited on the kitchen floor. I picked him up and placed him gently outside, cleaned up the mess, and went to my bed. I did not feel alone.

When the first light came into the room, I rose with anticipation. The desperate mewing outside the pantry door gave rise to an exhilarating confidence in her return. She wouldn't let Alf go hungry. I knew Morgan too well.

Each hour passed like a child's anticipation of Christmas. I took my coffee to the edge of the creek. The water was calm and deep in front of me, though I could see the dam clearly and hear its splashing song. Alf followed me and played impatiently, stalking insects and watching a frog he couldn't reach—displaying the same hungry yearning in his demeanor with which his new master studied the opposite shore.

The sun was high in the August sky when I saw her emerge from the log house, carrying a plastic bag. She waved and smiled, indications of the absence of both her sovereign and her repentance. She walked with the speed and urgency of a fugitive seeking sanctuary. I watched her lithe movements with loving admiration, then finally stood up and hurried to the dam to meet her. She laid down her wooden bridge and was across in moments.

"Hi," she said as she took my hand and jumped deftly onto the bank.

"Hi."

She looked happy and comfortable. Her actions were familiar and pleasant, as if we'd known each other all our lives. "I brought Alf his lunch," she held up the plastic bag, "as promised. It took me a while to get to town and back after Art left."

"It's a good thing you're here, he was driving me crazy," I said as she scooped Alf into her hand. "He was reduced to eating bugs."

"Ugh," she said and headed for the house. The familiarity of the action, and the ease with which we talked, after the intimacy of yesterday, had to touch a cord within her. After she fetched a bowl and filled it with the cat's breakfast, I feared she might leave, perhaps afraid to repeat yesterday's liaison, perhaps wishing to deny all that had transpired. Instead, she sat at the table, rearranged the wildflowers in their vase and asked for coffee.

She was wearing a simple blouse and shorts again, and it suddenly occurred to me that I'd never seen her wearing shoes.

"I'm sorry about yesterday," I said, twitching.

"Are you?"

"No."

"Me either."

There was a long silence between us as we stared at our cups. Finally, she looked up at me. "It won't happen today, though."

"Okay."

"Maybe never again."

"Okay."

Tears began to emerge at the corners of her dark eyes and flow along accustomed paths down her cheeks.

"What?"

"I'm afraid." There was a child's hitch in her voice as she spoke.

"Of Art?"

"Of my confusion. All I could think about since I left yesterday, was getting back here. How can this continue, Ben? My children would hate me! He's their father and he's always been good to them. He's never hit either one of them."

"Only you. And you think, somehow, that that doesn't matter?"

She lowered her eyes again to the table's surface and angrily interrupted the natural course of her tears with the back of her hand. The zircon caught a glint of sunlight and flashed surreptitiously, but I saw it wink at me. Her thick, vibrant hair glowed auburn in the morning light.

"You confuse me the most," she cried. "Should I give up being one man's punching bag to become a surrogate wife to another? What you want me to believe is impossible, Ben. Just because there are similarities between me and Morgan...don't you understand how insane that sounds?"

"Yes."

"But you still believe it?"

"Yes."

"Why?"

That single query was the beginning of her return. I told her of all the metaphors, the connections. She sat, listening patiently, to stories of thunderstorms and bridges, musical teddy bears, swans and rainbows, picnics and lost pets and rivers, hands and hearts. With each revelation, she would attempt to rationalize. I could always find a simple rejoinder that would stifle her argument. The morning slipped away unnoticed into afternoon. The heat drove us outside. Coffee changed to iced tea with lemon. I set up folding lawnchairs in the cave of the willow, still droning on like a solitary bee in search of his queen.

Every time I paused, whether from exhaustion or the tedium of my peroration, she would urge me on, as though the revivification of my memories resurrected her own. Her eyes never left my face. I didn't twitch.

When at last she let me stop, I was spent. There was more to tell, but a life, much less two, cannot be relived in the block of time called an afternoon.

"So you believe that all this is purposeful? That you've been 'guided' to this place, this moment, with me?"

"Yes."

"By whom?"

"God."

"So God speaks to you, tells you what to do?"

"Indirectly, yes. He speaks to everyone."

"He doesn't speak to me."

"Yes, he does. You're just not paying attention—or you refuse to listen."

I paused, seeing the fear on her face. "I've become involved with some nut who thinks he talks to God," it said. "This is a disturbed man who wants to be a new prophet." I knew the look. I'd seen it on my own face, reflected in my father's pale blue eyes.

"Have you ever read Plato's *Republic*?" I asked her.

"The Greek philosopher? No."

"In it, he described life as being like a cave, where humanity is trapped. From our position in this place, we can only see vestiges of what is real, like passing shadows—only images—because our mortal limitations don't allow us to see directly. It's like looking through those willow boughs. They obscure our true vision of what's real. Ironically, if we never leave this place, then this becomes real, the cave is reality, and we quit looking outside. But that doesn't mean that 'outside' doesn't exist anymore. It only means that darkness is easier to accept than half-light. The shadows, the metaphors, frustrate us, confuse us, often drive the most sensitive of us to despair. I suppose it's why artists and writers and clergymen populate the mental wards or drink themselves to death, while the engineers and politicians and chemists have accepted the darkness and gone about the pragmatic business of making it more comfortable."

"So God shows us the shadows."

"More appropriately, he provides the light. We can only see the shadows."

She sighed, then laughed. "Even a lapsed Catholic can remember her catechism: *And God said, 'Let there be light,' and there was light. God saw that the light was good, and he separated the light from the darkness.*"

"An interesting passage, but your allusion is to the first day's creation and the sun wasn't created until the fourth day. What was that first light, Sophie?"

"What do you think it was?"

"The creation of shadow, of metaphor, the voice of God."

"So the teddy bear, in the basement, that was the voice..."

"A foreshadowing. We're all integrated into the world, the structure of experience, but we can only be transformed through individuation. Sophie, you can't be afraid of your own shadow."

I think it was the word "afraid" that triggered her awareness of the descending darkness.

"Oh Ben, what time is it?"

I'd forgotten time too, or perhaps it hadn't existed. My heart pounded with alarm, with fear for her. "Almost eight."

She jumped up, sprawling the flimsy lawn chair behind her. "What have I done? Oh no!" There was a ghastly, wild panic in her eyes, the awful dread of the Serengeti antelope that has not, for the first time in its life, paid attention to the wind.

"Art will be home any minute!" She parted the willow ropes and ran for the weir. I watched her fly across the shadowed lawn in the mottled light. Then, suddenly, she went down. "Oh!" she cried. "Oh no!" I rushed to her as quickly as my bad knees would allow.

She was holding her foot. Her hands were covered with blood.

"What happened?"

"I stepped on something. I don't know what. Oh it hurts!"

I knelt down and forced her hands away. There was a deep wound on the inside of her left foot, perhaps two inches wide, where calluses often form. It was oozing dark blood. The quantity and color suggested arterial origins. Nearby, on the grass, lay the bloodied perpetrator—a broken mason jar.

"Help me up," she yelled. "Hurry!"

"You need a doctor. It's deep."

She struggled erect on one leg. The blood spurted gloriously into the grass.

She fell again. Her face was ashen. I picked her up in my arms. She was surprisingly light. "What are you doing?" she cried. "You can't take me home!"

"I'm taking you to the emergency room in Grenville. It's the nearest place."

"I can't," she screamed. She beat her hands against my breast in desperation, but I continued up the slope to the house. "Please, Ben," she sobbed, and lay her head on my shoulder. "You don't know what he's like, what he's capable of."

"It doesn't matter."

Inside the house, I sat her down for a moment, pulled a sheet from the linen closet and grabbed my car keys. She moaned softly as I picked her up again. "God help us," she whispered against my neck. The anniversary clock on the mantle struck eight times.

I made her as comfortable as I could in the back seat of the Cavalier, keeping the leg high and wrapping the wound in the sheet to stanch the blood. She was silent.

It took us fifteen minutes to reach Grenville, the only town in a thirty-mile radius large enough to support a hospital. I'd brought

Morgan here. They had flown her to Grand Rapids in a helicopter.

At 9:00, the doctor found me in the waiting room. "You brought Mrs. Hall in," he said, extending his hand. He was a young man, likely a new intern.

"Yes."

He had a delicate grip, like a man experienced in reversing pain. "She'll be okay, though the laceration was very invasive."

"Invasive?"

"Deep. She severed an artery, which also had to be sutured. Fifteen stitches in all. Different people react differently to this kind of trauma, Mr. Hall. She seems very distraught. I'm giving her sedatives and I think we should keep her under observation for an hour or so. Okay?"

"I'm not Mr. Hall."

"No?"

"I'm a friend."

"I see. Good thing you were nearby. She's lost a lot of blood." I sensed him studying me for a moment. "Has anyone called her husband?"

"May I see her? I'll get her home number and call then."

"Yes, of course."

She was lying on a too-narrow gurney, her hands folded across her bosom to prevent her arms from dangling. Her injured leg was raised on several pillows. Her foot was encased in cotton and gauze. Only her crooked toes protruded from the bandages. Color had returned to her cheeks, but her dark eyes betrayed the terror of the condemned prisoner who had lived the wrong life.

"Hi," I said, making a feeble attempt to be casual. "Feeling better?"

She managed a half-smile. She was squinting in the harsh glare of the overhead lights, artificial brighteners of a dark world. "What am I going to do, Ben?"

"I take you home, with me. You stay the night, and call a lawyer in the morning. You'll never have to be alone with him again. You won't have to be afraid anymore."

"And what do I say to my children?"

"They're adults. They'll have to adjust."

"I can't. I won't. I've known you for what? A week? Ten days?"

"You've known me all your life."

She stared at me, the black eyes fierce with longing. "I don't believe that."

"Don't you?"

"No."

"Then I'll drive you home."

"No. I want you to call Art, tell him you found me, brought me here."

"Have you told him anything about me?"

"No. He said someone was living in the old farmhouse across the creek when I talked to him last night. He must have seen you, or seen the lights. He doesn't know that I've been going over there. He ordered me not to after I broke my arm. You can't tell him I was there."

"Where do I tell him this happened then? In your yard?"

"Oh no. He'd expect to find the blood, the broken jar. You'll have to tell him that you found me coming out of the woods on the edge of Round Lake Road. That's the road I live on, the one our house faces. Tell him you were fishing at the lake that forms at the end of the creek. I'll tell him that I went for a walk, stepped on something, then managed to crawl to the road just as you came along. Can you remember that?"

"Yes."

She handed me a slip of paper with her phone number scribbled on it. "Then, once you've called him, I want you to get out of here and go home. I don't want him to find you here. Don't worry. He'll come and get me. He has to fill out the paperwork."

"When do I see you again?"

"I don't know. Maybe never."

I looked cautiously around, then kissed her. "You'll keep coming back. You have to. Look for the shadows. I love you."

She nodded, her eyes brimming with tears. She put one hand over her mouth to enforce a silence that went against her will and waved me away with the other.

In the corridor, I found a phone and dialed Art Hall's number. He answered immediately. His tenor voice made me think of him as being much smaller than I knew him to be. He didn't seem agitated or angry. His tone hummed of relief and gratitude. He said he would come right away. He told me of another fishing hole. He said the fishing was never very good down his road. He thanked me profusely. I sighed heavily when I hung up. I wanted to stay. I was sure that nothing would happen, but I obeyed Sophie's wishes and went to my car.

The bright moon illuminated the cornfields and apple orchards and cow pastures as I drove to Swan's End and turned down Creekpath Road. As I bumped along, the gravel ticked off the sides of the car. I pulled into the circular drive and went immediately inside. I almost fell as I stepped into the inner darkness, skidding on the wooden floor and regaining my balance only by grabbing the open door of the linen closet. I flicked the light switch. A spotted trail of blood led from the kitchen. I'd stepped in a pool of it, which had formed, I remembered now, when I placed Sophie in the cane chair under the Goya reproduction and fetched the sheet from the closet to wrap her wound.

A creeping rigidity shivered through my flesh, inhibiting all movement except for my mettlesome heart, which doubled its efforts, racing to restore the animation that distress had interrupted. The sheet! The last time I'd seen it was on Sophie's foot when they wheeled her into the examination room. It was still at the hospital, then. What had they done with it? They would assume it was hers. They might give it to her—or to Art when he came to get her. There was the hope that they might dispose of it, but that was unlikely. Why would a fisherman have a clean sheet in his car?

Alf's sudden mewing at the back door contravened my calculations and I forced my feet into service. As I followed the rusty trail of drying blood to the kitchen, another dissembling thought, a second discrepancy, enfeebled my previous sanguinity. Sophie had told me that Art knew nothing of her recent progresses across the dam. The boards that accommodated that passage must still be there! Art would see them when daylight came through the picture window that stretched across a full third of the back of his house; or perhaps he would notice them while inspecting his gardens.

I took a flashlight from a kitchen drawer and hurried outside as Alf dodged my feet and sneaked into the pantry. I made my way cautiously, although the moon was bright and illuminated the sloping yard in silver shadow. I entered the canopy of the willow and, with the aid of the flashlight, located the two glasses that had held the iced tea, lemon wedges still inside, only covered now with brown ants. Had I not changed the flashlight to my left hand in order to retrieve the glasses with my right, I never would have noticed it. But the light struck the boot print exactly. I possessed no shoes or boots to match the deep, rugged indenture of that sole. It belonged to a special kind of work boot that fit a foot slightly smaller than my own. I found another print, then another, before they disappeared into the unimpressionable lawn outside the cave of the willow. I found the pool of blood where she'd fallen. The broken jar still lay nearby in the dewy grass. I picked it up and flung it into the forest.

At the base of the dam, where the concrete abutted my shore, I found two more prints; one suggested movement toward my house, the other led in the opposite direction. The toe of the latter print left a deeper impression than the former, as he must have hoisted himself onto the surface of the weir.

I did the same thing, and with aplomb born of necessity, shuffled with Wallenda-like daring a few steps onto the surface of the dam, the water roaring almost invisibly in the darkness. I gripped my flashlight as if it were a balancing bar. I didn't need to move forward more than a few feet before the circle of light, advancing before me, revealed that the boards had been removed. The water rushed over and down, laughing in impedimentary delight.

I returned to the safety of the shore, fully convinced that Art Hall had been here. He'd seen the boards, come across, found the blood, the broken jar, the glasses with lemon, the lawn chairs under the willow. He knew. He knew when I called him. As I lied to him, he'd known. And yet he'd been so calm, so cordial. How much did he know? What did he suspect? Did he go in the house? See the blood on the floor? The open linen closet? She would lie to him too. The same lie. He'd recognize conspiracy. *The fishing is never very good down my road.*

I rushed inside. I moved frantically from room to room, searching for any evidence of intrusion. I found nothing. In the kitchen, the wildflowers were wilted in their vase. Alf, in the middle of the room, was happily licking the stains on the ancient tile. He turned to me with his bloodied muzzle as if to accept my gratitude. Instead, I grabbed him by the nape and placed him roughly on the landing outside, slamming the screen door.

And why should I be angry with you little Alf? Because she brought you food and now you lap up her blood? I knelt to the sanquineous floor with a wet rag and we bloodsuckers, being of one purpose, I began wiping up what Alf had left behind.

* * *

Dr. Kim Dong-Ho
Notes on the Riveridge Case
October 22, 2000

As Ben Riveridge has pointed out to me on several occasions, time is running out. He's due to be discharged on December 1st, and his lawyer has asked the court to consider an earlier release so that he might spend the Thanksgiving weekend with his family. It will require my approval, but he knows that I won't stand in his way. Belief in the supernatural isn't a reason for incarceration. If it were so, most of the world's population would be in places like this. The time is short.

One might ask what my interest (a better word would be absorption) is, in this case. I'm not sure yet. It fascinates me entirely, to the detriment of my other patients and duties. It's become very personal. Perhaps it's because of the Romantic in me (my undergraduate work included a minor in literature). That part of me has been long repressed and made subservient to the rational. God knows, romance is more fun.

Then again, Riveridge's notion of "Edenic time" is engrossing as well—from a purely empirical stance, of course.

I've decided to devote the greatest portion of my time to this case until Ben Riveridge is discharged, as I believe I will never have another opportunity to observe so closely what I've come to refer to as "metaphorical dynamism," his belief that we learn about, and are guided through life, by means of specific comparisons.

In order to force him to discuss his relationship with Mrs. Hall, I resorted to a kind of shock therapy tactic (minus electricity and insulin), in our interview today. I told him of her visit and her pleas for his release. For the first time since I met him, his attitude of swaggering confidence seemed to falter. He leaned forward in his chair and put his large hands on the edge of my desk.

"She was here?" he said. "She talked to you?"

"Yes."

"Did she look okay? I mean did she...."

"Look abused? No, she looked fine, although she walked with a slight limp. She's a very beautiful woman, Ben. It's obvious she loves you."

He pulled back into his chair, but the slouching nonchalance was gone. He lit a cigarette.

"How do you know that?" he asked.

"She told me." I waited for him to respond. When he didn't, I continued. "She also said that you two have had an affair, and that it was her husband who forced her to press charges against you.

She's very afraid of him. She's been a battered wife for most of their marriage."

"Yes," he said. "I know." I could see that my comments had affected him profoundly. His blue eyes brimmed with tears. The muscles in his jaw undulated as he ground his teeth together. "She has enormous courage," he said softly.

"She told me that you believe that she is your dead wife, Morgan."

He rose suddenly from the chair and glowered at me menacingly. I was reminded of a chest-thumping silverback, preparing to charge. I was no less fearful for the image, but I tried to remain calm and unintimidated. "Please, Ben," I said. "Sit down."

Although he did as I asked, his fists and jaw remained clenched. "So now you have me, Dr. Kim. In her desire to get me released, Sophie has given you the reason to extend my stay. Congratulations."

"Why do you say that?"

"You have proof of delusion. 'Poor, sick Ben. He misses his wife so much that he thinks this pretty woman is her. Poor fellow. Classic case of schizophrenia, your honor. We really ought to hold him for a while yet, say another six months or so? Runs in the family, you know. His father was crazy, too. Thought God talked to him.'" He banged his fist hard enough on my desk to make my little ivory elephant jump.

"That's not what I think."

"No? What do you think, Dr. Kim?"

"I think that schizophrenics don't hide their delusions, they wallow in them—celebrate them, because they don't believe anyone would perceive them as delusions."

Riveridge shook his head and lit another cigarette. There was a long period of uncomfortable silence that I was determined not to violate. Finally, he said: "What's going to happen now?"

"I'm going to sign for your release, the earlier date that your lawyer is currently pursuing."

He gawked at me in disbelief. His jaw unclenched. His mouth hung open. "What?"

"You heard me."

"Dr. Kim, I...."

"On two conditions."

His expression of open gratitude changed to dark distrust. "What are they?"

"I want you to write down your thoughts about Edenic time and what led you to believe what you do about metaphors, and how they've affected your behavior, your life."

"As evidence against me."

"No! This isn't any kind of trap. In fact, what I'm requesting is quite unclinical, really, and has no bearing on my diagnosis. You're quite sane, Ben. We both know that."

"Then why..."

"Let's say for the sake of intellectual curiosity."

"That won't do."

"What do you mean?"

"I need a better reason. There's something you're keeping from me."

I decided then, quite spontaneously, to tell him. I know now that truth isn't really truth, until it's spoken—and heard. "I told you I was born in Vietnam. Do you remember?"

He nodded.

"I said to you: 'As chance would have it, in the village of Tuy Hoa, where you were stationed.' And your reply to me was: 'No, Dr. Kim, not by chance.'"

"I remember that, yes."

"Why did you say that?"

"Because I don't believe in chance, or luck, or coincidence."

"You and I were 'guided' here?"

"Yes. I think so."

"Why?"

"I don't know, but I think you might be able to tell me."

"Perhaps. The Viet Cong murdered my mother, father, and three sisters, sometime in the late sixties. The assassins came in the middle of the night. My parents were killed while they slept. My sisters, who were twelve, fourteen and sixteen, were repeatedly raped, then shot."

"I'm so sorry," he said, and I could read the genuine sympathy.

"My brother and I slept in a separate room. He was ten or eleven. I was just a few months old. When my brother heard the shots, he knew that we would all die. While the murderers were preoccupied with our sisters, he picked me up and sneaked out. We went into the jungle and hid there all night. I slept through the whole thing."

"God!"

"The next day, my brother buried our family while our neighbors watched. Then he took me to a Catholic mission in a village a few miles away. The priest arranged for our adoptions: I by a family from Michigan, he by a family in California. We talk by phone regularly now. We see each other once or twice a year."

"He must be a remarkable man."

"He's a garbage collector for the San Diego Sanitation Department and, yes, he is. He paid for my extensive education. I pay for his sons.'"

"Dr. Kim, I don't mean to sound insensitive, but why are you telling me all this?"

I'm sure I must have smiled. I know I did. "The houses in our village were all huts, basically, made of thatch and bamboo—all one-room dwellings."

"Yes. I remember."

"Except ours. Ours was made of wood—plywood and two-by-fours. Our father had been an impoverished rice farmer before the Americans came. When they built the Air Base at Tuy Hoa, he got a job working on the base as a kind of handyman, or coolie. He polished the soldier's boots, did their laundry, cleaned their barracks. He made good money, but he really loved America. He wanted America to win. He believed they would. He wanted to live here someday. The communists saw him as a collaborator. They burned our first home to the ground, as a warning. My brother told me that our mother begged our father to quit his job on the base. He refused. The GIs on the base, led by your friend, Billy Borden, who my brother clearly remembers, built us a new home out of confiscated materials from the base. It was made of wood and had a corrugated tin roof. My mother was very proud of it, and dropped her demands. He'd won her over.

"It had three rooms. One served as a kind of general living quarters, my brother told me. One was a bedroom for my parents and sisters. The third was for my brother and me. That's why he and I are alive, because there were three rooms. The Cong would never believe a peasant's home would have three rooms. They never searched it." I stopped my narrative and watched comprehension creep slowly over Ben Riveridge's face.

"Papa-san," he whispered, his mouth and eyes opened by incredulity. "Papa-san was your father!"

"Yes. His name was Kim Quan-Trong."

"Then I met your brother too! Your father used to bring him to the base at times."

"Yes. To help him to learn more about Americans, to get him to pick up some English. I talked with my brother last night. He remembered you. The 'buku GI,' as our father referred to you."

"Papa-san died like that? He was a good man, a kind man, Dr. Kim. I'm sorry. He would have been proud of his sons."

Though I could remember nothing about my father, tears filled my eyes, perhaps in empathy with Riveridge's sorrow. "Is it chance, do you think, that the son of the man who used to polish your boots, now controls, to an extent, your destiny?"

"No."

"That's why I'm asking you to write about it. You believe that life is guided by metaphor, that we can understand and explain the world through the use of these implicit comparisons. I think you must regard our relationship as one of these, wherever they come from, whoever provides them."

"God provides them, we interpret—or we're supposed to. But most of us have lost the gift. If you watch animals in their natural surroundings, you begin to see what I mean. Like us, they live in this horrific world of tearing flesh and unbridled cruelty, where life continues only by death. What's the point of life? Only fodder for the strong? Those who are prey, they see a fellow brought down, and they learn to run. The next predator trips on a log and falls behind in the chase. The prey escapes. He who pays attention, learns to run among logs, nothing rational about it. Animals can read God and each other, even their enemies, with thoughtless intuition. Only humanity has outgrown imagination."

"That's what I want you to do. I want you to write these things down, to show me how they've applied to your life."

"Why?"

"In honesty? So that I can reexamine mine."

"Physician, heal thyself."

"Sort of, yes."

"Dr. Kim. Are you becoming a believer?"

I ignored the question. "And I want it done before you're released. I've asked for November twenty-second. That gives you about a month."

"That's rushing it, but okay. What's condition number two?"

I steeled myself and took a deep breath, though I tried to be the epitome of unflappability. "I want another interview with Mrs. Hall."

"Absolutely not."

"I can get it whether you approve or not."

"Then why bring it up?"

"Because I want you to be present as well."

"No."

"Why?"

Silence.

"Why?"

"I won't put her at risk again."

"Then you'll never see her again, and if you believe that she's Morgan, you'll have to. How can that be? Mr. Riveridge—Ben, I'm not your enemy. I'm *supposed* to be here. Remember?"

"I can't let anything happen to her."

"Why? Because you wouldn't be able to live without her?"

"Yes."

"So to accomplish this, you'll live without her? She loves you and—she's beginning to believe."

"Believe what?"

"Not what. Who."

He put his elbows on his knees and hung his head. It was only then that I realized how bald he was. His height disguised it. "You have to let her decide if she wants to risk it. We'll meet only if, and when, she wants to."

"Agreed."

I thought he would leave abruptly then, as he usually did when it appeared that the session was at an end, but he sat in silence for a long while, smoking and thinking. Finally, he said: "Forgive me, Dr. Kim, but how do I know this isn't all some elaborate hoax? You've managed to get what you wanted. Was your story just a ploy to advance your ambitions?"

"If that were true, how would I know about Papa-san, as you call him? And the wooden house with three rooms?"

"You could have called Billy Borden. I've told you about him. You know where he lives. He could have given you those stories."

"You must think me rather Machiavellian."

"No. I'm only considering the possibility. Believing as I do, I'm open to possibilities."

I reached in the lower drawer of my desk and extracted a paper bag. I pulled from it a pair of lime-green shower clogs with faded Mickey Mouse logos on each one.

"Those were Papa-san's."

"They were my father's. My brother kept them for me."

"Then it's true."

"Yes."

"I still can't understand what you have to gain from this. All I can see is that you're risking, possibly rejecting, what you've believed in—science, rationalism."

"Was Jung a rationalist? Perhaps there's room for magic in my profession, Ben. Perhaps we need fewer doctors and more shamans. It's something I want to investigate."

"I've misjudged you."

"Only by judging me at all."

When he left, I put my father's clogs back in the drawer and opened a window to get rid of the lingering smoke. I looked out at the maples and the glorious color of a Michigan autumn. With all my degrees and years of experience, this hour marked the first time in my life that I had ever felt wise.

Chapter Sixteen

Swain's Song

Our echoes roll from soul to soul,
And grow forever and forever.
—Alfred, Lord Tennyson, *The Splendor Falls*

I looked in the mirror and I knew I had become too self-absorbed. Even my great fear for Sophia's safety was egocentric. I was Narcissus by the water. I was Tantalus in the water. Indeed, this recrimination was itself, self-serving. Such vainglorious sadness destroyed my fragile nobility and diminished my existence to a hedonism worthy of any Sybarite.

I wallowed in a sty of self-pity that night. I watched the lights come on in the house across the creek, on the other side of the world. Would he hurt her? Had he already? Would such punishment drive the truth from her? Can pain be so bad as to send Morgan back to the garden? Pain had brought her here.

She'd lost so much blood. Did we get it all, Alf and I? Did she have anymore to give? The rags in the washing machine were enough to make the multitudinous seas incarnadine.

Would she ever come to me again? I felt it in the timeless rivers of my veins, but what would be the cost?

I sat in the cave of the willow all night. I was hungry, but wouldn't eat. I was thirsty, but wouldn't drink. I was a stranger, only a few feet from my back door. I felt naked and cold and sick. I was in the prison of my own anxiety. I felt good about my suffering. As with my joy, I felt I deserved it.

Long hours of darkness gave way to roseate light, creeping into the sky above her house. The cold mist that had gathered over the creek during the night now clung in dying refuge to the cattails and reeds, hiding in tatters from the consuming dawn.

Of course the swans came and poked their phallic necks among the accepting shallows, gulping night frogs who had stayed too long beneath the rags of mist to watch the unfamiliar sunrise.

I felt a strange love for them—the frogs, I mean; these slimy, bulbous-eyed, mud-dwellers, who gave their ugly lives to see, and perpetuate, beauty. I know what you must think, but what does it matter—in a world where death advances life—what kind of love there is? Can't a frog really be a prince?

Rays of sun crept across the roof of her house, spilled onto the lawn, then crept across the creek, silhouetting the real darkness of the swans. They became plucked and naked, exposing the black skin beneath the white down.

Then the light continued on, slithering up the slope toward my shelter, leaving the swans clothed again in its wake. I looked down at the boot prints in the dirt, kept dry by the umbrella of the weeping willow. Art had entered the temple with his sandals on. I spit on the prints, then erased them, crawling on my hands and knees, as if their obliteration, like her blood on my kitchen floor, could make consequence disappear and rid the heart of pain.

I looked out at the water, tumbling over the rift in the dam. It fell again and again, as if it were the same water, climbing, like Sisyphus, to the summit, before the stone rolled down again—the never-ending labor of water, the ceaseless motion of ambition without fruition, the cost of immortality. Oh, Morgan, Morgan!

There were some old boards in the shed. I'd seen them while putting the lawn mower away. With them, I could bridge the rift, be with her in moments, hold her again, reassure her. Morgan!

I stood up to go, but didn't move a step. I wasn't afraid, though Art was younger, probably in better shape, and certainly allied now with hate. I didn't care about that, really. He was likely gone to work anyway, tending to other properties. I simply sensed the *wrongness* of the idea. Morgan had to come to me, or it would all be meaningless. She would have to decide. Morgan must be wise, and find herself in Sophia's guise.

I took out a cigarette and fumbled in my jeans for a light. I felt a piece of paper in one pocket and pulled it out. It was the scrap of paper on which she'd scribbled her phone number. I felt a thrill run through me, no less intense than the anticipation of her kiss. I parted the willow boughs and jumped the steps in multiples, almost murdering little Alf whose mission, like all entwining cats, was the fall of man.

I went through the kitchen to the wall phone. Art must be at work by now, I rationalized. I had to know if she was all right. If he answered, I'd hang up. I dialed the number.

"Yes?"

"Sophie." I offered a silent litany of gratitude. "Are you okay?"

"Are you crazy, calling me here?"

"Is he there now?"

"No. He's gone out somewhere for a few minutes. He wouldn't tell me where, but he said he wouldn't be gone long. He took the day off."

"Did he hurt you?"

"No. He yelled a lot. Ben, he knows I've been over there."

"I know."

"You know? How?"

"The boards were gone last night when I got home. There are boot prints all over. It must've been him."

"He didn't say anything to me about that!"

"Nothing?"

"No."

"Was it the sheet then?"

"What?"

"The sheet! I wrapped your foot in a sheet to take you to the hospital. They never gave it back to me. Did they give it to you?"

"No."

"Then they either threw it away or gave it to him."

"Why would the sheet matter anyway?"

"It'd just seem peculiar, that's all, that a man would have a sheet in his car when he goes fishing. Rags, maybe, but not a clean, new, bedsheet."

"I guess so, but Art didn't say anything about that, either."

I paused for a moment, searching for other clues, other means of discovery. I could find none. "Then how does he know?"

"The cat food."

"What?"

"He stopped at the grocery store on his way home last night to pick up some beer. Judy, the cashier who works there, Judy Dunlop, asked him when we'd gotten a cat. He asked her what she meant and she told him I'd been there earlier in the day, buying cat food."

"How would he know from that? You could have picked it up for a friend..."

"He wouldn't. But he knows you have a cat. He told me. I couldn't figure out how he would know that, but I can now. Was Alf outside when you came home last night?"

I strained my memory. He ran in as I went out. I was sure. He was lapping the blood when I returned. "Yes."

"Then if Art was there, he saw the cat."

It didn't make sense. I felt adrift, unguided. "If he was here, Alf would have been the least of several incriminations. He most certainly saw the two lawn chairs and probably the glasses next to them; the pool of blood, the broken jar. For God's sake, Sophie, the boards were gone!"

"Please don't yell, Ben. I've had enough yelling."

I was immediately chastened. I felt base and brutal. "I'm sorry. I'm sorry. I'm afraid for you, that's all. Why wouldn't he tell you that he'd been here? How would he know otherwise?"

"He just told me that he knew you had a cat. I bought cat food. You brought me to the hospital. He put two and two together."

"Something's not right."

"Everything's not right."

"How's your foot?"

"It's sore. I won't be going anywhere for a few days. I can't risk..."

"Reopening the wound?"

"Yes."

"Can I call you again?"

There was a long silence, then a shuffling of paper. Don't call here. Give me your number. I'll call you when I can."

I gave it to her. "Promise?"

"Promise. I have to go."

"Be safe."

"You too."

I put the phone down in its cradle where it would sleep for too many days. I looked down at my soiled hands and knees. Concealment was a dirty business. Deciding that I should get cleaned up, I rose and headed through the living room to the stairs. I was halfway up, experiencing a strange composure for the first time in many hours, when I distinctly heard the door of a vehicle shutting in the circular drive outside. I couldn't imagine who it could be, but then, complacency stunts the imagination.

I turned around and went down a few steps in order to see through the sheer curtains that veiled the window's view of the broad porch. I recognized the thick black hair and military bearing. The window frame obscured the face, but I'd never seen it closely anyway. My neighbor paced nervously, his hands gripping each other behind his thick, firm waist. He knocked on the door, then began pacing again. My heart stopped. I held my breath. My hands clenched into fists. How do I handle this? What do I say? Will I even get a chance to speak? My brief observations and Sophie's descriptions of her husband led me to believe that this volatile man had no understanding outside the darkness of the cave.

There was no alternative. I moved quickly to the door and opened it.

"Mr. Riveridge?" The voice was pleasant, disarming. His thick hair grew low on his forehead, but he wasn't a homely man. He smiled engagingly. We were almost eye-to-eye.

"Yes?"

He pulled the screen door open. "I'm Art Hall, Sophie's husband." He extended a meaty hand, so callused that I felt as though I were gripping a hoof. "Sorry for droppin' in of a sudden like this. You look a bit flabbergasted."

I forced a smile. "Just a little tired, I guess."

"My Sophie gave ya a bit too much excitement last night, eh? Mind if I come in?"

"What? No, of course not. Please." He was standing in my living room and casually inspecting before I could compose myself and speculate both on the implications of his last remark and his intentions.

He was by the cane chair, studying my reproduction of *The Naked Maja*. "Beautiful," he said. "I like nudes, too. Who's the painter?"

"Goya."

"Ah." It was clear that he'd never heard the name before. He turned and looked at me. "Been working already this morning?" he said, pointing at my stained clothes.

I suddenly realized how disheveled I must look. "Yeah. I was working in the yard. I like to get it done early, before the sun gets too hot. I was just on my way to the shower when you knocked."

I kept waiting for the storm to break. I expected he would explode and charge me without warning. I began to wish that he would—that he would get it done.

His eyes were deep-set in his head. His nose was broad and flat. His thick lips were drawn back over flawless teeth when he smiled. Yet his features, strangely, didn't give him a brutish appearance. Rather, he bore a strong resemblance to a darker Spencer Tracy. He was deeply tanned, like most men of his profession, from constant exposure to the sun. He had more the appearance of the laborer than the CEO, though Sophie had told me that he owned both the construction business and a lumber-yard. "Would you happen to have some coffee?"

"Of course," I stammered. "Sorry. I don't get many visitors. Come into the kitchen and I'll make some. Only take a minute."

I was pouring water from the kitchen faucet into a glass carafe when Alf began mewing at the pantry door. I ignored him. Sweat fell from my brow and mingled with the water for the coffee.

Art Hall sat at the kitchen table. He was squinting at the vase of wilted wildflowers. "Sounds like your cat wants a meal," he said with dispassionate calm.

"Oh, I don't have a cat," I protested too hurriedly. "He's just a stray that I feed occasionally."

I ventured a quick glance at my antagonist. He seemed disinterested, preoccupied. I got the coffee going, then shut the heavier storm door to the outside, eliminating Alf's irritating mendicancy.

"I won't take up too much of your time, Mr. Riveridge."

"Ben, please," I said. I braced myself and sat down across from him.

"Okay. Ben." He smiled again, the white teeth flashing inside the tanned face like diamonds in a dark mine.

"I just wanted to come over and thank you in person for helpin' my Sophie last night. The doctor told me she'd been in real trouble if you hadn't happened along."

This is just the preface to rage, I thought. *He'll come after me now and rip my throat out.* "It was nothing, really, Mr. Hall."

"Art. Just Art."

"Okay. Art. Anybody would've done the same."

"I don't think so." His smile said: *I know, you stupid bastard. I know! How do you like this game?*

"How's she doing today?"

"Good," he said. "Much better. They got her on pain pills. She was kinda floatin' when I left a little while ago, if ya know what I mean." He chuckled.

The gurgling of the Mr. Coffee indicated that it was ready. I filled two cups and returned to the table.

"Thanks," he said as I slid his cup across to him. He took a long drink. "Your wife around?" There was a brief moment of terrible confusion, before I realized that the question was innocuous. "She's deceased."

"I'm sorry. What happened?"

"She had a heart attack. Four years ago now."

"But you still wear your wedding band."

I fingered the silver circle that had become a part of my hand. "I notice that you're not wearing one."

He laughed. "Couldn't afford one after buying Sophie's. We were young and didn't have as much money then. Cost me a damn fortune."

"It must've been difficult when she lost...." I realized too late the terrible blunder I'd committed; the howling mistake; the awful, bungling lapse in reason! I felt my face flushing crimson. The only excuse I had was that Morgan had lost the diamond from her ring twenty years ago. We'd looked for it for days, retraced our steps, to no avail. We'd replaced it with a zircon, too. It'd been buried with her. It was my only excuse for stupidity. I'd gotten lives confused. Now Sophie would pay. I lost it years ago, she'd said. I had it filled with this stone. Art's never noticed. He'd be very angry.

"Ben? You okay?"

My mind snapped back to the present. Art Hall's teeth shone in a feral grin.

"Yes. I'm sorry."

"You said something you weren't supposed to say."

"Listen Art, I ...."

"It's real."

"What?"

"The diamond on Sophie's finger. It's real. She didn't lose it. Is that what she told you? That she lost it?"

"Yes. She told me she replaced it with a zircon." Sometimes

truth is the only possibility.

"When?"

"Last night." I lied because I was still clinging to hope. "On the way to the hospital."

"No. I mean did she tell you when she lost it?"

"Years ago."

He laughed. "Well, it was still a diamond three weeks ago."

"What? I don't understand. She...."

"We had it cleaned and appraised in early July. It's worth over twenty thousand dollars. Pretty expensive zircon, huh?"

I was dumbfounded, utterly confused. Art appeared to be enjoying my discomfiture. "Why would she say that?"

Art sipped his coffee. His quiet composure rankled, like a stone in my shoe. "Sophie's not quite right," he said and pointed to his temple. "She ain't been right for a long time now. It's the main reason I built this house out here. Keep her away from prying neighbors."

I stared blankly at the wall behind him, hearing his voice from the bottom of a well, echoing down to me.

"Don't get me wrong. I love her dearly, but she lives in a different world, kinda like."

"Art, you were here last night."

"Yeah, I was. When I got home and saw she was gone, I checked. She thinks I don't know about her trips over here. Don't see how she could think it a secret. Damn near killed herself once. Fell into the crick and broke her arm. Can't stop her, though I've tried. Got a mind of her own. She loves it over here. She used to bug the old guy who lived here to no end. He used to complain. I think that's why he sold the place."

I felt dizzy and nauseous. I'd slept with this man's wife, but I was the cuckold. I could feel the horns growing from my head. I slid farther and farther down the well, drawn deeper and deeper into the comforting darkness at the back of the cave.

"She's been here a lot, I know. It's good of you to put up with her. She must've cut her foot on that mason jar, eh?"

"Yes."

"She's probably told you I beat her, too, eh?" I was alarmed that he should be so forward, so direct, like death itself.

"She intimated..."

"That's what I thought. Never laid a hand on her, Ben. She's been worse since you moved in. Can't seem to keep her focused on anything. She's on medication and I take her to Grand Rapids twice a month to meet with a psychiatrist. He wants me to commit her, but I don't have the heart for it. What can I do? I love her. I won't have her caged."

"How did you know she told me that you were abusing her?"

"She tells that to everyone. But everyone in Swan's End knows me. I was raised here. They know I don't beat her. Besides, you ever see a bruise on her?"

"No, but she's very afraid of you. That seems real."

"Probably is. She don't want to be caged up. She sees me as her jailer. Besides, she *believes* I beat her. I seen women afraid of June bugs, but what did the June bugs do to earn that fear?"

He pulled out a pack of cigarettes. "Mind if I smoke, Ben? I wouldn't ask in nobody else's house, but I see an ashtray over there..."

"What? Oh sure, go ahead." I got the ashtray and lit one myself. "How long has So..., Mrs. Hall, had this 'trouble'?"

Most of her life, I think, but it got worse after the kids were grown up and left. She has weird dreams—sometimes don't know who she is—especially lately. She had a brother who was kind of a half-wit. Brain trouble must run in her genes."

We finished our cigarettes and coffee in silence. I stared at the wilted wildflowers.

Art drained his coffee cup and set it hard on the table. "I should go," he said. "I do appreciate very much what you done for Sophie last night."

"I lied to you."

"I know, but only because you thought you had to." He laughed. "One good thing come of it."

"What's that?"

"Sophie ain't gonna be wanderin' around for a while. You can have a little privacy. After that, I dunno. I'll try to keep her home, but I can't put her away. Call me if she becomes a nuisance. I'll figure out something."

He got up and extended his hand. "You seem like a good man, Ben."

I took it. "Appearances are deceiving." He frowned a dark grimace of incomprehension. I laughed and his smile returned. "Thanks."

I escorted him to the front door. He turned to face me at the portal. "I almost forgot. I told the nurse at the hospital to throw away your sheet. Didn't look like it'd ever come clean. I'll buy you another one."

"Forget it," I said with surreptitious magnanimity. "Wish your wife well for me."

"Will do. Take care now."

"Bye."

He went down the steps and got into a blue Dodge pick-up truck. It had *Hall Lumber and Construction* printed in neat, white letters on the door. He smiled amicably and waved as he drove around the gravel circle and up Creekpath Road.

I went back into the kitchen and slumped in a chair. I remember feeling then like I did on the day of Morgan's funeral; despondent, desperate, utterly alone.

If all that Art Hall said was true, then this was greater punishment than any violence could inflict. It meant the triumph of chance, the absence of direction, the celebration of dumb coincidence, dead love. I heard Alf's muffled cries of hunger.

"Morgan!" I screamed, and hurled the vase of wildflowers against the wall. It shattered and I remembered the glass skittering across the tile as I crawled to the back of the cave. Darkness enveloped me in ragged arms of anonymity, and I slept.

Chapter Seventeen

Never Hero More

...We have undernourished our capacity for emphatic and magical participation in creation, we are both alienated and stunted by abstraction, removed from the profound and immediate apprehension, which is the hallmark of a whole person, of the dancing interpenetration of the physical and the psychic, their ultimate inseparability.

—Ian McEwan, *The Child in Time*

At first, I tried to ease the suffering of my heart with the industry of my hands. I bought an axe at the hardware, then went into the forest near my house and spent an entire day cutting wood. I told myself that I was stockpiling for the coming winter, that I would put the fireplace in my living room to good use, but it was only an attempt to work away the pain. I didn't really believe in winter anymore. By evening, my hands were sticky with blood and the water of ruptured blisters. The mosquitoes had roughed my skinscape with a thousand red, itching mounds. I was faint with heat and hunger and exhaustion. I returned to the house by moonlight. I showered and slept the night in welcome oblivion. I don't remember much else about that first day without her.

The phone woke me the following morning. It was Shelly. Her voice was comforting. I loved the way she still called me "daddy." I couldn't force myself to tell her about Sophia. How could I explain that her mother had come back to me, then gone away again? She'd think me mad. Perhaps I was.

In the early evening, Ty called as well, alerted by his sister that Dad "sounded depressed." I told him the same things. He seemed reassured. I was grateful that they cared, but felt peripheral, somewhat like a mutt whose loving owner has checked to make sure his chain is not twisted and choking him; the terrible assumption being that if he isn't dying, the old dog must be content. I was relieved to put down the phone. It was painful to grip the receiver with my bandaged hands.

As the sun left that second day in darkness, I watched the lights go on in the house across the creek. I fed Alf and listened to the rushing water. I felt dead. I thought of Morgan in her grave, waiting.

The next morning, a Saturday, Jack Csinos was sent to restore my faith.

Two years earlier, the tobacco industry, the Michigan State Legislature, Charley Rose's father and Frank Girty, had all conspired so that I might meet Jack.

Charley Rose and Jack had been friends for some time before I knew either of them. They'd met when Jack had been assigned, as part of the custodial staff at Swan's End High School, to clean the classrooms in the east wing of the second floor.

Jack came in every day at 3:00 P.M., shortly after the students were dismissed for the day, to clean the blackboards in Charley's classroom. Jack's intense intellectual curiosity would lead him to ask Charley (who, like most of his colleagues, hung around a while to get paperwork done), about words he'd written there, like Milvian Bridge or Second Triumverate.

Before long, they were engaged in a kind of cognitive sparring over the influence of the Romans on western culture or the importance of the Hungarians in saving Christian Europe from the Turks (Jack's ancestry was Hungarian on his father's side, and he was enormously sensitive about what he considered to be their "relegation to insignificance" in European history).

The relationship quickly became social, the two men being constant visitors to one another's homes. Although it was I who introduced Charley to Shelly, it was Jack who encouraged his friend to pursue her. In the process, Shelly and Jack's wife, Debra, had become fast friends. Jack had three sons, the youngest of which, Tamerlane (referred to simply as "Tam"), was Christopher's age. They too, became buddies.

Through all of this, I knew little of Jack Csinos. I saw him occasionally, but my classroom was on the ground floor and I was usually out of the building by four o'clock, while Jack worked the second shift upstairs until midnight. Charley talked about his friend a good deal, amazed that a man with so little formal education could be so intelligent. (My son-in-law had not yet learned that the terms were not synonymous—could even be antonymic).

When the elder Mr. Rose offered Charley and Shelly the home in Wawatam, Jack Csinos lost his intellectual companionship. Frank Girty, the head custodian, (mentioned here only as a pawn of God), retired. Jack applied for, and got, the vacancy. He went on the day shift.

I'd always taken my smoke breaks outdoors, on the south side of the building, where no students would be able to witness my depravity. But that year (1998), the Michigan legislature, in an attempt to save the lives of the corrupt, enacted a law prohibiting the use of tobacco anywhere on the grounds of any public school.

This measure, of course, affected the student smokers not at all, since they'd been defying the law for years and had learned to indulge their addictions clandestinely.

It did mean that I had to get in my car and leave school property to smoke a cigarette, making it obvious to everyone (impressionable youth included), that I was an enemy of public health.

I had to pass through the custodial area and out the loading dock doors to get to my car in the staff lot, and that's how I came to be friends with Jack Csinos.

He struck up a conversation with me one particularly difficult widower's day, as I was on my way out to lunch. He'd known Morgan. Her job in the kitchen at the high school had brought them into proximity and their mutually gregarious natures had done the rest. Jack told me that she'd confided her fears to him about Shelly's first marriage and had expressed her joy in grand-motherhood by sharing with him innumerable pictures and anecdotes of the Bean. He had, in turn, boasted about the infant Tam.

I invited him, on that day, to go with me in the smoking car, since he, too, was an addict. He accepted. In spite of my best efforts to the contrary, he always referred to me as Mr. Riveridge, even after we'd become close. Initially a token of respect for my position, he later confessed that it had become habit. Now, on occasion, he calls me "boss."

Our literary conversations began that day in the parking lot of the bowling alley across the street from the school. Our visits became a part of our daily routines. On my preparation period and during lunch hour, we would head for the car. Jack timed his breaks to coincide.

He'd once been a successful restauranteur, but he'd quit because, although he was making a good living, he had little time to spend with the two things most precious to him—his family and his books. So he left a lucrative position, trading money for time. He loves his sons and wife devotedly. He's custodial by nature.

He's a short but solidly built man. No taller than five-seven or-eight, his compactness and muscularity nevertheless, give those who meet him the impression of physical power. He disguises his creeping baldness by cropping his blonde hair very close. From a distance, his head appears shaven. He says the style camouflages his age, which is just short of forty. Outside, he regularly covers his pate with a billed cap that has the head of Mickey Mouse on it encircled by the words: Disney World, Orlando, Florida.

At work, he always wears navy blue work pants issued by the school and a navy blue tee shirt with the word *Jack* printed on one side of his barrel chest and *Swan's End High School Staff* on the other. As with all custodians, dozens of keys dangle from his belt.

He drives a rusty pick-up truck whose windshield wipers never work and whose heater always does, even on ninety-degree days. Like Morgan and Billy Borden, he believes in magic and metaphor.

He was particularly taken with the concept of Edenic time when I mentioned it to him. He asked me why it was called "Edenic" and I told him that it existed in that metaphorical paradise we refer to as the Garden of Eden, differently from time as we know it now.

He lit a Marlboro. "Go on."

"And there was evening and there was morning—the first day. Same with the second day and the third, etc. Time existed, if we're to believe the Genesis account. Days pass. But they had to be different."

"Why?"

"What's our time based on, Jack? Today, I mean. Scientifically."

He pushed his cap back and rubbed the blonde stubble, as if to encourage thought. "The rotation of the earth on its axis and our orbit around the sun; days and years."

"Yes. Still, the sun wasn't created until the fourth day."

"But there was evening and morning and light and days before that."

"Yes. Edenic time. Metaphor. The "light" isn't the sun. It dispels the darkness. It isn't defined statically, but dynamically. Not by position, but purpose. In the New Testament, Jesus says: 'I am the Light of the World. I have come into the world as a light. God is light.' He calls himself the 'Door, the Truth, the Way, the Good Shepherd, the Lamb of God'...all metaphors. Edenic time has to be looked at in the same way."

"How?"

"You know how time-lapse photography works?"

"I think so, yeah. They want to make a film of a flower opening, but it happens too slowly. So they photograph the flower at various intervals, then put all the shots together to make it look like a continuum."

"But there are lapses."

"What lapses?"

"I mean that when you look at the finished product, you aren't really seeing all of the stages of the flower opening, only the frames they shot. The other frames of time still exist, we just aren't aware of them. They become, to us at least, non-temporal, even non-existent. I think that's what Edenic time is—the lapses that we miss—and all those frames continue to abide in a kind of never-ending stasis. In a perfect world, like Eden, there is no time, and 'morning' and 'evening' are only metaphors to assist us in understanding purpose. In Eden, everything was of a moment, what can only be called 'immortality.'"

"Then why did it end?"

"Ah, Jack, it didn't. We were just removed from it. That was the true Fall of Man. The first bite of the fruit of the tree of knowledge was the world's first, real minute. We began to understand what 'yesterday' meant so we could rue it. We learned to remember, so we could grieve. We came to know the meaning of 'future' and 'ending' and 'death.'"

"In a perfect Eden, metaphor wouldn't be needed."

"No, not there. But here, it's the only method for understanding."

Slowly, over the next year, I began to reveal to Jack the metaphors that guided my life. He accepted the stories, sometimes with skepticism, often with enthusiasm, always with interest. He devoured the books I loaned him with the passion of the deprived bibliophile; the Brontes, Keats, Shelley, Rilke, Harrison, Helprin, Campbell, Kundera, Morrison, McEwan.

Every day except weekends and holidays, we'd sit in my car, now referred to as the "smoker," and discuss the thematic direction or motifs of a new book. The weather didn't matter at all. Jack is an amateur meteorologist and generally can predict conditions better than the professionals, but we held our tete a tetes, whether in two feet of snow, pouring rain, or searing heat. The cooks, who saw us come and go every day, believed we were seriously addicted. They were right, but it had nothing to do with tobacco.

In the summer, I was free to do as I pleased, but Jack had to continue to work. I would see him, of course, but not nearly as often. I had not, in fact, seen him since about a week before my first encounter with Sophia, so he knew nothing about the events that had transpired since, though he'd been to the new house.

His timing couldn't have been better. My terrible despondency over the last forty-eight hours could be eased, I was convinced, only through a confessor. So it was with a kind of desperate solace that I watched Jack's rusty pick-up pull into the circular drive in a cloud of dust and gravel spray.

He grinned broadly as I opened the door to greet him, but as he drew near, his expression changed to alarm. "Sorry, Mr. Riveridge," he said, "but you look like shit." He extended his hand. I held up bandages. "What the hell happened to your hands?"

"C'mon in. I'll tell you about it." We went into the kitchen. I got us some coffee as Jack slumped in a chair and placed a book on the table and slid it to my side. "I came over to return your copy of *Crime and Punishment*. Thanks. Good book. Nice idea Dostoevsky had, splitting Raskolnikov into Svidrigailov and Sonia. Good personification of his dual nature."

"I always loved it."

He lit a cigarette, a luxury Debra wouldn't allow him in his own house. "Damn it, Boss," he scolded. "What in hell have you been up to? Shelly and Charley are gonna have my ass for not lookin' after you, not to mention Ty. You look positively desiccated."

"I've had a rough couple of weeks. Haven't slept or eaten too much."

"Flu?"

"I wish." I handed him a cup of coffee and sat down.

"Tell me about your hands."

"Oh nothing, really. They'll be all right. I was chopping wood to work off some frustrations and got carried away. Just some bad blisters. This has more to do with the heart, really."

He glanced quickly at me, recognizing the allusion. "I'm taking a look at those before I go anyway." He pushed his Disney cap back on his forehead. "So what's going on? You look like one of those guys they find who've been lost in the wilderness. What the hell have you been up to?"

"I'll tell you. I will. But I need to know some things first."

"What kind of things."

"You know Art Hall?"

"Your neighbor? Does he have something to do with this?"

"Kind of. Do you know him?"

"Yeah. Everybody does. He was the big football hero in high school. I was just a little kid, but he was the icon of the town. Led the Knights to two consecutive state titles in Class B. He owns the lumberyard over on 28."

"Do you know him personally, I mean. Ever have any dealings with him?"

"No, not really. He's got a reputation for temper though. When he was a senior, he nearly beat a guy to death over some girl. Almost cost him his diploma, but he was a football god, so he got away with it. The O. J. syndrome, you know?"

"What girl? Sophia?"

"His wife? Naw. He met Sophie when he was workin' on some construction site on the other side of the state. They got married in a hurry as I recall. She was pregnant when he brought her back to Swan's End."

"What can you tell me about her?"

"Sophie? Nuthin' much. Better'n what Art deserves, though."

"What? Why? Why do you say that?"

"You ever seen her? She's a knockout. Even at her age, most men would jump her bones in a minute." He paused, and lit another cigarette. I did my best to conceal my raging emotions. "Besides," he continued, "the town scuttlebutt has it that he knocks her around."

"What?"

"Beats her, you know? Ever heard any kind of ruckus from over there?"

"No. Don't you think it could just be gossip?"

"I don't think so, no. But most people in this town would defend Art. He's home-grown, and a football hero."

"Why don't you think so?"

"I ain't into idolatry. Besides, Debra's got a cousin, a registered nurse, who works at the emergency room at Grenville Hospital. In the last ten years, Sophie's had a fractured rib, ruptured spleen, broken arm and kidney damage. Debra's cousin tried to get Sophie to turn the son-of-a-bitch in to Social Services, but she wouldn't do it."

"These injuries, they're all 'hidden.' I mean you wouldn't see them unless she was undressed."

"I guess so, except the broken arm. I remember that one. Saw her with a cast on it at the gas station. Sophie's a real nice person, too. Everybody likes her. Don't see her around much anymore though, since they moved out here."

He looked at me. He was reading me. "What is it?" he asked.

"You're such a mess, but you look like you just experienced an epiphany. You had a euphoric look, the kind you'd see on Old Testament prophets." He got up and helped himself to more coffee. "There's a pair of swans out there, in the creek," he said, looking through the window over the sink.

I smiled. "You forgot to tell me something."

"What?"

"He's a good liar."

"Who?"

"Art Hall." A good liar, a clever liar, and much more dangerous than I'd imagined.

"Listen, Boss," Jack said, resuming his seat. "I'm totally lost. You want to fill me in?"

I hesitated, but felt a pressing need to confess. If anyone could believe it, Jack might. If anything happened, someone had to know. "You got a couple of hours?"

"It's Saturday. I got all day."

"Morgan's alive."

As it turned out, it took all day.

Chapter Eighteen

Strays

Soft as an Incarnation of the Su,
When light is changed to love, this glorious One
Floated into the cavern where I lay,
And called my Spirit, and the dreaming clay
Was lifted by the thing that dreamed below
As smoke by fire, and in her beauty's glow
I stood, and felt the dawn of my long night
Was penetrating me with living light...
—Percy Bysshe Shelley, *Epipsychidion*

Jack restored my faith in God's voice, by forcing me to go through it all again. Explanations fostered justification. I became convinced, for the last time, that coincidence just didn't exist in any of it. You would think that a man who had spent most of his adult life in education would know that the best way to learn is to teach. But I'd always been wary of the obvious.

I know Jack accepted it too, particularly after I described Sophie's dream to him. He then told me of a dream he'd had, in which he saw hundreds of swans swimming wing to wing in a river, struggling against the current. The dream, he said, came to him in frames, and in each frame, the number of birds was reduced. At first they were so numerous that he, standing on the shore, could have used their backs as a bridge to get to the other side. He said he felt a deep yearning to do so, but his trust in the strength of the swans to hold him up, wasn't there. Their numbers decreased rapidly, frame by frame, until Jack's hesitation doomed him to remain on what he termed "the wrong side." Finally, in the last frame, there were only three swans left; the third merged into the second, and the remaining pair, trumpeting loudly, lifted into the

air, their plump forms thinning in the distance, until they were one
and evaporated under a rainbow, arched over the blue sky.

I didn't spoil the vision with analysis, but only listened, as I
was meant to do. Jack said the dream had brought him here. He'd
felt driven to tell me. Now he knew why.

The phone rang shortly after he left that evening. I was in the
pantry, feeding Alf. I lunged for the phone in the kitchen, desperate
not to miss Sophie's call.

It was Jack. He'd walked into his house, and the first thing
he'd heard was *One Hand, One Heart*. He said Debra was watching
West Side Story on television, with tears running down her face.
His voice was animated, full of excitement. I smiled. "You don't
think it could be coincidence?"

"No," he said firmly.

"Me either."

"When do you think she'll come back?"

"I don't know."

"But she has to, doesn't she?"

"Yes." I could hear Tam yelling for his dad in the back-
ground.

"Gotta go."

"Jack?"

"Yeah?"

"Thanks."

"Your hands feel better with the aloe?"

"Yes, but I'm not thanking you for that."

"I'm not a believer because you're my friend, Boss."

"That's why I'm thanking you."

"You don't need to thank people for something they can't
help. Keep me posted."

"I will."

"Bye."

I waited by the phone, almost literally, every minute of the
next few days. I slept on the sofa, since I had no phone upstairs. I

ran out of food, then coffee, then cigarettes, but I couldn't leave to go to the store. I controlled my bladder to bursting; I kept the TV, the radio, the CD player, off. I was afraid to sleep. Over three days, I received four calls, all but one from a salesman. I hung up on them. The fourth was from Ty, who I'm sure was mystified by my urgency to finish the conversation. I made a mental note to call him back.

I watched across the creek continually from my kitchen window, but saw no sign of either of them. I noticed the boy cutting their lawn and watering the roses, the same one who'd been there when they were on vacation. Yet each night at dusk, the lights went on and I saw shadows of movement through the picture window. They were there.

Finally, on the morning of the sixth day, she called. The sound of her voice made me euphoric.

"Art came to see you, didn't he?" she asked.

"Yes. Are you all...."

"Did you believe him? He can be convincing."

"At first I had my doubts. Not now. Can you walk?"

"I'm limping, but it's healing well. I have an appointment to get the stitches removed this morning, then I'm going to drive over, okay? Art's on a job site until five or six tonight."

I was transported, transfigured in an instant to wild enthusiasm. I felt rapturously, ecstatically, whole. "How long before you're here?"

"A couple of hours."

I heard her breathing. She was gathering strength—or courage. Finally, she said: "Morgan lost her engagement diamond, didn't she?"

The question took me by surprise. "Yes, she did." I waited for her to tell me what she was thinking.

"Why didn't you tell me that when I told you that I had lost mine. Of all those similarities between us, you never mentioned that one. Why?"

"I don't know. It didn't feel right somehow. I sensed something was wrong there. It didn't fit."

I waited for a comment, but there was just the quiet rhythm of her breathing. "Art told me that you didn't really lose yours," I finally blurted. "He said you'd just had it cleaned and assessed. He lied, didn't he?"

Silence.

"Didn't he!"

"No. Not about that."

"Then you lied to me?"

"No, that's not true either. I lost it in a parking lot somewhere, when the kids were small, near a school, I think. We retraced our steps. My husband even took a flashlight and checked the tires on the car to see if it might have become embedded in the treads."

I remembered then, being on my hands and knees, on the cement, studying the tires, while members of Ty's soccer team looked on. Morgan was in tears. How could it be possible? How could Sophie know?

"I told you about losing the diamond after my dream, Ben, the dream of the garden, remember? It was real to me then. I could see it happening in my mind. I told you that Art didn't know, and he didn't, couldn't know. That's why I said I'd kept it from him, when really there was no secret at all, because it didn't happen to me!"

"What...what are you saying?"

"That was the first of several memories I have now, Ben, things that never happened to Sophia Hall. She's fading."

"Morgan?"

"I'll be there soon." She hung up. I heard only the pleasant buzz of disconnection.

I think that perhaps the difference between great men of God or art—men who change the world—and the rest of believing humanity, is that the former didn't just believe, they knew.

Somehow, they were privileged to know, a kind of hallowed sancti-
fication; a lighthouse in a sea of lost time.

That's a poor way to describe a miracle, but miracles defy
description, at least in a few sentences. It takes chapters, volumes,
the life experience of a million writers, searching for the single
comparison that will bridge the gap from fairy faith to insightful
wisdom.

I had followed the path, and God had led me back to Eden. I
dropped the phone, covered my face with my healing hands, and
sobbed—the terrible, wild, unconstrained, blubbering prayer of a
creature's gratitude to his Creator.

I went upstairs and took a long, hot shower. I'd washed and
shaved in the kitchen sink for days, unable to risk not hearing the
phone. The soothing, wet heat only served to heighten my exhila-
ration.

I felt eulogistic, swollen with appreciation. I sang off-key and
laughed at myself. Four long, grieving years were drawing to
finality.

It was at that moment of frivolity, of giddy joy, that I saw the
obstacle, the final impediment. I knew that Art Hall would not
simply disappear. We'd have to go far away, perhaps to another
country. Does Morgan have her suitcases with her? Is that why
she's driving here? Why did the image of that car disturb me so? A
machine out of place.

Art would follow us. His path was dark, but he'd stay on it,
play it out. I couldn't leave Ty and Shelly and Christopher. Morgan
wouldn't either.

I dressed hurriedly and rushed downstairs. I waited for
almost an hour, wishing very much for a cigarette. At last, her car
pulled into the yard. I embraced her as she stood up and I smoth-
ered her face with kisses.

"I love you, Ben," she whispered, and held onto my neck to
steady herself against my raging affection. She gave me one, long,
passionate kiss, then put her arms around my waist and laid her

head on my chest. I kissed the back of her head. Her hair smelled of lilac.

"Ben," she said, her voice muffled against my shirt.

"Yes, Morgan?"

She released her grip and stood straight, her dark eyes burrowing. "Don't call me that!" Her tone softened. "Not yet. I'm too confused."

"We name a thing to make it real."

Her forehead wrinkled. She closed her eyes. The long lashes caressed her cheeks. She was remembering. "Not yet," she repeated. "Not until it fully exists. You don't name a child before it's born."

"Then what do I call you? Sophia?"

"For now. Even the dying have a name." She took my hand and limped up the porch steps. "Let's go inside."

She was wearing a dress. It was the first time I'd seen her in a dress. It was blue, dark navy, and scattered with tiny, white dots. I think I remembered it.

She sat on the sofa and placed her injured foot on the coffee table, gingerly. I sat across from her. I could see the purple scimitar of her scar.

"I haven't much time," she said.

Her comment took me by surprise. I'd expected, at the very least, to spend a few hours with her. It was clear that she had no luggage. I must have frowned. I don't remember. She read my discomfiture.

"What is it?"

"Why did you use your car to come here?"

"What?"

"Your car. Why did you drive?"

"I was coming from the doctor...how did you expect me to get here, by crossing the dam? I can hardly walk, Ben." She could see my perturbation. "What's the matter?"

"I don't know. A feeling...you're sure Art was gone?"

"Yes. He left at six. He called on his cell phone at seven and eight, and again at nine. He knew I had the appointment with the doctor at ten." She glanced at her watch. "It's almost eleven now. He'll start calling again. That's why I have to get back—soon!" She looked lost, stunned. "What are we going to do, Ben?"

"I don't know."

"I'm willing to divorce Art now, but I don't think he'll abide that, do you?"

"It won't stop him, no."

"I'm so scared, Ben, and not just of Art. I get confused. I think, sometimes, that I might be going crazy!" She brushed away a tear.

"Why?"

"I see images flashing in my mind, like still frames from a film. I don't recognize the images, though. They don't mean anything to me."

"Like what? Can you describe them?"

"They don't seem to have much significance. In one shot, for example, I'm simply standing and looking out a window. All I see is a brick wall, only a few feet away. There's faded lettering on it, but I can't see all the characters. I think it says something about the ocean. What can that mean? I'm not even asleep. It's not a dream. Wouldn't that make you think you were losing your mind? It happens frequently now. Almost hourly."

"I think I know what it means."

"What? Tell me," she asked

"Could the letters spell Atlantic and Pacific Tea Company?"

I could see her reaching back, sorting.

"Yes. I think so," she hesitated. "How...how could you know that?"

"It was the view from our apartment window when you... when Morgan and I lived in Kansas. Only a little alley separated the house from the grocery store next door."

She shook her head, as if recovering from a blow. "It's real then," she whispered. "Oh Ben, I'm so scared! It's like dying. I'm disappearing."

"No, you're coming back."

She stared at me for a moment. "How much you must have loved one another!" She stood up and winced a bit as the blood moved to her foot, bringing with it messages she didn't want to hear. "I have to go."

"But we haven't talked about how we're going to deal with all this, Sophie."

"It'll have to wait. I'll come back again. You know I will—and much sooner than the last time—maybe tomorrow. I can't think now. I've forgotten a lot, Ben, but not how I pissed blood for three days. I still remember fear."

"If he touches you again, I'll kill him."

"No." She put her hand on my cheek and kissed me. "You and I weren't made to kill."

I helped her to her car. She got in and fastened her belt. She had to lean out to grab the handle and shut the door. For some reason, I didn't want to touch it. I felt revulsion.

"I'll call you this afternoon," she said. "Okay?"

"Sophie."

"Yes?"

"Why did you wait so long to call before today? I was dying over here."

For the first time she noticed my hands—without the bandages, they weren't as obvious. "What did you do? Oh Ben, what happened?"

"I took my frustrations out on the forest."

"What?"

"With an axe."

"Oh."

"Why didn't you call?"

"You took me to the hospital on Wednesday night. Art took the day off on Thursday. That's when he came to see you. I tried to call you on Friday, but you weren't here."

"That was wood-chopping day. Why didn't you leave a message, let me know you were all right at least?"

"Fear, I guess. I don't know. I wasn't thinking rationally. I'm lucky I can think at all. Then Art was at home for the weekend. Yesterday was spent sorting things out. Art called me every hour all day. I was a mess. Today...well, I knew I could get out today." She smiled. "I'm not going to have to deal with two jailers, am I?"

"No."

"I'll call today. I promise."

She pulled away and disappeared in a trail of dust. I remember feeling that something had gone very wrong, that the path had been strayed from. I got my keys and wallet and drove to Burger King in town. I hadn't eaten for a long time and I was feeling weak and dizzy. I stopped at the gas station too, for cigarettes. I came home immediately, praying that I hadn't missed her call. There were no messages.

I fed the ever-demanding Alf. He was grateful enough to climb into my lap and commiserate. We sat there, on the sofa, for an hour. I found myself nodding. I stretched out, after feeding the long-starved tobacco demon. I fell immediately into dreamless sleep.

When I woke, it was dark. I was sure that I hadn't slept that long, and yet the room was veiled in shadow. I looked at my watch—three-thirty. I went to the kitchen and looked out the window. The willow branches whipped in the wind. Flashes of lightning briefly illuminated a gray and violent world. Thunder crashed and rolled, vibrating the floorboards beneath me like a timpani. Curtains flapped wildly over the other window, and a puddle of water had already formed on the table and the floor beneath it.

Then, above it all, I heard Sophie's scream! I saw them instantly. Art held her tightly in his grip. They were standing in their yard, among the roses that were being decapitated by the wind. He had a choking hold on her neck and had twisted her arm behind her back with his free hand. Like all sadists, he knew her phobia, grown worse now with double memory. He'd pulled her out of the house into a nightmare of fear. Each time she struggled to be free of it, he twisted her arm, forcing another scream that pierced the howling anger of the tempest.

I rushed outside. They both saw me immediately. There were expressions of fear and relief, but they appeared on the wrong faces. Although I couldn't hear him above the wind, he was laughing. He pushed her closer to the swirling waters of the creek. He waited, until he was sure I was watching, then he punched her hard, in the back, and sent her sprawling onto the bank.

He stepped down to her and put his work boot on the back of her head, forcing her face into the mud. He was yelling at me, taunting, but his words were lost in wind and water.

This cruelty was for my benefit, to draw me over. He lifted his leg, and she raised her head from the muck, gasping for air. He yanked her to her feet and, with one arm around her neck, he tore the top of her dress and ripped her bra away, exposing her upper body to the angry elements, and shame. She saw me then, and held her hands out, palms first, with fingers splayed, as if to motion me away. Then he thrust her down, kicked her, and again buried her face in the ooze.

He would kill her if I didn't do something now. I ran to the dam and climbed upward. The force of the wind and driving rain almost toppled me before I could reach the surface, but I held on and gained the walkway. I peered through squinting eyes against the stinging blast. He was motioning me to come, jumping up and down like a depraved gorilla.

Then I saw the boards! I couldn't cross without them. He had placed them there. He wanted this. He wanted me.

He came toward the dam, leaving Sophie. If I went back, he would too. A terrible rage overtook me. Grief and pain, love and fear, exploded inside me, adrenalizing my limbs. I crossed the boards and neared the descent on the other side. I could hear him now as he shouted over the gale. "You want her, you bastard? You want to screw the slut-pig? C'mon, you sonofabitch! Wallow with her in the mud! I'll even watch!"

Sophie had gotten to her feet and was limping toward us, squelching one fear to feed another.

It was at that instant, watching her hobble toward us like a mud-caked scarecrow, the tatters of her dress wind-whipped behind her, that all reason left me. I hurled my hate at Art Hall. It was an unexpected show of acrobatics and I saw, with no small pleasure, the surprise on his face as he went down beneath me. I remember rage and hate and the blood that spurted from his broken nose. I pummeled him with my blistered, arthritic hands.

I heard Sophie's voice, far away. "Stop it! Stop it, Ben!" I felt her pulling at my shirt. Then the police were there, and it was over.

Art had called them, of course, before he'd pulled her out into the storm. Jack Csinos has sinced informed me by letter that one of the cops works part-time for Hall Construction Company. The other was an offensive lineman on those two state championship teams. They testified that they had discovered me beating Mr. Hall as he tried to defend his wife against my advances. Sophia signed the affadavit and Arthur Hall benevolently dropped the charges. A restraining order was issued. I was not to have any contact with Mrs. Hall.

I broke it the next day. I tried to call her. I didn't know the phone was tapped. She pressed charges to keep me from harm, not knowing that harm was all I wanted.

So I am here, Dr. Kim, in the Palace of Cracked Heads, and this is the document you requested. It contains what I know and what little I understand.

I have made copies for Shelly and Ty to read later. I can only hope they trust me. I love them more than anyone on earth. I would die for their happiness, but I have only been in love with one person in my life, as you now know. I hope you'll help them to understand. I will try.

So, it's finally November, Dr. Kim. Tomorrow, I'll see Morgan. We'll talk with you. You will have this manuscript. Bargain done. It's Sunday. On Wednesday, I will go home!

* * *

Dr. Kim Dong-Ho
Notes on the Riveridge Case
November 22, 2000

I read the final pages of Ben Riveridge's manuscript on Monday morning. I was appalled. If all that he's written is true, and I believe it is, then his detainment here has been a great injustice, despite his controversial theories.

Shortly after, I talked with his friend, Jack Csinos, by phone, and although he was reticent to discuss Mr. Riveridge's personal circumstances, he did confirm all that Ben had written, at least as much as had happened within the realm of his experience.

On Monday afternoon, I met with both Mr. Riveridge and Mrs. Hall, which they had agreed to do, as the final condition of his release.

She arrived first. I showed her Ben's written statement concerning his arrest and the events leading up to it. I asked her if it was true, especially the description of how her husband had openly abused her in order to draw Ben into a confrontation. She was embarrassed, I could clearly see, but she substantiated his story. I told her it was my duty to advise her that she should press charges against her husband. She had suffered a great deal at Art Hall's hands over the years; abuse that hospital records would confirm. She didn't respond, because at that moment, Mr. Riveridge entered my office.

Mrs. Hall stood up and faced him. Neither of them moved, but they only stared at one another. It was obvious to me that they were completely enamoured and that the strain that had been placed on their relationship by separation and injustice, had not altered that fact.

After an uncomfortable silence of some duration, Mr. Riveridge stepped forward and embraced her, whispering some endearment as he did so. She returned his attentions. I cleared my throat to remind them of my presence. They immediately separated and took their respective seats, Mrs. Hall crimsoning somewhat in her abashment.

Ben's immediate concern, as might be expected, was her safety. He wanted to know how she had managed to come here without her husband's knowledge. She explained that Mr. Hall was supervising the construction of a museum in Patterson, New Jersey. He'd been gone, she said, for two days and was scheduled to remain there for at least the rest of the week, straight through the Thanksgiving weekend.

"Since you've been locked up here, Ben," she continued, "he doesn't call to check on me when he's away."

Mr. Riveridge appeared somewhat reassured, but it required no great insight to understand that his concern for her welfare had not entirely evaporated.

After this initial exchange, we all sat for a while in uncomfortable silence. Ben lit a cigarette. It was he who finally initiated the dialogue that follows, transcribed from my recordings.

"You've read the manuscript I gave you, Dr. Kim?"

"Yes."

"All of it?"

"Yes."

"I'm still to be released on the 22nd?"

"Yes."

Mrs. Hall reached over and patted his arm. It was, I believe, unconscious—the kind of reassuring gesture that one observes between people who have been together for a long time.

"Mrs. Hall," I began, but she stopped me.

"Sophie, please."

"All right, Sophie. I want you to know that my inquiries today will be directed primarily to you."

"Me? Why?"

"Because I've a written manuscript from Mr. Riveridge which is, at best, phenomenal. At the worst, it could be construed as schizophrenic. I'm releasing Mr. Riveridge, regardless of your answers, so I want you to be completely honest with me. I need to thoroughly document this to cover my own tracks. Agreed?"

"Yes, okay."

"In this manuscript he prepared for me, Mr. Riveridge maintains that you have had, shall we say, 'visions' of certain events that occurred during the relationship between Mr. Riveridge and his wife, Morgan, events of which only she, that is his deceased wife, or he, would have knowledge. Is that true?"

"Yes."

"Like the brick wall of the grocery store?"

"Yes."

"Do you remember how many times you've met with Mr. Riveridge?"

She looked at me as if she were calculating. "This is the fourth time, I think." She seemed amazed by her own admission. "Can that be?"

"Four times, yes," Ben said.

"Have these phenomena continued since Mr. Riveridge's incarceration?"

"No."

"I see. Why do you think that is?"

"I don't know."

"Sophie, do you know what a subliminal message is?"

"Isn't that some sort of suggestion or information that's planted in a person's mind without their knowledge? Like playing tapes during sleep to help a person learn a language?"

"Yes, it is like that. The brain is stimulated to retain information below the threshold of conscious perception. In other words, you're learning without knowing. It's easily accomplished through hypnosis and other means."

"What are you trying to say, Dr. Kim?"

"I'm suggesting the possibility that these 'visions' could have been, in effect, been planted in your subconscious."

"By whom? Ben? Why would he do that?"

"To convince you that you are Morgan. Do you think it could have happened that way?"

I must pause here to interject my observations of Ben Riveridge during this interrogation. I had expected him to protest vehemently, to accuse me of betrayal, to defend himself against my allegations. He did none of those things. He merely sat there, quietly, his eyes fixed on Mrs. Hall. I think that, as much as he detested my insinuations, he wanted to hear her answer as much as I.

It was firm. "I don't believe he would do that."

"Even though you've only been in his company for four days?"

"That's right." There was no hesitation. She looked at him and I could see his eyes filling with tears. He smiled at her. I didn't exist at the moment. "Besides," she said, turning back to me, "I've known him all my life."

"Then you really believe that you're 'becoming' Morgan Riveridge?"

She looked back at Ben. I was ignored.

"Mrs. Hall?" That associative appellation served to draw her back so that I might regain her attention.

"Yes?"

"Is Sophia disappearing?"

"I don't know, but I wish she would."

"It's only natural that you should feel that way. Your life with Art Hall has been brutal and...."

"What about all those things that have happened? Ben must have told you about them?"

"Coincidence? Interpretation? We see things the way we want to see them. We communicate in this world by comparison. A bridge, for example, is a symbol of connection, union. It's not an uncommon metaphor; neither are rainbows or swans. It's how we apply them."

"What about my dream?"

"Whom did you go to for interpretation? How many dreams have you had since, or before you met Ben, for that matter, that made any sense to you?"

"It can't be. It's too overwhelming."

"Perhaps, just possibly, that in your desire to be loved, to escape an abusive husband who could batter you about freely in the absence of your children...maybe, Mrs. Hall, fear drove you to accept all of this."

"No!" She rose from her chair and began pacing nervously. "I don't understand this, and I don't care. The 'why' of it doesn't matter anymore. I've almost died three times in my life. Why am I still here? I don't know. I think it's because I'm supposed to be with Ben."

She stood behind his chair and placed her hands on his shoulders for a moment, then began pacing again. I pressed on. "Mrs. Hall, people die every day. It happens, that's all. We try to discover meaning in it because we can't stand the idea of meaninglessness. We see what we want to see."

"Ben taught me that in order to see, you have to look. Twice, Dr. Kim, Art almost beat me to death. I survived. The doctors told me that my recovery, particularly the healing of my transplanted kidney, was nothing short of—and it was their word—miraculous. And it wasn't the first miracle of my life!"

I remember looking over at Ben Riveridge. He seemed as startled as I by this latest revelation. "You said 'transplanted kidney.' Did Mr. Hall damage your...."

"The transplant had nothing to do with my husband. It happened five years before I met him."

"How did...why did you need it?"

"As a child, Dr. Kim, I lived on a farm with my parents and my older brother, on the other side of the state. My brother was...deficient, mentally. His intelligence was very limited. My parents did their best to raise him, but he became so unstable as he grew older, that they had to institutionalize him. He had a fascination with fire, you see. He poured gasoline on several of our sheep and set the poor beasts on fire. When he burned down the neighbor's barn, they finally realized that he would have to be 'put away,' as my mother termed it. He was fifteen at the time, and I was about to be born. My parents feared for my life, as well as their own. They had to do it.

I grew up not knowing he even existed, until my own troubles began. When I was ten, my kidneys began to fail. I had to start dialysis treatments at a hospital in the city of Flint, about ten miles from our farm. At first, it was once a month, then once a week. Still, both kidneys became more and more dysfunctional. Listen, I don't see why I'm bothering you with this story, it doesn't apply to anything you've asked me about."

"Please continue," I said. "I'd like to hear this. Your own history, as Sophia, is very relevant."

Ben nodded encouragement. She continued. "The doctors told my parents that a transplant was imperative. I wouldn't survive to adulthood, otherwise. They put my name on a waiting list for organ recipients. I was far down the list, and as my kidneys continued to fail, it became apparent that it wouldn't happen in time. Neither of my parents was considered a suitable donor. My father had had a kidney removed when he was a young man. My mother's tissue samples were judged incompatible. It was then that I learned that I had a brother. They ordered tests. He was healthy, physically at least, and his kidney tissue matched mine. He refused."

"Then how did...I mean...I'm sorry, please continue." I upbraided myself for being unprofessional. Every basic textbook on psychotherapy argues for the physician to interject as seldom as possible, to maintain the subject's discourse and his own distance. My only excuse was, of course, that Mrs. Hall wasn't my patient. I bit my tongue and waited for her to continue. Ben Riveridge said nothing, but I could see that he was as deeply engrossed in the story as I.

"You have to understand, before condemning my brother too quickly, that he had, by that time, been institutionalized for fifteen years. He hated it there, and no doubt associated my entrance into the family with his exit. His name was Ajax. My parents, who were still his legal guardians, went to court to force him into it. Though he had been declared incompetent years ago, the judge ruled that they couldn't make this kind of decision for him. In a final effort to save me, my parents offered to take Ajax home again. They would allow him to live with us, they told him, if he would agree to the procedure himself. He signed the consent form.

The night before the scheduled operation—it was in February, I think—they brought him to the house. We passed an uneventful evening. Ajax was very quiet, but seemed composed and content. As we were preparing to go to bed, a winter storm came up suddenly. The wind howled and snow and sleet buffeted the clapboards outside.

After we had all retired, sometime after midnight, I think, Ajax sneaked out of his room and left the house. My father heard the door slam and hurried downstairs. The tumult had grown in intensity. The snow was so thick in the violent wind that he couldn't see past the porch. Ajax had left without even wearing a coat. The temperature was easily sub-zero. My parents were frantic. Ajax's death, you see, would have meant the loss of both of their children."

While she paused to take a breath, I noticed that Ben Riveridge was smiling, a strange expression, given the dramatic intensity of Mrs. Hall's narrative. It wasn't an affable grin either, but a wry pinching of the corners of his mouth, denoting an uncomfortable (for me, at least), smugness. It was as if he knew what she was going to say and, of course, he did.

"My parents called the state police," she continued, "but they gave little encouragement there would be any assistance, especially since the storm was overloading their capacity to respond because of stranded motorists and power outages. Then, one of the miracles of my life happened."

She seemed entranced for a moment, lost in her own memories. "Please, go on," I said.

"Probably about the time we were giving up hope, the state police called us back to inform us that a motorist had called from a gas station's public telephone. The young man and his new wife were traveling to Detroit for their honeymoon, when they almost struck a man, they said, who was wandering around on the interstate without a coat, in the middle of the blizzard. Because of our previous phone call, the desk sergeant had made the connection. The caller had given them the location, and they told us they were leaving to check it out. They found my brother, unconscious and half-frozen. The transplant had to be delayed for several days, but it took place, and I'm alive because of it. If those people hadn't called..."

"When did you say this happened, Mrs. Hall?" I asked.

Ben Riveridge broke his long silence. "February 19th, 1966."

The expression on Mrs. Hall's countenance was indescribable. Elation, intoxication, ecstasy, fear, frenzy, madness and glee were all present each, in its turn, struggling for supremacy.

As for myself, I still hadn't fathomed the significance of Ben's statement, though I should have, since I'd just finished reading his manuscript. "How would you know that?" I asked.

"One doesn't forget one's wedding anniversary, Dr. Kim."

"What you're suggesting is..."

"More coincidence?"

Mrs. Hall interrupted. "What he's telling us, Dr. Kim, is that he and Morgan saved my brother's life and, by extension, saved me. To what purpose, I've often asked myself, especially since Ajax made my parents' lives a living hell after that operation. The year following my move to Swan's End with Arthur, he set the house on fire. He and my parents burned to death."

"I'm terribly sorry," I said. Ben reached over and took her hand as she resumed her seat. She smiled at him, as a child might smile at her father who, standing below her with open arms, had just told her to jump from a dock into the water, trying to get her to swim for the first time. It was trust and fear combined.

"I spent a good portion of my existence," she said, "trying to figure out why my little life was more important than the three of them. I actually enjoyed it when my husband first began to beat me. It was a kind of purging of my guilt. In the absence of purpose, punishment seemed the only alternative. But now I know. I *know* why I'm supposed to live and I won't let it go, Dr. Kim. You may need some further proof, but I don't, not anymore."

"I don't think I do either," I told them. "Ben wrote of the incident in this manuscript." I held it up in front of me. "I believe this. As incredible as it is, I believe it all. I did even before this interview."

Ben looked startled, taken aback. "Then why all this insinuation of manipulation—this business of invading her subconscious?"

"I needed to know what she believes. So did you."

Sophia turned and smiled calmly at me. "I was baptized Carla Sophia Gianetti," she said. "Art didn't like 'Carla,' said it sounded too masculine, so he began to call me by my middle name. But I'm not Carla Gianetti, or Sophia Hall. I'm Morgan Riveridge, Ben's wife. That's all I ever want to be."

With tears running down his cheeks, Ben lifted her hand to his face and kissed it.

I told them then that I was going to leave them alone for a while. They needed the time to sort it all out, and so did I. I told them they could have an hour, then I'd return. I asked them not to leave my office. They agreed and seemed grateful for the time alone.

I wish I could say that there was a rational explanation for every incident, every "metaphor" of Ben's life, but there is no accounting for it—at least not through traditional, scientific, analyses. My own life, I believe, is inextricably tied to his, and not by chance. No other doctor in this place would have let him go. However, there is a power beyond science here, the kind of power that prophets and poets avow. It's nothing short of miraculous—and miracles, though not antithetical to reason—require faith.

After a brief lunch in the cafeteria, which I left mostly uneaten, I took a brisk walk around the grounds and then, almost exactly an hour after I'd left, I returned to my office.

They were standing by the window, each with an arm around the other's waist. They resumed their seats, as did I. For some odd reason, I felt taller. The once-imposing desk in front of me seemed inconsequential.

"I guess the question I have for you now is this," I said. "Where do you go from here? I can assure you, based on both of your descriptions of Arthur Hall, that he's psychotic and, obviously, dangerous. What do you intend to do about him?"

"I'm to be released the day after tomorrow, correct?" Ben said.

"Yes."

"My son's coming to get me. I just called him from your phone. I hope you don't mind. Ty and I are going to drive to Swan's End, pack a few things, then travel up to my daughter's home in Wawatam. We'll celebrate Thanksgiving together there, as a family, on Thursday. Sophie's going to do the same with her children. Her daughter, Erica, is having Sophie and her brother there for a turkey dinner. Art won't be there, of course. He's working in New Jersey at least until Monday. We're going to try to explain to our children about us. Then, we're going to meet back in Swan's End on Saturday and leave together."

"Leave? For where?"

"We don't know yet, but we're sure that we'll be guided. Certainly far enough away to be safe while Sophie begins divorce proceedings and brings criminal charges against Art for his abuse. Once he's safely in custody, we'll come back to testify, then move to some other place and start over—together."

I saw Sophia Hall squeeze his hand, as she looked at me, nodding in agreement with each sentence.

"I wish you well," was all I could manage.

"Dr. Kim?" Ben said.

"Yes?"

"If anyone ever discovers the truth about all of this, they'd laugh you out of the profession. I can't help but think that you're taking an enormous risk with your career, by letting us go. I guess I need to know why you're doing it."

"Oh, academic curiosity has a great deal to do with it. I'm fascinated. I'm in love with the whole notion of Edenic time. I want to see it played out," I replied. "Then, too, it's a tribute."

"Tribute?"

"To Kim Quan-Trong."

"Who?" Sophie said.

"My father. Ben will tell you about it. Perhaps it's a tribute to George Washington Riveridge as well."

Thirty-six hours later, I said good-bye to Ben Riveridge on the steps of Ypsilanti State Hospital while his son loaded suitcases in the car. "You believe I'm sane, then?" Ben said, as he shook my hand.

"Does it matter anymore?"

"It does to me."

"You're an enigma, Ben," I told him, "but you're not crazy. If you are, then the world isn't right."

"Thanks," he said, and skipped down the steps to the car.

That was the last time I ever saw him.

July 31, 2021

Ty called Dr. Kim in Ypsilanti and requested a copy of his notes dealing with the interviews with both our mother and father, and his knowledge of their "reunion." He was, as always, understanding. I have included them with Dad's manuscript, interjecting them chronologically whenever possible. Ty divided the manuscript into chapters, and gave them titles. Jack Csinos added the quotations. It's complete now and ready for publication.

I've just finished reading it again. Still, I can't begin to comprehend what I know to be true. I've lived it for two decades. It's a wonderful, frightening story. It begs for some conclusion, some tying of loose ends. This task has fallen to me.

Twenty years ago, on the day following his release from Ypsilanti State Hospital, Dad told us, his family, over Thanksgiving dinner in my living room, that after twenty-eight years of teaching, he was going to resign and run away, "somewhere," with Sophie Hall. He would leave Swan's End permanently, he said.

The peaceful gathering erupted in a flurry of vehement objection. I couldn't see him surrendering something he loved so much. My Charley, a teacher himself, couldn't understand why Dad would resign only two years short of retirement. Ty argued against wasting his "exceptional talent."

Where would they go? We wanted to know. Did they intend to marry? They hadn't known each other long. We hadn't even met her. She was already married. Was she going to divorce her husband? What about her children? What did they think of all this? What was he going to do about his house? His possessions? When would we see him again?

I began to cry. Charley tried to reason with him. Ty grew angry, then silent, then morose. Collette, Ty's new wife, said nothing—but her face betrayed what we were all thinking—that Dad shouldn't have been released.

I could see the pain on Dad's face, his regret at having disrupted a lovely day; his remorse at having caused his children such consternation. But beneath his sad exterior, I sensed an indomitable resolve, an unshakeable determination that, I believed, could only be thwarted by death. Knowing what I know now, I'm not even sure that would have stopped him.

His answer to the general outcry was to hand each of us a copy of his manuscript. He forced us, almost literally, to sit down and read it. He cleared away the remnants of our feast and washed the dishes. He took Beanie for a cold walk on the frozen beach. He put him to bed; said prayers with him, tucked him in. We read on into the long night.

Many times, as he sat in a chair and watched us, one of us would ask another question. His response was always to tell us to continue, and that he would discuss it with us when we were finished. It was early morning when we did so. None of us had put it down except to visit the bathroom or get something to drink.

Of course Dr. Kim's notes were not included then, so Dad had to fill us in orally, being especially detailed when he related the last interview at which Sophie and he were both present.

The insinuations contained in the manuscript were too much for Ty to accept. He threatened to call Dr. Kim and have Dad legally committed. Dad responded quietly and calmly to my brother's outburst, knowing that Ty's only motivation was love. He knew that it was difficult to believe in the magic, even when assured by an adoring father. He'd had the experience himself. He gave Ty Dr. Kim's home phone number.

My brother snatched it from his hand and made the call. When he finished his half-hour conversation with the sleepy psychiatrist, during which time he said very little, the sun was beginning to rise across the bay. Ty hung up the phone and stared blankly at us. He shrugged and shook his head. Dad merely smiled. It was the dim beginning of our reluctant acceptance.

We continued our interrogation well into mid-morning. Dad countered every negative argument. He was convinced that Sophie Hall was our mother, somehow returned from death. Nothing could shake his faith in this premise.

For us, acceptance would mean, as it had for Dad, the super-fluity of four years of awful grief, and the embracing of an impossible hope. Gradually, over the years, it happened.

After a tearful separation, Dad returned to Swan's End. We didn't hear from him until almost a week later, when he called from Eagle Harbor, a tiny village north of the bridge, on the shore of Lake Superior. This town, my brother has already described. Dad and Sophie Hall were living there in a little, rented cabin and had decided to look for property.

Within a few weeks, his house in Swan's End was sold. Jack Csinos arranged everything. Dad had given him power of attorney so that he would not have to be present for the closing. My brother and I cleared out everything else and drove the rented moving van, filled mostly with furniture and books, to Eagle Harbor. It was then that we both met Sophie Hall for the first time. She appeared to recognize us and warmly embraced us. Her resemblance to our mother was uncanny. Eventually, whether by mere proximity and fading memory, or actual change, the differences would become indistinguishable.

We helped them to find the property they wanted and moved them into the house/bookstore where they would live for the twenty years they would have left together.

Sophie's husband would never have the chance to cause any trouble. He called Sophie at their daughter's house on Thanksgiving Day as she was trying to explain her metamorphosis to her children with considerably greater difficulty than Dad had encountered with us.

Erica and Carl Hall talked with their father that day by phone. Sophie pleaded with them not to say anything about her planned betrayal. Charley believed that their silence had something to do with their knowledge of their father's propensity for cruelty. I think it was because they were supposed to.

Art Hall told his children that he was working in Patterson, New Jersey, on the construction of a new museum for "some damn, dead, Puerto Rican poet," and that he wouldn't be able to get back to Michigan, it looked like, until Christmas.

The next day, he disappeared. The consensus opinion, offered by the men who worked with him (although no one saw it happen), was that he fell into a thirty-foot deep, upright cylinder that was being filled with concrete that morning. It was the mold for one of the four pillars meant to support the second floor of the museum. Mr. Hall's remains are, to my knowledge, still there.

When Ty learned of it, two months later, he told our mother. She cheerfully replied that she couldn't recall having known anyone by that name.

Strangely, or perhaps logically, depending on one's perspective, Erica and Carl never questioned their mother's disappearance. They never tried to contact her, nor she, them. I don't know what's happened to them.

A year after the exodus to Eagle Harbor, Dad gave us their addresses, which he found in Sophie's old purse. He asked us to try to contact them. Being the loving parent that he was, I think that he carried a good deal of guilt around concerning this lapsed relationship. My brother did his best to find them, but both had moved and left no forwarding addresses. Dad believed that they had lost the memory of their mother. They were, in all this, his only regret.

Art Hall's palatial home, across the creek from Dad's old place, was sold, Jack Csinos informed us, for non-payment of taxes. No claim was ever made on the rest of Mr. Hall's estate—neither his businesses nor his bank accounts.

I was informed, several years ago, that Sophie Hall was declared legally dead. I don't know any more about her past. She couldn't tell me. She didn't exist anymore.

Our mother's memory was slow in returning, but with our assistance, she began to talk of camping trips at Straits State Park; of Ty's bout with Legg-Perthes; of the move from Saginaw to Swan's End; of Beanie's birth. She would come to remember everything of her life with dad, but nothing of her own childhood or the four years, which as Dad put it, she was "away."

I learned to call her "Mom" and really believed that she was. Ty had a more difficult time because he feared, so greatly, losing her again. He always called her "Morgan." That was as far as he could accept. She didn't seem to mind.

Dad's sister and brother and their children, of course, had to be told. One visit to Eagle Harbor erased their doubts. Mom remembered everything, passed every test of experience and memory. Like us, they know the story now, but the amazement has never left them. When visiting Eagle Harbor, my Aunt Ruth and Uncle Tommy continued, until the end, to look unconsciously at our mother with wondering incredulity.

Jack Csinos, Debra, and their boys visited once or twice a year. Jack, retired from long service at Swan's End High School, was a pallbearer at Dad's funeral. It was the first time I'd ever seen him cry.

Dad had kept up a regular correspondence with Dr. Kim, whose book on Edenic time caused him to suffer considerable ridicule from his more rationalistic colleagues. Perhaps the publication of this manuscript will serve as vindication. I hope so. He was always so kind to Dad.

The little doctor never came to Eagle Harbor, though I'm certain he wanted to very much. When I asked Dad why, he talked again of boundaries and other things I didn't understand. Ty would later observe that Dr. Kim was the only person involved with this phenomenon who had not known the "first" Morgan. Perhaps that's the reason. I don't know.

In a black hearse, Dad made one last trip south across the Mackinac Bridge. He was interred in Bethlehem Cemetery, beneath the rose-colored headstone, next to his beloved Morgan; the intertwined rings of one hand and one heart floating above them like halos.

Old friends, former students and long-forgotten acquaintances came to pay their respects. They were full of curiosity about Dad's twenty-year hiatus. Many had believed that he was already dead. Only Billy Borden, widowed, stooped with age, and barely able to walk after his plane flight from Kansas, had no curiosity and shed no tears. On the day we left to return home, I was leaving flowers at my parents' graves, when I found a Zippo lighter with Billy's initials, 'BB,' engraved on it, lying on the rose marble headstone. At first, I thought I should take it with me and mail it back to him. I suspected that he had forgotten it. But on further reflection, I came to believe that it was no oversight. I left it.

I don't know what happened to Mom. She disappeared which, of course, she had to. I'm sure she was holding Dad when he went away. I believe she went with him. Ty was right, though. Grieving is just as hard the second time through.

A few weeks ago, I was going through Dad's few personal belongings at the house in Eagle Harbor with Ty. In his wallet, we found the faded, dog-eared slip of paper, torn from a TV Guide in a motel room long ago. It read:

Dear Ben:

I love you so much. I have all my life.

It was unsigned, but we recognized our mother's handwriting.

We'll never solve the mystery. Miracles don't have solutions, they *are* solutions. This miracle required a special kind of devotion; an unconquerable faith in the power of God, love...something. I don't know if it's happened before; I'm not sure it should again. But it was a high romance, an assurance of the triumph of what is rare and good.

I'm fifty now. My strawberry-blonde hair is turning gray. Christopher is twenty-six and I haven't called him "Beanie" for a long time. His sisters are adults now, too. Time passes. I write this as I sit in my Adirondack chair on the back porch of our house, looking out at the water and the bridge beyond and I remember my mother, Morgan Riveridge, reading to me, only a few months ago, a passage from her favorite book, *Wuthering Heights*. They are Catherine's words:

"Nelly, I am Heathcliff—he's always, always in my mind— not as a pleasure, any more than I am always a pleasure to

myself—but, as my own being..." I think she knew the end was coming, as she did the first time. It was her way of comforting—her way of explanation.

So am I guided to end this narrative. So have I come to believe, with my brother, that we are not the children of two parents, or three—but one.

About the author:

David Turrill lives in Grand Rapids, Michigan. He has been a teacher in Michigan high schools for thirty years. He is also the author of *Michilimackinac, A Tale of the Straits.*

CEDAR FORT, INCORPORATED
Order Form

Name:_____

Address: _____

City: _____ State: _____ Zip: _____

Phone: (   ) _____ Daytime phone: (   ) _____

A Bridge to Eden

Quantity: _____ @ $13.95 each: _____

plus $3.49 shipping & handling for the first book: _____

(add 99¢ shipping for each additional book)   _____

Utah residents add 6.25% for state sales tax: _____

TOTAL: _____

Bulk purchasing, shipping and handling quotes are available upon request.

Please make check or money order payable to:
Cedar Fort, Incorporated.

Mail this form and payment to:
Cedar Fort, Inc.
925 North Main St.
Springville, UT 84663

You can also order on our website **www.cedarfort.com**
or e-mail us at sales@cedarfort.com or call 1-800-SKYBOOK